dream me home

A STORY OF BETRAYAL, INFIDELITY AND LOVE

LAURIE ELIZABETH MURPHY

First edition: March 2023

Library of Congress, September 01, 2022, TXu2-333-910, Registration issued pursuant to 37

CFR, 202.3

Print ISBN: 979-8-35090-390-4

eBook ISBN: 979-8-35090-391-1

The book was published by Book Baby in 2023

To contact the author go to www.lauriemurphy.net

A MYSTERIOUS RECKONING OF

CELESTIAL PROPORTIONS

ACKNOWLEDGMENTS

I WOULD FIRST LIKE TO thank my children, who've been a blessing to me every day of their lives. I would not be who I am without them. I also wish to thank every patient I have ever had the privilege of knowing, whose stories reverberate in my mind, whose heartfelt losses were entrusted to me through blind faith. Their experiences allowed me to reach past my own view of the world, into theirs. My family and friends have been unwavering in their support of my writing, and without them, I might not have had the courage to continue.

I'd like to thank Glen Fetzner, editor of My Living Magazine, who gave me the opportunity to connect with his readers through my bi-monthly column for the past six years. Their positive feedback has proven invaluable.

Thank you to Gisela Tuller, a former English teacher, who held my grammatical feet to the fire.

Huge thanks to Patrick O'Neill who saved me with his technological wisdom, and to my grandson Max, who has an understanding of the internet that I will never have.

Last, but not least, I'm grateful for my first love, who continues to be instrumental in my life. Thank you for the memories of more than fifty years, hilarious laughter, invaluable teachings, life-long friendship and forgiveness. This book would not have come into being without knowing you, then and now.

As always, I am thankful to Divine Intervention, placing us where we need to be, when we need to be there.

CHAPTER ONE

I AM WELL AWARE THAT this is the last time I will ever lay eyes upon my home, my belongings, and my children. For that, more than anything else, I am truly saddened.

My body has been placed in back of the windowless van on a ride to my final destination. The temperature inside is cool, almost cold, yet I feel comfortable in a way I've never before experienced, content inside my own skin. I have a certain freedom now, that until this moment, I hadn't known was possible. Although I am traveling alone, I sense that I am accompanied by hundreds of souls who have passed before me, their energy palpable, their emotions still raw. Some seem relieved to have left this earth, the infirm, the aged, those who were ready to leave, who begged to die, but my sense is that the majority of my fellow spirit-travelers have experienced untimely, unexpected deaths, those who were abandoned and misunderstood, those whose lives were cut short by careless circumstances of unthinking strangers. They all seem to be immersed in fear, stuck between the here-and-now and the hereafter. I wonder what energy I will leave behind. Hope, perhaps. That would be fitting.

The air is stuffy and midnight-dark. The trip is tedious, with only the sound of the driver's voice echoing inside the hearse. It is intense, seductive, as he whispers into his cellphone. He thinks I cannot hear him, so he speaks openly. I imagine the person on the other end to be his girlfriend, by the things he says, by the clandestine plans he is making, sexual plans. He sounds confident that his careful discretion will protect the woman he is married to, even as he is inexplicably drawn to the woman he is not. I understand. These plans are not unfamiliar to me. Soon, this trip will come to an end and a new beginning will emerge, a mystery unsolved, though the answer is in plain sight. I expect that the medical professionals will put their heads together in an attempt to make sense of what lies before them, unraveling clues to explain my demise, struggling to draw what should be a logical conclusion. That, of course, will not happen. Regardless of their efforts, they will be wrong. They cannot possibly fathom the events leading up to today, or begin to comprehend the extent to which I would go for love.

CHAPTER TWO

GROWING UP, I WASN'T ALWAYS rich, but I prefer to tuck memories of more difficult times away forever. My mother named me Margaret Elizabeth, because she thought it sounded like royalty, as if bestowing a royal name would bring the fame and fortune wished for me. In the end, she was right. Though she was still alive to witness my marriage to Dr. Robert Prescott, the money arrived after the early years of his internship and residency. The fame only came yesterday, and not in the way my mother could have imagined. To our friends, all wealthy as well, we are simply Peggy and Rob, a loving couple, married twenty-five years, and living in the Florida Keys. As it turns out, I have taken up another name, and residence, but that story will have to come later.

Rob and I met in Boston, a thriving metropolis of culture and grit, of sensitivity and toughness, a place I loved, a place where our story began. In my opinion, if we had remained there, perhaps we might have continued to be happy, but Rob had other plans. Rob made most of our decisions. No, that's not accurate. The truth is, Rob made all of our decisions, and I allowed it. Our relationship strangled me with his opinions, drowning me in his narcissistic neediness. I will take responsibility for marrying a man who borrowed my heart, but never owned it. There's enough blame to go around, but certainly the realtor who seduced him toward the path of no return should be held somewhat accountable. To hear Rob tell it, she made an incredible sales pitch, and one that he fell for. Before her, we were happily residing in Massachusetts, braving the winter cold, basking in the summer heat, marveling at the spring blossoms and raking the fall leaves. That's when Rob decided to take a continuing education seminar in the Florida Keys. To be fair, the Keys is like a mistress who will flirt with a man until he finds himself begging for more, and Rob did.

The conference was held in an historic hotel located only steps from the Atlantic Ocean, and Rob got more than an education in Facial Reconstruction. After only three days, while he basked in the sun and walked the beach, never giving a moment's thought to how I was faring, nursing our two young daughters back to health, one with a cold, the other with a stomach bug, he was a changed man. It is doubtful that he attended the conference at all, but he certainly found the time to accompany the realtor on house tours, complete with her depiction of what his future could hold, what he deserved after long days in the operating room. She loaded him with Chamber of Commerce brochures to dream about while he slept after a day of swimming and room service, and before he knew it, he had put money down on a home in a gated community, safe enough to leave your doors unlocked. At least that was the headline on the brochure of Sunny Isles Community, situated on an eighteen-hole golf course, less than a mile from the beach. Anyone might have fallen for the beautiful pictures of turquoise waters and brilliant orange sunsets, laced with happy couples strolling the boardwalk, tanned bodies, stress-free faces. The residents of Sunny Isles consisted of the independently wealthy, professional golfers, and physicians with wives and young children who certainly weren't employed. There was a clubhouse for fine dining, an Olympic-sized community pool, tennis courts, pickleball courts and racquetball courts. There was a playground for the young children nestled far enough away from the homes that even the loudest crying would not be heard. The brochure's greatest moment was its finale, located on the back cover, which simply stated, "Sunny Isles, why would you want to live anywhere else?" Whatever the advertising agency was paid, should have been doubled, because in less than two months Rob returned home to pack us up, secure a moving van, and move me and the children to our new, sight unseen home.

I never saw it coming. I knew that Rob was tired of the harsh winters and dreary Boston scenery, as well as our drafty two-story walk-up that served us well, until the children came along. But lately, he was forever complaining about the cramped quarters, tripping over highchairs and playpens, and boxes of disposable diapers stacked high. It simply became too frustrating for a man who viewed himself as worth more than just making do. That's when he sat me down, and said, "I've had enough."

I thought he meant that he had enough of the rattling windowpanes in winter nor-easters, and the dampness of days of freezing rain, of stained carpets left over from previous tenants, and the screaming of profanities through the apartment walls from our inebriated neighbors. Looking back, I wonder if he meant that he's had enough of us, me and the children, or to be more specific, the chains that accompanied a growing family. I was too busy making formula and changing dirty diapers to notice the chaos that comes with two toddlers and a tired wife, but in hindsight, he wasn't wrong. His hours in the operating room were followed by a family in daily crisis, with teething, rashes, fevers, and temper tantrums, both the children's and mine. So, I couldn't imagine the possibility that life would be easier in Florida, with no snow to shovel, and picture-perfect sunsets. I couldn't have known the degree to which I would resent him for pulling me away from a city I loved, from the quaintness of the cobblestone streets and history that Boston held. I always imagined that when Rob was finally making a decent salary, and there was money building in our bank accounts, we would enjoy a babysitter and elegant dinners before the theatre, not pulling up stakes and leaving our home. That move was eventually going to become the line that divided us, although you might be surmising that I could have resisted his unilateral decision, but there is something you should know about me. I have a fear of controversy and great powers of denial, the degree to which probably border on psychopathology. Some, those who didn't dig deeper, might say I was an eternal optimist, but they would have underestimated me. Everything in due time.

Sunny Isles was exactly as it sounds, a posh, planned community of homes, large and well-manicured, on winding roads that are all named after fruit. We lived on Orange Blossom Lane. The residents were alerted through the neighborhood newsletter of our arrival, complete with family pictures and biographies of our status. We were greeted by a group of neighbors, all of whom took it upon themselves to latch onto Rob and me, hugging us as if we were long-lost friends. That's the thing I noticed first about Florida. No one is considered a stranger, and no one is entitled to any personal space. Hugging is not only reserved for close friends and family, but also, down-home hospitality from which there is no escape. My insecurities about voicing any displeasure, and therefore perhaps presenting an image of snobbishness, brought me into the fold immediately. This desire to please people has not only made me quite popular, but it has also robbed me of myself. In a city such as Boston, people tend to keep to themselves, or in close-knit groups of friends, but in the warm and sunny Florida Keys, there is no anonymity and therefore, any secrets one has, must remain unspoken.

Rob became an instant celebrity in Sunny Isles, and at the Keys Memorial Hospital. His biography and the gossip about his surgical expertise made us the new, must-know couple. There was no doubt that he was a talented physician, but what others could not have guessed was that his real talent was his ability to manipulate others so skillfully that they were often unaware how quickly they became aligned with his every thought and action. He fooled most people by his charitable endeavors, but he never fooled my mother, from the day she laid eyes on him. "He will rule your life," she said, "and your own voice will be silenced." She made lots of profound statements depicting his character, most of which I chose to ignore when I married him, but in her declining years, she didn't do much talking. We moved her down here with us and placed her in an expensive, decorator-showcase nursing facility, which, if she was able to think clearly, she would have despised. Money was never her master, nor was it mine. I married him because I loved him, pushing away other haunting thoughts that had no place in our marriage.

Rob's entire life was successfully laid out, his attributes taking center stage, his accolades only a few seconds shy of the next brilliant offer, and the next rave review. Our family life seemed happy, at least from the outside looking in, and why wouldn't it? I was the dutiful little housewife, he was the brilliant plastic surgeon, and his daughters closed the circle of the perfect family. When he was gone, working late, patching people up, consulting on emergencies, with the children long asleep, I would often stare at myself in the mirror, and wonder how my life had gotten so far left of where I was once headed. My face, without makeup, was burdened with secrets, lines that threatened to one day reveal themselves like a roadmap of my unhappiness. But for all Rob's planning, he couldn't have anticipated that on the second day of August, at 5:45 a.m., his life was about to become completely and forever irreparably changed.

Rob's daily routine never wavered, not even on weekends when he didn't have to make rounds, or see his patients. There were two other plastic surgeons working at Keys Memorial, but none that compared to Rob's gifted hands, although they were reasonably talented men who shared calls and rounds. Still, on his days off, even without an alarm clock, he awakened at the same time each day, by some internal signal that beckoned him to jump from our bed fully awake, ready to start the day. In the early days of our marriage, he would linger sometimes, rolling over to kiss me, and make love. But those days were far behind us, left over memories of what we used to be before he was owned by the hospital, to whom he vowed undying loyalty.

On this particular morning, had he given me even a moment of his time, he might have recognized that something was wrong, but his mind was headed in a different direction, and not one that included me. We fought the night before, something silly, perhaps the late hour he came home, or my unhappiness with his inattentiveness, or even the way his eyes looked over my head to stare at the television set, while I spoke to him. Then, as we always did after an argument, he needed the reassurance that I would never leave him, laying aside any concern that there might be someone else. But there was.

He couldn't have known that before I met Rob there was a man whose soul entangled with mine, a man I left one day, even as I loved him, because I didn't know I would need him with such pain that it nearly broke me. I dared not utter his name to anyone, except my mother, but although he had not been with me for the past twenty-five years, he spoke to me in dreams, and I told him things I would never have shared with anyone else. My memory of him, and of us together, was still as vivid and detailed as the day I left, and those memories were what made the rest of my life bearable.

My secret remained locked inside my heart, threatening to break free, sometimes actually visiting me in my loneliness, but afterward, it was days before I could find myself. Then, weeping, I would vow to never think of him again, until the pull to be with him was too great, and I was weak. The only way I continued to exist in my marriage, was to live a lie, and recite words in the script I read, written by an imposter, whose name was mine.

Rob never missed an opportunity to have his face plastered on the latest edition of Plastic Surgery Top Doctors, or any other photo op that might come along, charity events, golf competitions, and country club who's who. He's in for a different type of photo op today, and not one that he's going to be pleased about. Today his face will find its way past small-town news and into the big time, ranging from cities like Miami and New York.

Rob, freshly showered and shaved, made his way back to the bedroom to dress, still oblivious to the fact that I had not gone downstairs to make his breakfast, as usual. When he finally became aware that I was still in bed, his face was laced with annoyance, but as he yanked the covers off me, he took in an unimaginable sight. My lifeless body was contorted stiffly, with my leg twisted and broken underneath. My face was black and blue, and my lips were stained with dried blood. My front teeth were missing. My hair was matted around my face, and my eyes were swollen shut. The expression on his face quickly shifted from irritation to disbelief, and his mind scattered in disjointed memories of what it was attempting to process, struggling to piece together the details of the previous night. The bottle of wine he drank during our argument snuffed out any recollection of the chronology of events, although he was certain there had been an argument.

His reaction to my dead body was very disappointing. At the least, I would have expected him to make even a marginal attempt at performing CPR, but instead, he kept staring at me with horror, recoiling as he paced the floor, back and forth, his hands running through his hair, shaking his head, trying to jog his memory. I suppose one never really knows their spouse, until the person who professed his undying love is more concerned with his own situation, so absorbed in the moment, that he makes no attempt to revive me, already so disconnected, that all he can think of was to concoct any story that would clear him of what would surely become accusations against him. By the time he decided to call the emergency number for help, more than fifteen minutes had passed.

The dispatcher answers on the first ring, "911. What's your emergency?"

Rob stammers, "It's my wife. There's been an accident of some sort. She's not responding."

"Not responding?" she asks. "Is your wife breathing?"

"I don't think so."

The dispatcher's system has already connected with the address from the cell phone tower. "Sir, I have police and an ambulance on route." Her voice is calm, as if she's done this thousands of times before. "Listen to me. I'll give you directions to perform CPR on your wife until they arrive. First, place her on a firm surface, such as the floor, then--"

Insulted that an underling such as herself would have the audacity to give him instructions, he says, "You don't have to instruct me. I'm a doctor. I know how to administer CPR."

"And you are?"

"I am Dr. Robert Prescott, Chief of Plastic Surgery at Keys Memorial Hospital."

"Yes, of course, Doctor. Have you begun performing CPR?"

Rob's voice raises to the level of controlled annoyance, "Yes, of course." He doesn't sound at all convincing, but the dispatcher probably assumed that he was in shock. She couldn't have been more wrong. I know him. Even at a time such as this, he is indignant and arrogant. Nonetheless, because he hasn't yet attempted CPR, and knowing his words were being recorded, he reiterates, "I am performing CPR right now, but it's useless, she is already gone."

"Okay, sir, just stay with me. Help should be arriving soon, please don't hang up the phone." But, in fact, Rob did just that, and instead, continued pacing, his eyes averted from the sight on the bed. To his defense, nothing he could have done would have changed anything, but still, a little effort would have been reassuring that our years together were not in vain. In minutes, sweat begins dripping from his body, staining his scrubs under his arms, and down his back. This is summer. Even with air-conditioning turned up to full strength, it was no match for the Florida heat. The month of August is especially unbearable. It is one of the worst months to live here, and certainly one of the worst months to die. Rob's legs give way to the adrenalin pulsating through his veins, and he collapses on the floor, his back propped up against the mattress, my tangled hair resting on the back of his neck. Selfish tears stream down his face. He is terrified, and why shouldn't he be? His entire life is about to change.

Soon, Rob hears the sirens approaching our street, and he drags me onto the floor, furious that I have ruined his day. He bends over me and begins life support, reinforcing his image as the doting, heartbroken husband. The approaching noise alerts the neighbors to grab their robes and run to the street, where they are about to witness human tragedy in real time.

CHAPTER THREE

IT WAS ANYONE'S GUESS WHO I might have met and married after college graduation, but Anne Prescott didn't like to wait for fate to intercede. She wanted a hand in my future, and she found her chance when she introduced her brother Rob to me. Anne was as good a student as she was a party girl, always on the arm of someone new, while most of my time was spent in the university library, studying to keep my grades, and my academic scholarship, on a steady course. Anne was wonderful in many ways, but her uninvited involvement changed the entire trajectory of my life. Rob was a blind date, if you could call it such, but more to the point, she bribed her brother into setting up a chance meeting with me at the park on the campus of Riley College. He was a senior at Harvard Medical School, and to hear him tell the story over all the years we've been married, the plot was so exaggerated, you'd think I was sentenced to a life of spinsterhood, if not for being saved by Prince Robert Prescott. The storyline sounded cute many years ago, when he told it with tears in his eyes at the meeting that set the rest of his life in a forward motion, but it began to lose its luster when he intimated that he rescued me from what would have been a free-fall of financial and romantic catastrophes. The greater his audience, the more unrecognizable the facts, until I actually visualized myself slapping him into reality.

Anne knew the truth, knew that I was pretty enough to find my own partner, when I was ready, when the time was right, but the farther his story veered from the truth, the more silent his own sister became and I realized then, that no one would ever stand up to Rob, not if they wanted to have any credibility. If she knew her blunder had set up a domino effect of disappointment following disappointment, she never let on, finally fading away after moving across the country, keeping little contact. I wonder how she will feel now, when she receives the news of my death, with Rob the last person to have spent time with me. Even she couldn't imagine he was capable of murder, but then again, when pushed, we are all capable of unimaginable things.

Anne inserted herself into my life at a time when I really needed a friend, and her extroverted personality won me over immediately. She was the antithesis of me, open and outgoing to my shy and quiet demeanor. Within minutes of meeting her in our dorm room, she grabbed my arm, leading me to the cafeteria, convincing me that I was starving. The cafeteria had just closed down after lunch, but she bribed a worker into reopening the kitchen, saying we were new on campus, and without nourishment. At that point, I had known her for less than fifteen minutes.

"Okay, okay," the tall lady in the pink uniform said, "Hold your horses, there's still plenty left in the back. We're not going to let you starve to death." Then looking past Anne, she added, "Who's your friend?"

Anne turned to me, and said, "This is Peggy. She's new, like me. We're roommates, and we're already best friends."

"Is that so?" the woman said, chuckling. "How long have you known each other?"

"Just a few minutes," laughed Anne, "but I love her already."

Her statement was prophetic. We were inseparable for the next four years, and she was not about to graduate without securing that I had a man on my arm.

On the first day of spring, in our senior year, with only two months until graduation, Anne woke up early, dressed quietly, and made her way to the bus stop, on a mission to visit her brother across town. As far as she was concerned, there was no need to call him first. It was Saturday, which meant he would be at home, studying.

Rob Prescott lived in an old building on the campus of Harvard University, neglected by years of inconsiderate and entitled students. He had the same cramped third-floor walk-up apartment that he shared with his roommate Arnie since the day they first arrived. It was a quick two block stroll from the bus stop to his apartment, and before Anne had time to formulate her words, Rob opened his door, wiping sleep from his eyes, still in his boxer shorts. Shocked to find his sister at his door, he said, "Anne, what's up? No call, no advanced notice? How did you know I'd be home?"

Anne casually draped her sweater on the back of the beer-stained couch, "Where else would I find you on such a beautiful day, but holed up in your room, either sleeping or studying, and from the looks of you, I'd have to guess, sleeping." She opened the refrigerator, thirsty, hoping to find some orange juice or bottled water, but the shelves were bare. "Just like always, no food, nothing to drink. How are you still alive?"

Rob smiled, saying nothing. Anne paced herself, taking her time to formulate her words carefully, as she rifled through a stack of mail on the counter, mindlessly tossing advertising inserts into a nearby garbage pail. Without making eye contact, she got right to the point, "Do you want to meet my roommate?"

Rob stopped smiling. "No. Absolutely not."

Continuing haphazardly tidying up the counter, she cast Rob a disapproving look. "Why not? She's a great girl. Pretty. Sweet. Fun, well sort of fun, probably more fun if she met the right guy, or to put it another way, any guy."

"Well, that guy is not going to be me. You know I can't afford to waste my time getting involved with anyone. Anne, this is medical school, this is Harvard! I'm still amazed that they let me in the door of this place, much less kept me all these years."

Anne was not to be deterred. "Okay, genius, I never said anything about getting involved with her. God, Rob, it's just like you to always get ahead of yourself. All I'm offering is the opportunity to meet a nice girl, have a casual cup of coffee, maybe a little lunch." Pointing to the refrigerator she added, "You do eat, right?"

"I have all the company I need with Arnie." Anne gave Rob a blank stare. "My roommate? Arnie Stimmel? The guy you hate. Besides, your roommate sounds a bit hard-up. No dates, she has to solicit my sister to beg me to take her to lunch. A definite no thanks!"

Anne rolled her eyes and said, "Don't flatter yourself, Rob. She doesn't want to meet you either."

"Your lame roommate said that? Why not?"

"No, she never said a thing. She doesn't even remember I have a brother, much less one as stubborn as you. She hasn't dated the entire time we've been roommates. Almost four years. Her face is permanently imprinted with textbook ink."

Rob started to laugh. "No date in four years, she's sounding better every minute. A real catch. What's wrong with her, bad breath, bald, rotting teeth?"

Anne swiped the last of the junk mail into the trash. "So, yes?"

Rob quickly rescued the pile of mail filling the trash can and put it back on the counter. "Are you deaf? I said no, and that's final."

Anne walked within inches of her brother's face. Punching him in the arm, she said, "You owe me."

"No, I don't. For what?"

"Look, I don't have time for this. I have to get back, if I'm going to make my afternoon classes. Just do it, okay? Her name is Peggy. She's usually in Lincoln Park, the one next to campus on Broad Street, on Saturdays, around twelve. If it's not raining, she'll be there. You could set your watch by her."

"Let me get this straight. You want me to drive all the way to your side of town, stalk some girl among the other hundred girls who might, or might not, be studying that day, walk up to her and ask her out? Am I getting this right?"

"So, you'll do it then?" Before he could answer, Anne stood on her tiptoes and planted a loud kiss on his cheek. "You're the best brother I ever had."

"I'm the only brother you ever had," Rob smirked.

"Thank you, thank you, thank you! You won't be sorry." Anne opened the door, turned back and said, "I'll call you next Saturday as soon as she leaves and tell you what she's wearing." Rob hadn't won a debate with his sister, ever. If he was going to salvage the rest of the day, he might as well placate her, but not cave entirely. "Never said I'd do it."

Anne chuckled and closed the door behind her, saying, "Never said you wouldn't."

As the rest of the week dragged on, Anne was tempted, after a few glasses of wine, to tell me of her plan, but miraculously she kept her secret, exhilarated by the possibilities of an unexpected afternoon. Finally, Saturday arrived. "What are you wearing today, Peggy?" she asked me.

"I don't know. Jeans, I guess. Maybe a sweatshirt, if it's not too warm outside."

Anne knew what my jeans looked like, baggy, unattractive, farmer jeans, and the worn gray sweatshirt a mile too big. "I think you should wear a sundress, the yellow one, it really livens up your face."

"Why?" I asked without paying much attention to the clue before me.

"l don't know. It's spring. Our last semester to study in the park. Seems like we should be celebrating in style."

"You're coming to study?" I asked.

"What? No. Why?"

"Because you said we should celebrate spring and we should enjoy studying in the park. What's wrong with you, today?"

Anne caught her mistake too late, and now had to rectify it. "Yes, I'm coming, but I've got an errand to run first. You wear your sundress, I'll wear mine, and I'll meet you there in a little while. In fact, we'll celebrate with a late lunch. My treat."

"Okay." Back then I was an easy target, a person without conviction.

It proved to be a perfect day. The sun was warm, and the chill that hung in the air all week was nearly gone. I left the apartment, predictably on time, carrying two books and a thermos of coffee. "See you soon," I said to Anne.

"Okay," Anne said. Probably not, she thought, not if things go the way I hope they will.

Anne waited until she spotted me through the window, and then telephoned Rob. "Hi, it's me. Okay, she's wearing a yellow sundress, yellow sweater. She has a yellow ribbon tying back her ponytail. She's carrying a red plaid blanket."

"Who?"

"Rob! Pay attention. Peggy, my roommate, the girl you're going to meet today."

"Oh, her. Sorry, I'm not going."

"But you promised," Anne pleaded.

"No, I didn't."

"I waited all week for today. Please, just this one time, one teensy little favor and I promise I'll never ask you for anything ever again."

"Oh, but you will," Rob laughed. "You always do."

"I won't. Just do it, please?"

"And, if I go, you'll leave me alone after this? It's less than a month before finals. This is crunch time."

"Okay, Rob, I promise. But you aren't going to have anything to worry about. You're the smartest guy I know. You need to live a little. Dad's still taking up space in your head, huh?"

"Something like that," Rob said, pressing back the memories from emerging.

I never tired of that story, and the way she told it, with such imagery, it was as if the clock turned back all those years. I wonder what would have happened to my life, if not for the tenacity of Anne Prescott.

Rob arrived in his old car, littered with used coffee cups and fast food wrappers. He parked close to the mound, where most of the students gathered. After several minutes of searching, he concluded there was no girl wearing a yellow dress anywhere to be found. As he pulled his car to the back lot, he stepped on the brakes and stared. "There she was," he would tell people later, "perched on the red plaid blanket, sitting underneath a budding oak tree. Strands of blonde hair escaping her ponytail, framing her face."

Even from a distance, according to Anne, he found me exquisite. He turned off the ignition, stepped out of the car, and walked slowly to a nearby bench. He hadn't thought about what he was going to say, but now random words swirled in his head, his hands were wet and clammy, and he felt paralyzed with fear. His wool sweater radiated heat, clinging to his body, and he tugged at his neckline to loosen his collar. He walked toward me and stopped just feet away, just as I looked up, saying later that my eyes danced like sunlight on a deep blue ocean.

I caught him staring at me, and I knew he would be in my life for more than one afternoon. I made the first move, introducing myself, and all he could say was, "Hi. I'm Rob. I came here to meet you."

I didn't understand, of course, but he explained, "My sister, Anne. She made me come to meet you. Well, not made me, of course. No one can make someone meet someone else." Rob stopped to take a deep breath and regroup. "She practically begged me. No, that's sounds awful." He shifted his weight. "Sorry, I'm not making much sense. Let me start over."

I laughed out loud, and Rob, with newfound confidence, said, "Anne, your roommate, is my sister. She thought I should take you for coffee, so, she set this up. I have to admit I didn't want to come, but you know Anne, when she gets something in her head, she won't let it go." He stopped talking to take a breath, then went on, "I'm rambling again. This isn't going well, is it?"

I looked at him and said, "I think it's going just fine."

From that day on, we were a couple, stealing kisses, taking nothing for granted. I loved everything about him, the way he spoke, the way he walked, the quiet way he breathed in and out when he slept. I wanted to be in love, desperate to block out the memory of another man who stole my heart so long ago.

CHAPTER FOUR

IT'S DIFFICULT TO PINPOINT THE exact time when our relationship began to erode, at least for me. In hindsight, I loved the idea of being married to Rob, more than the reality of the day-to-day duties of being a wife and mother. I mean, he was a dedicated father, a loving husband, a loyal friend, and a stupendously talented physician, so, I can't define when a small crack found its way in. When Rob was an intern, the girls were barely out of diapers, and I didn't have time to worry about whether I was happy or not, but I think I was. Then, as they became toddlers, and slept through the night, Rob was well into his residency program, and I had evenings to myself when he was on call. I'm fairly certain I was happy then. I had lots of friends, other wives whose husbands spent much of their time at the hospital, so we raised our children together, trading everything from recipes to sexual experiences, followed by howls of laughter and camara-derie. We planned daytime excursions to the playground, and afternoons window shopping, pushing carriages in and out of boutiques, longing to afford new clothes, but money was tight on an intern and then resident's salary, and all we could do was dream. I think I was happy then.

Still, my husband was slowly becoming a stranger, gone most days and evenings, missing the developing woman I was becoming. I formed my own opinions, made judgment calls, and raised the girls as a married, but single, parent. By default, Rob was phasing out of the man I fell in love with, as he dedicated his time to everyone and everything else, but me. Our friends were my friends, and, with the exception of Arnie Stimmel, he had none. I might have predicted various scenarios to befall us, but in my wildest dreams, I could not have envisioned the grotesque scene that was playing out right now.

"What do we have, Sheriff?" The sergeant asked, arriving a few minutes behind his superior.

"Something strange, that's what we have. Husband says he woke up to find his wife dead. Then, he says he didn't find her body until after he showered and dressed, or maybe it was before he showered. Can't keep his story straight."

"A guy wakes up next to his wife and doesn't know she's dead? Where is he?"

"Downstairs, got Crandall interviewing him. He couldn't wait to get out of the bedroom. I don't know, but if I was him, I'd think I'd want to stay with my wife until someone threw me out."

"You think he killed her?"

"Hard to say. From the looks of her, she has a couple of facial bruises but nothing that indicates a fatal wound. A couple of missing teeth, no trace of them on the bed. The paramedics are on their way. I told them not to rush. She's definitely cold."

Minute by minute the bedroom walls close in, as every cop on duty cram inside. Rob's pajamas lay where he dropped them, and they all walk on them as if they're part of the carpet. I usually tidy up after Rob, but under the circumstances, I hope they understand.

With the exception of the sheriff, most of the deputies look young and inexperienced, staring wide-eyed at the outline of my body on the floor, underneath a makeshift covering of sheets. They no more want to be here than I do, and they are relieved to step aside when the paramedics arrive, eager and hopeful, burdened down with ventilators, backboards, heart monitors and life-saving drugs, their adrenalin pumping, all set to save me. It isn't long before they shake their heads, defeated, packing up their equipment in silence. They don't bother commenting about my situation, instead empathetic toward Rob. "Poor guy."

"Great guy," another one joins in.

The sheriff takes out his notepad. "Ya'all know Dr. Prescott personally?" His voice has the distinct tone of skepticism.

A couple of paramedics quickly come to Rob's defense. "He's called in for our accident cases regularly. He's a genius with a scalpel and sutures. A precision tailor who can sew together shreds of human skin. A really nice guy, always taking the time to shoot the bull, always going out of his way to thank us for doing our job."

The sheriff wasn't impressed. "Don't let this "nice guy" feeling get in the way of your judgment. There's been plenty of nice guys who don't think twice about murdering their wives." The men give each other sideways glances but know better than to disagree with a superior. "I hate to do it, but I'm going to have to put Detective Harvey on this case. He's either going to sink or swim. Rumor has it that his reputation has gone sideways, so a lot of his cases have been given to the younger, more aggressive guys. The way I see it, he'll have plenty of time on his hands to dedicate to the Prescott file."

The paramedics seem to have the same opinion as they pack up to leave, still voicing among themselves as to what a great individual Rob is, what a shame something this awful should happen to him and his children. When they meet Rob downstairs, now released from his initial interview and getting ready to go down to the station for a formal statement, they hug him, with tears in their eyes. The first responders don't notice the bulging veins in Rob's neck, or the twitching of his right eye. Even if they had, they wouldn't know that it was a dead giveaway to Rob's controlled, but seething anger. When they look at him, they don't see the burden I had become, but I know him intimately, the way any wife knows her husband, and I know that he had reached his limit. He feels empty without me, but I believe, deep down, he is finally relieved.

Before long, my ride appears, a shiny black hearse, newly washed and waxed for just such an occasion. Two men in black suits and ties, crisp white shirts and cuff links, let themselves in. After a whispered conversation with the sheriff, they are escorted upstairs, and the next leg of my journey to the Medical Examiner's Office, more commonly known as the morgue, is about to begin. They speak quietly as they secure my limbs, nodding their heads as they whisper "one, two, three" and just like that, I am off the floor and sprawled atop the gurney, my body covered with a red wool blanket. Meanwhile, Detective Harvey, a paunchy, balding man with bad hair implants, arrives with a bluster. He had already predetermined that I was murdered sometime in the pre-dawn hours, and there was only one person to pin it on. He ordered them to escort Rob to the station, in handcuffs.

"Okay, Prescott, get in. Watch your head, and make it snappy."

Rob wasn't used to being spoken to this way, and the air around him was thick with accusatory glances. One deputy sat in the driver's seat, one in the passenger seat, and there was a wire cage separating the front and back of the car. "Am I under arrest?" Rob asked. "Because if I'm not, I demand to have these cuffs removed, and I can certainly take my own vehicle."

One of the men answered curtly, "No, you're not under arrest. Should you be?" The intonation in his voice was laced with sarcasm. The other one joined in, "It's just that at a time like this, with your wife deceased and all, it must be quite a shock to your system. You might not be able to keep your mind on the road."

"So, I can drive myself, right?"

Both cops stared him down. One of them said slyly, "Makes you look guilty as hell, if you don't want to comply, but, hell, it's your call."

Rob got into the back seat, uncuffed, and almost immediately regretted it. "You're a pretty big deal, I hear, Dr. Prescott. At least that's the word around the station. Heard you helped out a few of your patients who were not exactly pillars of the community. Folks that would be better off without getting patched up."

"I'm just doing my job, boys. I don't select my patients based upon their standing in the community."

"That's right, you're a big shot."

Those words brought Rob Prescott back to his college days, the words of his father still gave him palpitations. He hadn't heard the words "big shot" since then. It was the night his acceptance letter came, when he and his buddies decided to go to the corner bar with fake ID's and have too much to drink. He came home to his father slinked back in a living room chair, his eyes bloodshot, his speech slurred. "Where you been, boy?"

"Just out celebrating a little."

"Ha! Celebrating what? That you can break the law? Not even legal age. Thank God your mother isn't alive to see this!"

"I'm sorry, but I've never done anything wrong before, in my entire life. You know that. Didn't you ever drink too much when you were a kid?"

"You think that's the problem? Drinking? No, that's not the problem. The problem is turning your back on the family, leaving your sister and me to fend for ourselves, taking off without a care in the world, and after all I've done for you." His eyes narrowed, and his mouth snarled as he put the bottle of whiskey to his mouth. Then he reached underneath the cushion of the kitchen chair and pulled out Rob's acceptance letter and a lighter. The flame flickered momentarily, and before Rob's eyes, it ignited the corner of the letter, spreading quickly. Rob watched in silence as his father tossed the ash remnants into the sink.

"So, you decided to go, huh, big shot? My son, the disappointment of my life, the one who knows everything, the one who is going to spit on the family business. You have no respect for my father, your grandfather, the man who started this business with ten dollars in his pocket, who worked fifteen-hour days to make something special, something to be proud of, something to pass down to the family. You shit on his grave with this Harvard crap, but you don't care, do you Mr. Big Shot? You and your big ideas, don't insult me. Let me tell you something, you leave and you know what this means? It means when I die, the business dies with me. But do you care? No!"

Rob watched him drink what was left of the whiskey, and slouch back into his chair, his paunchy stomach threatening to burst through the buttons of his pajama top. "Pop," Rob said. "That's not fair. I do care. I'm grateful for what you've given to me and Anne. We have everything we ever need, more than we could want, but I just can't be a plumber. My heart's not in it. I've always wanted to be a doctor, you know that."

"Yeah, well I want to go to the moon, but you don't see me flying off into space, do you? No. Instead, I'm here, being a mother and father to both you and your sister."

"I know that, and I'm grateful, but my calling is to help people."

"Ha! You want to help people, help me. Pick up the phone and call the funeral parlor, tell them we have a dead business because of you. We should have a wake."

Rob lowered his voice respectfully, "Maybe you could give the business to Anne. She's got a good head on her shoulders."

"Anne? I should give my business to a woman? Your grandfather just rolled over in his grave! I want you to tell Harvard thanks, but no thanks. You stay with the business, where you belong."

Rob squirmed in his chair and wondered if he was going to get the belt, like he did when he misbehaved as a child. Still, he stood by his convictions. "I'm sorry Pops, I can't do it."

Rob's father's face flushed a bright crimson, hot with liquor and anger. "Just like that? Sorry Pops? What's the matter, you're too good for this life? The life that supported you with braces, a new car, and gas money? You weren't embarrassed that your old man made a living under sinks all day when you needed money in your pocket, but now you're such a hot shot!"

Rob knew better than to defend himself, but still, he couldn't help taking the bait. "Pops, you're not spending time underneath sinks anymore. You haven't worked out in the field for years. Look at what you've done. You have a fleet of trucks with your name on them and twenty guys working for you. I'm proud of you, proud to be a Prescott, but Pops, I'm talking about Harvard. I got into Harvard!"

"Of course, you got into Harvard. What do you think, they should turn down my money? Plumbing money? Ha! I remember when you couldn't even spell your own name, just three letters, R-O-B, such a hard thing to remember, I begged you, for God's sake, just say it, R-O-B, but you were a moron then, and you still are."

"I was five years old."

"You were in kindergarten, the dunce of the classroom, a kid who couldn't put three letters together, and now you're suddenly such a brain? Now you remember how to spell your name? Well, here's something else you should remember. When you flunk out, don't think you can come crawling back to me. You turn your back on me now, it's over. After graduation, if you pack up your car and get on that highway, you're done, finished, kaput!"

"I'm going to study hard and make you proud, you'll see."

"You want to make me proud, roll up your sleeves, get on your knees and snake a clogged toilet, then I'm proud. You collect money after a hard day's work, then I'm proud. But reading books? That means nothing to me. College, huh? That's a fancy way of saying beer parties and orgies. I know what goes on in those places, I hear things, with those fancy-schmancy college girls climbing all over you. The first pretty girl you meet, you'll get her pregnant, and then you can spend the rest of your life writing out child support checks. How's that for a future?" The alcohol still swirled in Rob's head, but he needed to make this right. He got up from the table, arms open, and walked toward his father, who quickly turned his back, stumbling as he started to climb the stairs to his bedroom, turning before he reached the top step, and said, "Here's a graduation present for you. Free advice. When you get yourself a girlfriend, you get yourself misery. All women want the same thing, your money, your freedom, and your life! Someday, you'll be sorry."

His words eventually rang true. They always did.

CHAPTER FIVE

Rounding the corner, the hospital came into clear view, and with it, the street lined with news vans, reporters and curious onlookers. Rob couldn't believe how this day was evolving, finding his wife dead in bed, and then enduring the sarcasm of the officers on the ride to the station. His hospital scrubs were soaked with sweat, as he mentally rehearsed an alibi that would steer him clear of further scrutiny. If only he could recall the specifics of the previous night. He remembered there was an argument, and a bottle of wine, his wife upset that he was never home anymore, his voice raised, her telling him he was going to wake the neighbors, but that's it. He couldn't be sure of anything else, other than the fact that he was fairly certain he didn't murder his wife. Not that he hadn't thought of it over the years, imagining what life would be like without the responsibilities of being a husband, but he certainly didn't have it in him to kill her. At least he didn't think so. He tried to pry himself away from the wetness of his own perspiration, glancing momentarily in the rearview mirror. He barely recognized the image before him, his face beet red and blotchy, his eyes wild and frantic. He wore the face of a criminal. Further down the street, the patrol car came to an abrupt stop directly in front of the sheriff's office. People were coming and going with their own set of tales. None, he thought, could be any more shocking than his. As Dr. Prescott was escorted into the station, his wife was being wheeled into the morgue.

After the hurricane in 2004, and catastrophic damage to the area, insurance money was put to good use, reconstructing the hospital closer to department headquarters. The morgue was located in the basement of the hospital, with an elevator operated only by a single key, given to those who would be traveling there, law enforcement, medical examiners, and of course, families of victims needed for identification. In this case, there would be no need for identification. The sign in black block letters on the glass window of the morgue door identified the Senior Medical Examiner as Dr. Walter Scott. Underneath his name, in slightly smaller block letters identified his son, Junior Medical Examiner, Dr. Harold Scott.

Because this town was a mix of locals and tourists, most of those admitted to the hospital were heat stroke, heart attacks, and the occasional car accident, but none ended up in the morgue. In fact, the last victim was a drowning, during the aftermath of the hurricane, in rough surf. That was more than fifteen years ago. No one, as far back as anyone could recall, knew of anyone who was the victim of a suspected murder. Not until today.

Harold Scott, Junior Medical Examiner, was summoned to the morgue. The outside temperature was well over one hundred degrees, but the sweat building on his forehead, was due more to anxiety than heat exposure. This was Dr. Scott's first autopsy since he graduated from medical school, two months earlier. Harold donned his white lab coat, and washed his hands for five minutes, scrubbing from his fingers to his elbows. His body stood immobile as his eyes wandered to the refrigeration unit marked number one. He took two steps forward, and realized he was experiencing a sudden migraine headache. Breaking sterility, he walked backward toward the desk, opened the center drawer, and shook out two extra strength Tylenol, washed down by a paper cup of filtered tap water. He returned to the sink, and began his ritual again, washing his hands, fingers to elbows, and drying them in sterile towels. He could think of nothing else to do, except to begin. His hands shaking, he opened the unit that housed the body of Mrs. Peggy Prescott, and wheeled her to the awaiting metal table. Then, he opened the sterile packages of surgical tools, including a saw, and lined them up alongside the body.

He was well aware of the importance of this moment. Not only would it be his first solo autopsy since he left school, but it was a high-profile case, with all eyes and ears awaiting his findings. He took a deep breath and pulled the sheet from the victim's face. She was breathtaking, even in this state. He forced himself to focus. It was clear she had suffered some type of physical trauma from both eyes, blackened, with petechiae hemorrhage, indicating some form of asphyxiation, although, when he quickly glanced at her neck, there were no outward signs of strangulation. One eye orbit had been fractured, yet the other eye orbit remained structurally intact. Her nose angled unnaturally toward the right side of her face, and her ears showed no signs of trauma. There was no food lodged in her trachea that might have caused choking. Her top lip was swollen, covering what were wide gaps where two front teeth should be. He mentally reviewed his teachings. Begin from the head down, examine the skin for bruising or needle marks, for trauma, or dislocation. If there was no visible trauma, begin using the saw, cut open the cranium, in search of aneurysms or pressure on the brain. It was all coming back. The thought of it made Harold wretch, leaning over the sink, dry heaving. Her missing teeth and fractured eye socket would eliminate the need for that, but just the thought highlighted all the misgivings his father had, when Harold announced he wanted to become a medical examiner and work with his dad. He bent underneath the faucet and rinsed his mouth. Taking some slow, deep breaths, he felt somewhat better. He walked back to the metal table and continued.

He noted there were no scalp lacerations, no missing hair, no bumps or bruises on her head, and if he jumped to conclusions, he would think she had been beaten. He shook his head violently, as if to rid himself of jumping to any conclusions. That rule was elementary in his education. Her shoulders were aligned properly with no indication of dislocation. Her chest showed no signs of bruising, although the husband allegedly performed cardiopulmonary resuscitation. He made note of that in his paperwork but didn't think much about it. Her enhanced breasts were firm without outward signs of bruising. There were no fractures to her arms, or hands, and her fingernails were intact. Curiously, her arms, hands and fingernails were unnaturally darkened.

Lowering the sheet to below her feet, he stared at the body before him. She was truly a magnificent specimen. He attempted to focus professionally but found it difficult not to wonder what it might be like to marry someone as beautiful as Peggy Prescott. Her torso showed no outward signs of foul play, nor did her hips or right leg. However, the femur and tibia of her left leg was displaced, the fracture severe enough to reveal a fragment of bone cutting through the skin. As well, her left knee was dislocated, as was her ankle. All four limbs were discolored in a manner that could not be mistaken.

Her hands and feet were dark blue, with blackened fingertips and toes. The body was nearly frozen, too cold to be from refrigeration. He made note of the physical examination thus far but was careful to underline the discoloration of her limbs. Finally, he examined her skin from head to toe, checking for any bruises or needle marks. He swabbed underneath her fingernails, for blood or any evidence that she might have scratched the skin of her aggressor. He found a vein and drew a small amount of blood for DNA and to check for drugs or insulin administration. Then he turned her over, examining the back of her neck, torso, arms and legs in the same manner. He found nothing that he hadn't already noted. Repositioning her on her back again, he turned on the power saw. He felt his breakfast coming up to his throat and tried not to think about what he was about to do.

The power saw left an odor of burning skin that made Harold gag. He had learned to breathe through his mouth rather than his nose, but the mask did little to obliterate the smell of burning flesh. He opened her skull and removed her brain, searching for signs of blood clots or aneurysms. He found none. He worked his way to her chest, splaying her ribs wide open, examining her arteries and veins, pulling her heart and lungs through the opening, and again, he found nothing. He placed the organs alongside her now-mutilated body, and began again, searching for clues as to what had happened to the doctor's wife. Upon vaginal exam, he found semen. He took a sample for DNA, but assumed it was from her husband. Looks like they had a night of intimacy, he thought, unless it was rape. Murder, he surmised. What else could it be? Harold was going to have to find hard evidence before he could give the cause of death. So far, he didn't have any. He repeated his examination to the letter and came up with the same result. Nothing. Eventually, he had to face it. He was going to have to make the phone call he'd been dreading.

After two rings, his father answered. "Hello? Harold, is that you?" His voice was laced with expectant frustration, coming from a man who stood by his feeling that his son was not cut out for the job of medical examiner.

"Yes. Hi, Dad. Umm, I have a bit of a problem. I don't know if you've heard, but Dr. Prescott's wife was found dead this morning, and her husband's been arrested. Every reporter in the town is standing outside the hospital, waiting for some sort of explanation. The sheriff told me to call him first, and he even gave me his private cell phone number."

Dr. Walter Scott, Senior Medical Examiner, had passed the baton to his son only last week, hoping to take a much-needed vacation, and ease into semi-retirement. His confidence in his son's ability was skeptical at best, but he did pass his medical boards the first time around, somewhat ramping up his father's hopes. This phone call proved his initial instinct to be correct. "Of course, I heard. Every living person within a hundred-mile radius is glued to the television. What seems to be the matter, Harold? Don't let the local celebrity status cloud your medical expertise. Treat this case as you would any other. Just examine the corpse, find the cause of death, fill out the death certificate and go home. It's Saturday, still time to salvage some of the weekend."

"That's just it..."

"What's just it? What's the cause of death?"

"I don't have one. Well, I sort of have one, but it makes no sense, so I guess I don't have one."

The frustration in Walter's voice ramped up an octave. "Are you nuts? You can't determine a cause of death? How is that possible. Am I hearing you say that you can't do the only job you are trained to do, on your first time out of the gate?"

"I don't want to mess up. Please, Dad, I'm begging you. I'm freaking out right now."

Dr. Walter Scott turned off his television set, sat upright in his chair, and gave his son his full attention. "What have you done so far?"

"I examined her head to toe, twice. I checked all her organs for signs of poisoning, damage, decay, illness, opened her skull, checked her brain, cracked open her chest, removed her heart, her lungs, her liver, her spleen, her kidneys. There is no sign of heart disease, her arteries are clear, no enlargement of her thyroid, but it's her extremities that have me puzzled."

"No one died because their arms and legs didn't match your idea of perfect limbs. Only so many ways to die, boy. Organ failure, accident, murder, suicide. Pick one."

"It's hard to explain. You need to see this for yourself."

"What do you expect me to do?" The question was rhetorical, because it was painfully obvious that Dr. Scott, Senior would not be enjoying the rest of his day off. Putting on his shoes, he was already out the door still speaking on his cell phone, while Harold continued speaking.

"So, if you wouldn't mind just overseeing what I've done. I mean I wouldn't bother you if it wasn't important. Can you come soon?"

"Harold, I'm already in the car, but I can tell you, there's probably every news reporter camping out on the hospital lawn, and when they see me coming, they're going to assume either the autopsy results are headlines, or that you're incompetent. My guess it's going to be the latter."

It was a fifteen-minute drive to the hospital morgue, and in that time, Harold reassessed Mrs. Prescott's body again. It was the color of her limbs that stymied him, and although he had a hunch, it was ludicrous at best, to even consider the thought. He panicked. Ruining this case would be the lynchpin that would dismantle his entire career, before it had barely begun. He sighed deeply as he pulled the drape over Mrs. Prescott's body and waited. His eyes had missed nothing, he was certain of it, but they could not believe what they saw.

Walter Scott was nearing his seventy-fifth birthday, but that didn't mellow him any. Being Florida-born and bred, he was a native who was as comfortable gigging frogs as he was carrying the title of doctor. In these parts, he was famous for making swift decisions and pinpointing causes of death, quickly and accurately. He was also famous for his moonshine, an illegal public secret, protected by his best friend, and drinking buddy, Sheriff Maxwell Ronan. Driving in the stop and go traffic, he shook his head in disbelief. No cause of death, he thought, that's nuts. Harold had to be leaning toward something, drowning, gunshot, stabbing, heart attack, suffocation, the usual drug overdose, but his son sounded knotted up, like a youngster who just peed his pants in his kindergarten class. "Damn kid," he said out loud, "Sensitive, just like his mother. No balls."

Twenty minutes later, Dr. Walter Scott pushed through the shiny metal doors that opened into the air-conditioned morgue. He was feeling especially old, cranky and gruff. His once fit body stooped at the shoulders, his lab coat humping over them, stained brownish-yellow from too much bleach. His girth had widened considerably now that he had weekends free, and the moonshine didn't help. He looked at Harold, then at the covered body, and back to his son. "This had better be good." The sweat continued to pour from his brow, his body still overheated from unbearable Florida humidity. He said out loud, "This summer's been a scorcher. One for the books."

Harold shifted his weight from his right foot to his left, nervously. His father always made him feel inadequate, but this was different, worse. He spoke in a low, and respectful voice, "Sir, you know I wouldn't have bothered you if it wasn't an emergency. It's just that we have a bit of a dilemma."

"We?" Dr. Scott said. "I believe the only dilemma I have, young man, is trying to figure out why I'm standing here with you, instead of getting drunk in my swimming pool."

Dr. Scott sauntered over to the semi-draped body and looked at Harold and repeated, "This had better be good." Wiping the sweat dripping from his brow, he said, "I gotta tell you, it's hell out there. So, where do you want to start?"

Harold squirmed as he mumbled, "The corpse is cold. And stiff."

Walter stared down his son. This was worse than he thought. "Of course, the corpse is cold and stiff. Refrigeration, rigor mortis. Any of that ring a bell?"

"Well, sir," Harold continued, "that's just the point."

"What's just the point?"

"The corpse was stiff when she arrived."

"Of course, she was stiff. She's dead."

"Not that kind of stiff, sir. The kind of stiff you get when you're frozen solid."

"You sound like someone who's either drunk or crazy. Which is it?"

Harold was not to be dissuaded, "Sir, if you'll just take a good look at her."

"What I see, Harold, is every organ from her brain to her spleen is perched on the side table, like we're expecting company for dinner. This place looks like you just got done carving the turkey with a dull knife. What in the hell are you doing, hunting for treasure?"

Harold's ears burned and he began stuttering. "I never had this much trouble performing an autopsy in school. You know that, Dad, you know that."

"Okay, okay, don't get all soft on me. Let's just get the job done and salvage what's left of a once-promising day. Let's take it from the top, and take our time. Besides, she's in no hurry and I need to get up to speed. From what I hear, the lady went to bed alive, and was found dead in the morning. Her husband, Dr. Prescott, discovers her. He calls the police, gets questioned and taken down to the station house, and she arrives at the morgue. Nobody knows anything more than that, nobody in the neighborhood heard anything, no fighting or gunshot or the like, and the police are counting on us to make sense of it. Did I leave anything out?"

"It's not that simple. Take a look for yourself, Dad." His next words are all but buried in the collar of his lab coat. "There is a cause of death, but it's not reasonable. It defies all odds. It's impossible."

The Senior Dr. Scott whipped his face around until it was two inches from his son's face. "What the hell are you talking about? Stop mumbling. Spit it out, what's the cause of death? If you are going to tell me you don't have one, that's rich! You do realize that's what we do here, right, Harold, determine the exact cause of death?"

"Yes sir, but it's crazy, I mean, really, it's nuts."

Walter Scott continued, "What you mean is that you're nuts. You want me and everyone else on God's green earth to believe that this lady's death defies all known human intelligence. That perhaps she's a mutant? Sent here on a spaceship? Unable to return to her planet?"

Harold looked as if he was about to cry. "You don't understand, sir."

The elder Scott was shouting now, his voice echoing off tiled walls and metal lab tables. "I understand plenty. I understand that apparently you must have been missing in school the day they explained how to make a determination of death." Scott's face was contorted in anger, and beads of sweat rolled down his face and onto his collar.

"Sir, Dad..." Harold stammered, "I've gone over the body from every angle, but..." He looked for a sign of sympathy, with none offered. "If you'll just uncover the rest of her, you'll see what I mean."

Dr. Scott Senior removed the entire drape, and suddenly his face turned white. There was no other explanation, but then again, the explanation that popped into his head was impossible. "So, you're telling me that this woman--"

"Mrs. Prescott."

"Yes, Mrs. Prescott. You're telling me that this woman just up and died in ninety-nine-degree Florida heat from what you and I both know can't be true?"

Harold hung his head. "So, you agree, right? That's why I called you in. I know it's crazy, but there it is!"

Scott Senior, buddied up to his son and whispered, "Listen, Harold, we have to come up with something better. I can't even think it, much less say it. There's a front lawn full of reporters waiting for answers and a sheriff who's holding his breath. Let's find something else, anything else, because there's no way we're selling what I'm seeing." Dr. Scott's mind was racing. Impossible to believe, every extremity of Mrs. Prescott's had frostbite, it was unmistakable. He stared at the corpse again, then at Harold. "Notice anything about Mrs. Prescott's face?" he asked, once again in disbelief.

"Like what?"

"Take a good look. Her expression, Harold. The corpse is smiling!"

Harold took a few steps back, shivering. The air had been sucked out of the room, and he wanted to flee with it. "What the hell?" Harold asked. "What's going on?"

Dr. Scott couldn't take his eyes from her face. "I thought I'd seen it all. Expressions. They tell the story. The dead speak. Mouths formed in a silent scream, grimaces from inflicted pain, eyes wide open in shock, but I swear, I have never witnessed anything like this. I have never seen a smiling corpse."

Harold moved close to the exit, his clammy hand reaching for the doorknob. It was disconcerting to see his father, a man of logic and reason, circled in confusion. "I feel like I'm going to be sick. I can't stay here any longer."

"That so, boy? You're not going anywhere, there must be a hundred reporters out there, waiting to eat us alive. We gotta get our story straight. All I can say is, it must have been one helluva night. And one helluva murder."

Harold's voice rose up several octaves. "Murder?"

"What else, if not murder?" Dr. Scott asked. "The bigger question is, how are we going to explain this in court?"

Harold blurted out, "Who said anything about court? I can't go into a courtroom unprepared, and you know that I've never testified before. I'll mess up everything!"

"Look, I know you're new in the field without much experience, but you do own a television, don't you? You must watch crime shows and such. Think about it. The lady goes to bed with her husband, and wakes up dead, no marks, no bullet wounds, no stab wounds, nothing. Toxicology reports hopefully will identify some sort of poison. Did you check for needle marks?"

"I didn't see any."

"Well, look again. Could have been an injection of insulin, hard to detect, one shot drops her blood sugar so low she's comatose within minutes. Hard to prove. Her husband's a doctor, right?"

"Right, but listen, I'm telling you, he's a really nice man."

"Nice? Oh, I beg your pardon. Then the really "nice" man did it. Everybody knows the husband's always the first person they finger for murder, and usually for good reason. The last known person to be with her, he's the one. And for my money, they don't have to bother looking any further. I don't think the good doctor will be going to work today, or any other day for that matter. Not unless he can build a clientele in prison, suturing chewed off ears and broken noses." Dr. Scott laughs at his own joke, and Harold laughs with him, eager to earn points.

Harold makes another attempt to state his case. "I know it looks bad, Dad, but you know him. Dr. Prescott is a reputable surgeon. He's done work on your own sister, for Pete's sake. Salt of the earth. Didn't even charge her. There are a hundred stories of how he's saved people, sewed their faces back together after car accidents, repairing cleft palates on babies and doing much of the work pro bono. He's like the goodwill ambassador of the ugly and grotesque. Besides that, he had a beautiful wife. I mean look at her. Even dead, I'd..."

Dr. Scott cut him off and cast a disgusted look his way. "You know Harold, sometimes you're pathetic, like you're stuck in some adolescent nightmare, but I'll give you this one, you're not a half-bad doctor. If you're thinking what I'm thinking, then your cause of death, unbelievable as it is, is hypothermia with a severe onset of frostbite. I don't know how he did it, but mark my words, the husband's good for it."

Dr. Scott's compliment gave Harold the confidence to continue the rebuttal. "Hell, Dad, they've been married over twenty-five years. They just had sex last night, according to the semen I collected."

"So, they had sex. Sex is sex. That doesn't mean anything today. Maybe the truth of it is, he was sick of her. Twenty-five years is too long to live with anyone. He's probably heard every story she had to tell a thousand times over. Faked interest until he couldn't do it anymore. Maybe she turned into a nag, maybe she was never satisfied, maybe the sweet girl he once married turned into a relentless shrew. Before he knew it, he couldn't do anything right. Twenty-five years? Hell, I know I couldn't do it."

"You were married to Mom longer than that."

"Don't get smart with me, frat boy. Your mother was a saint, and you're still wet behind the ears. How old are you, twelve?"

Harold was used to his father's sarcasm, but it stung every time. He mumbled, "Thirty last month and you know it."

"Okay, okay, don't get all defensive. I'm just stating a fact. The husband did it. So, he's been a good leader in the community, and has a great reputation as a doctor. That doesn't make him immune from being human. Who knows the mind of a killer? Who knows what makes a sane man go nuts? Maybe he came home from work tired, worn out, had a few drinks, maybe more than a few and maybe the good wife started talking shit, whining about this and nagging about that. The guy finally had enough. All he can see is her mouth moving, talking, talking, talking. Then he snaps. Just like that, he kills her. He panics. He needs to hide the body while he thinks. He rolls her in a blanket, tosses her into his trunk, and drives around until he finds a fish freezer somewhere by the wharfs and shoves her inside, is my guess." He wipes his brow for effect, "Then he carries her back in his trunk early in the morning, positions her in bed, and pretends he wakes up to find her dead. Calls for help before he goes to work with some cockamamie story of how he just found her. What he didn't count on is her body taking so long to thaw."

"So, I'm off the hook, right? You'll sign off on the death certificate?"

"Nope."

"Don't you see, Dad? If you sign it, what's the worst that can happen? But if I sign it, with the cause of death impossible to fathom, then my career is over."

Walter thought about it for a minute. "You do make a good point. The worst that can happen for me, sonny boy, is that I get forced into early retirement, which isn't a bad idea. Besides, you're a good kid, even if you haven't reached puberty yet. Okay, I'll sign it." Dr. Walter Scott looked around the morgue with emotions of both sadness and relief. He removed his lab coat, threw it in the dirty bin, and headed for the door. "Clean up this mess, Harold. I'll talk to the press. But, between you and me, there's a freezer somewhere in this town that could really tell a tale."

When both medical examiners called the sheriff into the lab, they were ready for the barrage of accusations that would surely come their way.

"Frostbite?"

"Yessir, Sheriff. The lady died from exposure to some type of cold, barring any other lab findings. Her arms and legs were mottled, black and blue, the way frostbite looks when it starts eating at a body, a scavenger of the elements, tough and unrelenting. Her hands were nearly black, and her toes were so brittle that when I touched them, one fell off into my hand."

"This is impossible! What are you going to tell the press?" the sheriff asked. "If word gets out, they'll mop the floor with us. Your job will be over, and I'll be right there with you. Say anything, but don't say that."

"Sorry, Sheriff, but I'm afraid it's too late. I just faxed the death certificate to the courthouse. Had to. Cause of death, hypothermia with frostbite, plain and simple. It's going to be up to some poor schmuck detective to figure out the how's and why's."

CHAPTER SIX

THAT POOR SCHMUCK ENDED UP being none other than Detective Harvey, a below average student and lifelong deadbeat who managed to squeeze his way into the police academy with some help from his uncle, a big police supporter, to the tune of twenty thousand a year. His uncle had a seemingly endless supply of money from unknown sources, and used plenty of it to buy his less than desirable friend's freedom from an otherwise lengthy prison term. He even managed to get his daughter's drug record expunged. It turns out that his nephew, Glen Harvey, was a man who failed at nearly everything he attempted, not so much because of a lack of intelligence, but rather lack of motivation and sheer laziness. To make matters worse, he suffered not only from asthma, but also bilateral bone spurs which essentially made him useless as a street cop. He eventually was hired to work in the county jail as a warden, but even then, his carelessness and lack of detail to paperwork, summoned him in front of his superiors more times than he could remember. He was moved to work as a bench cop in the police station doing mostly meet and greets, until he got the big break. His uncle, still flexing his monetary muscles, helped him to file a grievance with his union, stating that after being a cop for more than fifteen years, he had not been promoted. He then skyrocketed from a desk job to a junior detective, to the chagrin of anyone who knew him. He was the laughingstock of the station house, having bungled the few cases he was given, on technicalities, that allowed most criminals to walk away scot-free, including an earlier Prescott home invasion.

To say the Prescott case was the biggest case in his career was an understatement, and given his record of insufficient closures, it would never have landed on his desk, except for the recent rise in crime trickling in from Miami. With half the staff overloaded with cases, his name came up as the lead detective. For the police force, this was an embarrassment, but for Detective Harvey, this was just the case he needed to solve, and regain whatever shred of reputation he had left.

Unfortunately, Detective Harvey didn't have the front-row seat that I have. Being dead gives me three-hundred-and-sixty-degree vision, ranging from past to present and back again, but Harvey is only able to piece together facts as they become available. Some of those facts would lead to the mindset of Arnie Stimmel, culminating to Rob Prescott's overwhelming need to be liked, and to Rob's sister Anne, whose sharp instinct, could not protect her own brother. In my ringside seat, I now understood that no secret is ever kept indefinitely. I also realize that the emotion of jealousy is more destructive than any weapon. Arnie Stimmel possessed that type of jealousy.

CHAPTER SEVEN

THE PAIRING OF ARNIE STIMMEL and Rob Prescott could only have been explained by a universal crossing of wires, a faux pas of destiny, where steady, methodical, and conscientious Rob Prescott would become best friends with Arnie Stimmel, an unconscionable leech whose toxic envy of Rob could barely be contained. Raised in an immoral family, Arnie quickly made his father proud by preying on his kindergarten schoolmates as young as five, stealing crayons and knocking over their milk cartons. The more they cried, the more he laughed, enjoying their torment, with his misdeeds escalating through grammar and middle school. By the time he got to high school, he was expelled for theft and insubordination. Without skipping a beat, his proud father sent him to a number of private schools, most of which he was also asked to leave, until his graduation. Those prestigious schools and his father's money were enough clout to get Arnie into Harvard University, then Medical School, and finally Internship. Rob's story was quite the opposite, and in an ironic but somewhat predictable moral shift, the two spent the next nine years together, with Rob studying and applying himself, and Arnie reaping the benefits. As might be expected, Arnie had no respect for someone who could be so easily manipulated and would say to his father, "Poor, stupid Rob, I'm practically stealing everything but his identity and he never sees it coming." Rob, to his defense, did know that Arnie was plagiarizing his work, and copying his tests, but he shrugged off rumors, and continued his one-sided unconditional friendship.

"He's just mixed up," Rob would tell his friends, "Lost, without direction. He'll sort himself out someday, mark my words." College was tough, and medical school was grueling, with Rob studying long into the night, every night, leaving his work hidden in plain sight, where it took no effort for Arnie to memorize pages word for word. Arnie was clever enough to make certain that he and Rob never shared the same professors, and his cheating remained undetected. Rob's sister, Anne, was furious about her brother's friendship, and Arnie knew it. He taunted her with her own words.

Imitating her voice, when Rob was out of earshot, he said to her, "Arnie, you are unbelievable, you're a liar and a thief. You think Rob is going to let you steal from him forever, but one day, you'll be sorry." Then he laughed, from a place deep inside, where his evilness resided.

Anne believed Arnie to be the most manipulative, conniving, vile and backstabbing man on campus, but Rob continued to make excuses, citing Arnie's lack of commitment in his earlier years of education, but now, believed that he was scrambling to make things right by becoming a physician and serving the public. Anne saw right through Arnie and the covert control he had over her brother, but nothing she could say was powerful enough to penetrate his wall of denial. Arnie was not only smug in his treachery, but was blessed with incredibly good looks, causing women to flock to him, and his appetite for women was never satiated. He was street smart and had he applied himself, could have had almost any opportunity he wanted, but his downfall was unabated jealousy toward anyone who prospered. This abominable trait was never more pronounced than when he met Rob. From the beginning, Arnie plotted to destroy Rob's very foundation, brick by brick, until his future would someday come crashing down. He despised everything Rob stood for, and fantasized about destroying him in due time.

Arnie assumed there wasn't a woman anywhere who wouldn't be able to succumb to his charm, deluding himself into believing Peggy Prescott was wildly attracted to him. However, over time, as his confidence teetered, he began devising a plan, so sinister that even he was shocked to the degree he would stoop to win the prize. Arnie flirted with Peggy at every chance he got, even if Rob was in the adjacent room, using the bathroom, paying the pizza delivery man, or taking out the trash. Meanwhile, Anne's hounding needed no sugarcoating. "Why don't you just move out, Rob? He's not good for you. He's going to jeopardize your reputation, sooner or later."

"I can't do that, Anne. Give him a break. He's not such a bad guy, he's just different, a harmless party animal. Sleeps all day, plays all night. But he gets decent grades."

"His decent grades, as you call them, are the grades you hand him on a silver platter. He doesn't have one original thought in his head. You're just as guilty as he is, by enabling him."

"That's not entirely true. Yes, he copies much of my work, but his test scores are exemplary. He can cram just about anything into his brain. He has a talent for memorizing facts straight out of a textbook and regurgitating them later."

Anne shrugged her shoulders in exhaustion. "Memorizing a fact is the cliff notes of learning. He might be able to spit out information on a test, but can he apply it? We're not talking about working on a factory line where everything is redundant, we're talking about the life and death of his potential patients, presuming he gets that far."

Rob was patient but firm, having had this conversation endless times before. "I'm not kicking him out. I couldn't do that to him."

"So, you're never going to be rid of him?" Anne asked.

Rob's voice lowered to a whisper. "Actually, we'll probably be parting ways sooner than you think. On the QT, Arnie doesn't know this, but I've applied to Massachusetts General Hospital for my residency in Plastic Surgery. They only have one spot available, so if I get in, and that's a big 'if', then we'll be separated by default."

Anne admonished, "So let me get this straight, you're leaving your entire future to chance? If you don't get in, then what? He'll shadow you for the rest of your life."

"Then I guess I'd better get in," Rob said grinning, giving her arm a brotherly love punch. "Besides, I'm his best friend."

"Well, I certainly hope that's not true."

Rob sat down on a living room chair, rubbing his neck, strained from studying. "In some ways, it is kind of true. Now that I think about it, he really is my only friend, certainly my longest, present company excluded."

Rob knew deep down Anne was right, but his loyalty for Arnie ran deep, and he watched over him like he was a rogue brother in need of guidance. This was the first time Rob ever kept anything from Arnie, and although he felt guilty about the betrayal, he really wanted that Plastic Surgery spot and he knew that Arnie would try to steal it for himself, given the chance. He would have to shed Arnie's shadow, or it eventually could jeopardize his career. While Rob slept restlessly with this secret preying on his conscience, Arnie slept just fine, hiding a little secret of his own.

Arnie not only stole Rob's essays, but he made a habit of scrutinizing Rob's personal mail, bank accounts, stashed money, and letters from the Dean, all of which had gone on for years, not necessarily for the purpose of stealing money, although he wasn't opposed to putting a little money in his pocket from time to time, but more importantly, to keep abreast of Rob's every move. This time it paid off.

Arnie's family had a hefty bank account, but enough was never enough, and the pile of money accumulating wasn't the motivating factor. The real high came from manipulating unsuspecting people, even friends, and swindling them out of money they could ill afford to lose. Arnie was one of three children, and the only one who immersed himself in the art of the con game. He was a fast learner and became the prodigal son. By the time he reached his teens, he had amassed his own fortune, having stolen cell phones, gift cards, and even a laptop computer. Once Arnie was accepted into Harvard, his father wrote promissory notes to pay for tuition, which, of course, he had no intention of paying. His parting words to his son on his send-off to college was a reminder to ride the coattails of an unsuspecting patsy until graduation, making him believe "he is like a brother to you."

"You know I will, Dad. In fact, I just might end up being better at this game than you are." He wasn't wrong, and it wouldn't take long to project that the student was on track to surpass the teacher. If Charles Stimmel went through life without much of a conscience, his son Arnie had none at all.

Arnie couldn't have found a better roommate if he had chosen him himself. "Fate is certainly looking out for me," he'd tell his father. Rob was a creature of habit, making Arnie's goal that much easier. Rob took an afternoon nap after his morning classes, he stayed in the library for hours whenever after school, and walked five miles daily even in inclement weather.

That gave Arnie all the opportunity he needed to rifle through Rob's wallet, dresser drawers and mail, securing his date of birth and social security number, to be used at a later date. After all, he thought, why steal for petty rewards when the big jackpot would come after graduation from medical school, and he was nothing if not a patient man. Rob's absence also gave Arnie plenty of time to pull up Rob's history on the computer, reading assignments he had submitted, and after changing a few sentences, was able to craftily turn them in as his own. In fact, if it wasn't for Rob's meddling sister Anne, he would have had an unobstructed path to the perfect crime.

One day, Anne made an unexpected visit to Rob's apartment, using her key to enter. Her plan was to do some surprise housekeeping, but instead, when she entered, she caught Arnie pilfering through Rob's personal items, laying them on the bed systematically while he photographed his personal affects including his passwords, license, and passport. Anne demanded, "What the hell do you think you're doing?"

Arnie, caught off guard, had thoughts of punching her, but quickly thought better of it. "If you must know, I'm cleaning up Rob's room. He's so busy studying, he keeps this place a pigsty. Not that you need any explanation. I believe you owe me one, such as, why are you trespassing into my apartment?"

"This is my brother's apartment also, and I'm helping him get organized."

"I can call security right now and tell them you had no permission to break into this place, but I'll give you ten seconds to leave right now, and we'll forget this ever happened."

"Why are you taking pictures of his things?" Anne demanded.

Arnie walked toward the phone, "You have exactly one second left. Either leave or I'm calling the police, and by the way, I don't know what you're talking about. I'm not photographing anything. You must be reading too many mystery novels. Now get out."

Anne opened the door to leave, but said, "I'm going to report this to Rob."

Arnie laughed in her face. "I don't give a shit what you do. It's your word against mine, and trust me, my word weighs heavily in Rob's mind."

Anne did call Rob later that day. "Hey, Rob. I stopped by your place to do some light housecleaning, and I found Arnie going through some of your things. He said it's fine, that you're cool with it."

Rob didn't have anything to hide, and he certainly didn't want Arnie as an enemy at this stage of their educational career. Besides, he thought, what harm could come of a little snooping. "Anne, Arnie and I are like brothers. We don't keep secrets from each other. You haven't liked him from day one, and sorry, but I don't need this right now. If you make him angry, he'll take off, and then I'll be stuck trying to get another roommate, which by the way, I don't have the time or inclination to do, so as much as I appreciate your concern, just let it be."

One month later, Arnie's snooping paid off. Shortly after dinner, only two months before graduation, Arnie logged onto Rob's computer history, and came across a stunning piece of information. He had filled out an application for the only available slot of the Plastic Surgery Residency program, at Massachusetts General Hospital, one that was nearly impossible to even hope for, and one that very well might ruin Arnie's chance to continue riding on Rob's back throughout the next several years. As far as he and Rob had discussed, Rob had applied to several local hospitals in general surgery, but never mentioned the big-ticket item of Mass General. "So, he's playing me for a fool," Arnie thought. "Well, we'll see about that." Arnie promptly went next door to one of the freshman students who moved in recently and asked to borrow his computer, with a sob story of how his was on the fritz. He downloaded the application, filled it out, and rather than sending it by email, he decided to hand-deliver it the next day, directly to the head of Plastic Surgery at Mass General.

When Rob came back to the apartment, Arnie feigned a sore throat and said he was going to have to miss classes the next day. Rob brought him dinner in bed on a tray, complete with a bottle of water and Tylenol. "He'll never see this coming," Arnie thought. Rob left the next morning bright and early, looking in on his roommate who pretended to be asleep. Ten minutes later, Arnie was catching a bus to the hospital, his application in hand. He sweet-talked his way past the front desk and managed to get a nurse to escort him to the Chief Resident in charge of Plastics. Arnie shook his hand while he begged forgiveness for his unscheduled meeting. "This will only take a minute, sir. I realized that my computer never sent my email application that I filled out several months ago, and I didn't want to miss the deadline. I hope you'll forgive my enthusiasm, but Mass General has always been a dream of mine." The Chief Resident accepted his apology and with a handshake, took his application with the promise that he will look it over himself. He smiled, and gave Arnie a head nod, which Arnie took to mean that he was as good as in the program.

He managed to get home before Rob, threw his clothes off, and plopped himself under the covers. When Rob inquired as to his health, Arnie said he was weak, but feeling much better. Smiling to himself, he whispered under his breath, "You have no idea how much better!"

For the next three days Arnie ate all his meals in the hospital cafeteria at Mass General, buddying up to the Plastic Surgery Residents, buying them meals, telling them jokes, and setting them up with some of his female discards. "Now, don't forget to put in a good word for me with your superiors," he said. Then, he handed each of them an envelope stuffed with five hundred dollars, a present from his father to sweeten the deal. "Just a little something for your trouble," he winked.

Arnie was scheduled to meet with Dr. Levin, Head of Plastic Surgery on a Saturday, the same Saturday, as luck would have it, that Rob was scheduled to meet his sister's roommate in the park. "I don't want to go, Arnie, but you know how persuasive Anne can be. It's just easier to get this over with. What do you have planned today?"

Arnie was cagey, but believable. "Oh, just a little of this and little of that." When Rob left, Arnie quickly showered and dressed, taking a cab to meet with Dr. Levin. The meeting, scheduled for fifteen minutes, lasted more than three quarters of an hour, with both of them sharing plenty of camaraderie and laughs. "I'm in!" he thought, pleased with his performance, and even more pleased that Rob, the golden boy of surgery, would not be scoring any points this time. He even came home to the apartment with a large pizza, and a six pack of beer, but he was surprised to find Rob still gone. "He must be at the library," he thought. "Well, that's just great. Keeping up with his grades right until the very end." Arnie laughed out loud. "Wait until he finds out that the rug is about to be pulled out from underneath him!"

The pizza was stale by the time Rob came home. It was past midnight, and Arnie should have been worried at this historically unusual behavior, but his emotional makeup didn't allow for caring about anyone else. Still, when he heard the door slam, he rolled out of bed to see what had kept him out so late. "Hey, man," Arnie said. "Late night, huh?"

Rob's face was flushed with excitement, his words nearly falling out of his mouth. "I met a girl. Her name is Peggy. She's beautiful! She's a senior at Riley. You won't believe it, but she likes me. She even kissed me goodnight, twice!"

"That's super, Rob. Nice going. Why didn't you bring her back here? I'd take the hint. A quick one tonight, and one in the morning before you send her packing. Good for you."

"It's not like that, Arnie. She's not that kind of girl. She's the kind you bring home to Mom."

"I thought your mother was dead."

Rob's expression went from excitement to anger, "That's a hell of a thing to say. You need to watch it, Arnie. Sometimes, you can really be an ass."

You have no idea, Arnie thought to himself, but you're about to find out. "Now we'll see who's going to be the plastic surgeon and who's going to be left behind," he muttered under his breath.

Less than one week later, two identical looking envelopes postmarked from Massachusetts General Hospital arrived in the mail, one addressed to Rob Prescott, the other addressed to Arnie Stimmel. Gus, the mailman, who was no novice when it came to sorting out the latest gossip, brought the envelopes to the door instead of placing them in the mail slot, knocking loudly. When Rob answered Gus said, "Looks like you boys are applying to the same hospital, huh? Couldn't get enough of each other, yet?"

"What do you mean?" Rob asked.

The mailman grinned. "I like to try to figure out what's what. Keeps my job interesting. From where I stand, it looks like Mass General either wants both of you, none of you, or one of you." He held the envelopes high above Rob's head. "For my money the fat envelope is usually the winner, and the skinny one is nothing but bad news."

"Gus," Rob said, "quit fooling around and give me my envelope."

"What about your obnoxious friend? Want me to lose it in my bag?"

"What? No! I can't believe Arnie applied to the same hospital. He indicated he was going to Lakeside Community Hospital to teach for a year. He hates touching patients. It must be a mistake."

"Nothing's a fluke with that loser," Gus said, handing over the mail. "You should know that by now. Well, good luck to you."

Rob held both envelopes in his hand, his, bulky, Arnie's thin. He laid them on the kitchen table, waiting for Arnie to finish showering.

"You're up early," Arnie said. "Getting a head start on studying to make the rest of us deadbeats look bad, as usual?"

Rob looked at Arnie, eyes half-opened despite his shower, his breath still vile from the odor of stagnant alcohol, his voice slurred. "You're hung over," Rob said.

"Yeah, so what? You gonna call the booze police and report me?" Arnie started to laugh, until he spotted the envelopes on the table. "This for me? Guess we both got one, huh, Robbie-Boy?"

"I didn't know you were going to apply to Mass General," Rob said. "Are you hoping for a teaching position there?"

"Nope. I guess there's a lot you don't know about me." He couldn't wait to see the look on Rob's face when the plastic residency opening had Arnie's name all over it. He reminded himself to look humble, but the temptation to gloat was rapidly building.

Rob opened his envelope slowly, his hands shaking. It read, 'We are pleased to inform you...'

Arnie's letter began, 'We regret to inform you...'

Rob was elated. "I made it! I got in! I applied for the Plastics residency. I got in! Which specialty did you apply for?"

"Plastics. The one you stole from me."

"You tried for the Plastics rotation? I can't believe it. You told me you hated that rotation. I'm sorry, Arnie, I wish you would have told me."

"Oh, yeah? What difference would that have made? Would you have bowed out?"

"I don't know. Maybe. I don't want us to be in competition."

Arnie measured his words, keeping his anger in check. "You know, Rob, you're really something else. Sometimes, I think this holier-than-thou attitude is just a dramatic stunt."

"Don't be mad, Arnie. I can imagine how you must feel. I'm so sorry about how things worked out, but Plastics, well, we both know that was never your thing."

"Again, a lot you don't know."

"You hated the hours, the intensity. You've said it a thousand times, you called it tedious and boring. You called it a thief in the night, that nothing good ever happens after midnight. That's a direct quote."

"And that it is," Arnie sneered. "But it's also where the money is, and I love the smell of money. Look, I don't give a crap about saving lives or sewing people back together like you do, and I don't mind admitting it, but I do care about a big, fat bank account. I want my wallet to be so thick that it splits my pants open."

Rob felt sorry for his friend, but there wasn't much he could do about it. Still, he felt burdened with guilt, and he stifled any excitement he might have felt so as not to make his roommate feel worse. Arnie, in the meantime, spent the next several days racing through the halls of Mass General, hoping for any position that might still be available, but with no contacts, and the place beginning to slow down for the summer, he was having no luck. For the first time in his life, Arnie felt panic. Without a position in the same hospital, he and Rob couldn't be roommates. The only hospital that did offer him the teaching stint was more than one hour away. Still, he applied to every residency position in every specialty at Mass General, hoping that there might be a last-minute dropout. There wasn't. One by one, the rejections poured in, and graduation was right around the corner. Finally, much as he hated the compromising position, he begged Rob to help him.

"You have connections. You're such a goody-goody that everybody likes you. You've got to help me, put in a good word, threaten them if you have to, but come on, Rob, I need something and fast. I turned down the teaching position a month ago, and now I'm desperate." Arnie was repulsed by how low he had stooped, begging for a favor, making him despise Rob all the more.

Rob shook his head. "I don't think I can do that, Arnie."

Arnie forced himself to contain his anger, deciding he would get to Rob's sympathetic side by wiping his eyes and managing a few sniffles. "Please, Rob. You've got to help me. You're my best friend. My only friend. If you don't help me, who will?"

Rob knew it was true. Without his influence, it was unlikely that Arnie would be placed in any specialty, or even on a waiting list, but as much as he wanted to help him, he remembered Anne's words. "You're never going to be rid of him." Still, Rob's kind heart ached for his friend.

He couldn't bear to see him suffer, so he put in a good word for him in the Dermatology Program, a rotation that just opened up, a specialty that most doctors don't want, considered to be near the bottom of the barrel for physicians, perhaps not as low as Psychiatry, but a close contender.

The next week Gus delivered a thick letter addressed to Arnie Stimmel. Rob had already gone to the library, but when he came home for dinner, Arnie said, "Well, Robbie-Boy, looks like I'm going to spend the rest of my days popping pimples, but at least I got something." There was no thank you, no gratitude, just entitlement, but that's how it always was with Arnie. Regardless, Rob was so relieved he felt giddy with joy, the burden of guilt removed from his shoulders.

Rather than feeling happy, the next few days found Arnie becoming more disagreeable by the moment. His sarcasm was aimed directly at Rob, and when Rob attempted to avoid his nasty comments by steering clear of him, Arnie accused him of thinking he was too good to talk to a lowly Dermatology Resident. "I see how it is, Rob. You think you're a big deal, but in the end, I'm going to win." Arnie was furious. He couldn't bear the thought that Rob had Peggy devoted to him, hands down the most beautiful girl in Boston, and now this, passed over for the coveted Plastics position, and after he put in so much effort manipulating the Chief of Plastics, not to mention the money he gave away. He felt no professional sorrow, just the worry of how he would break this news to his father, a man who had spent so much time grooming Arnie in the world of covert manipulation.

Arnie's moods vacillated between jealousy and anger. As far as Arnie was concerned, it was only a matter of time before Peggy would realize how boring her life with Rob was, and leave Rob for him. How that was going to happen, or when, remained a mystery, but with only weeks left until graduation, and the impending termination of their apartment lease, Arnie felt off center. Rob hadn't mentioned looking for a new apartment with Arnie, and Arnie didn't want to appear overly anxious, but one night, after a few drinks, he blurted out, "So what's on the agenda, Robbie-Boy? What are you and your sweetheart doing tomorrow?"

Rob looked up from the newspaper. "Arnie, I've asked you not to call me Robbie-Boy. It's degrading and insulting."

"Don't be so sensitive. You're just like a girl, Rob. You're going to need to grow a pair if you want Peggy to stay with you. Beautiful women like her want a real man."

Rob gathered up the newspaper, tossed it in the trash, and headed for the bedroom. Halfway down the hall he turned and said, "I wouldn't worry about that, Arnie. As a matter of fact, Peggy is going to stay with me. I proposed to her this afternoon, and she said yes."

Arnie steadied himself against the kitchen counter, a queasiness rocking his stomach. He was stunned, not for one minute having believed that Rob would be able to close the deal, and yet, somehow, he did. He stole Peggy right out from under him, or at least that's the way Arnie saw it. Arnie's hand balled up into a fist. He wanted to punch Rob into unconsciousness, but instead, he walked down the hall and gave Rob a congratulatory pat on the back. "You're the man, Rob. You've got it all."

Rob, believing that Arnie was truly happy for him, relaxed and said, "Thanks, buddy, I appreciate that. Life is really something, isn't it?"

Arnie, no stranger to rage, forced himself to swallow his words. He used to beat his classmates up for sport when he was younger, many assuming after several years of court-ordered counseling that his anger was under control, but the underlying rage hadn't dissipated after all. Arnie was nothing, if not a patient man, deciding that he would wait for as long as it took, and maybe, he would eventually sucker punch him into misery by grabbing Peggy right out from under him. That's my plan, he thought suddenly. Steal Peggy. Arnie looked at Rob and said kindly, "Good for you, Rob. You deserve it. You got your rotation and your girl all in the same month. Lucky guy!"

Rob looked at Arnie, "I was thinking, I'd really like you to be my best man, Arnie. We're not going to have much of a ceremony. Justice of the

Peace sort of thing, maybe a few of Peggy's friends, and Anne of course. What do you say?"

"What about your old man? Is he going to come, or is he still holding a grudge because you won't stick your arm into somebody's overflowing toilet? Maybe he could give you a snake and some hip boots for a wedding gift." Arnie knew that was a low blow, but what the hell. He needed to have a little fun at Rob's expense, despite his escalating hatred.

"You might not believe it, but my father made it big. Like a damn empire."

"No kidding?" Arnie said mockingly. "There's that much money in plumbing, huh?"

Rob bantered back good naturedly, "Hey, everybody's gotta take a crap."

"So, is he coming or not?"

"No, I didn't invite him, but he wouldn't come anyway. He's completely done with me. So, will you be my best man?"

"Best man, huh? What are you kidding? Of course, man. Who else loves you like I do?"

Rob gave Arnie a hug. "Thanks, man."

"Anytime. So, I guess our plans for getting an apartment together aren't going to pan out, now that your plans have changed. Getting married and all. That's a big step. Good for you. Sounds like you and Peggy will be getting an apartment together, instead of me and you, right?"

Rob laughed. "Yeah, that's usually how it works."

Arnie quipped, "Unless you want a third party sharing your marital bed."

Rob stepped back. "What the hell does that mean?"

"You know, it's not a bad idea. You get her for a while, then I'll take over when you're tired. This way, she'll always be serviced."

Rob raised his voice. "You're a jerk, Arnie. Even when you're kidding, you're not funny."

But Arnie's underlying hostility took over, "All I'm saying, is that when you're busy in the operating room sewing people back together, I can keep her off the streets."

"Don't be stupid. I told you, Peggy's not that kind of girl."

"Every woman's that kind of girl, given the right circumstances."

Rob inched closer to Arnie, menacingly. "I'm serious Arnie, not another word about Peggy."

Arnie was smart enough to recognize when he had gone too far. "God, Rob, take a breather. We're just having a little fun. It's just that we've been together a long time and all of a sudden, I'm odd man out. We had plans. We were going to go into business together. Stimmel and Prescott, but you messed that up by getting the Plastics specialty."

"Arnie, we never talked about going into practice together," Rob said, his voice kind, absorbing some of the tension, "but if we had, it would have been Prescott and Stimmel, alphabetical order."

Arnie mustered a smile. "You know what I'm going to do right now, Robbie-Boy? I'm going out and getting laid. Maybe even married. Maybe I'll beat you to the altar. At least then I'll have someone to live with, too."

True to his word, that is exactly what Arnie Stimmel did. That night, he met a blonde barfly, stacked, at the little joint on Fourth and Elm and within four hours, had her on her back, leaving the bedroom door wide open. When Rob walked past Arnie's room the next morning, Arnie poked his head out from under the covers and said, "Can you give us a little privacy, Robbie-Boy? The lady and I are still getting acquainted, if you know what I mean." Three days later they were married in a chapel in Vegas. "After all," Arnie thought, "My days of taking a backseat to Rob Prescott are just about ready to come to an end."

CHAPTER EIGHT

ARNIE IS THE LAST PERSON anyone would want to keep their secret, and yet, Rob confided in him, not knowing the consequences the future would bring. Arnie's timing has always been impeccable, instinctively knowing when to strike, when his blow would do the most harm, but that is getting ahead of ourselves. For now, it is time for the secret to be revealed.

Arnie's first wife was one for the books, but it was the night before his second marriage that brought the rewards. Arnie's bachelor party was held at a corner dive, a bar that had seen its share of misfits, drunks, and down on their luck individuals whose dreams were never going to be granted. The venue was just a few blocks away from the hospital where both Arnie and Rob worked, and with some pleading, and favors owed, Rob gathered enough doctors to fill the place, with promises of bar tabs to be paid in full. Rob didn't have much money at the time, still working with wages less than high school dropouts could make, but it was his best friend, and he wanted Arnie to feel as though people liked him. It was in that seedy joint that the secret found its way out of the crevices of Rob's mind, and wormed its way toward daylight, inching quietly on a path to self-destruction.

It was late. The bar should have closed hours ago, but the beer never ran out, and neither did the bar tab. That night, Arnie was not only about to get married for the second time, he was given the gift of a lifetime. He was given Rob's secret. Finally, around three a.m., when the last of the guests had stumbled out the door, and Arnie was thinking of calling it a night, another round on the house was supplied by the bartender. "Come on, Rob. We're not leaving free beer on the table. One more drink for the road, and then we'll go."

The bartender cleaned up around them, then sat down to tally the money. That was the moment that presented itself, the moment that Rob would regret for the rest of his life.

"I did something really bad, Arnie," he slurred.

Instantly, Arnie was revived with a second wind, and hailed the bartender to keep them coming. Then, he looked at Rob with sympathetic eyes and said, "What's up, big guy?"

Maybe it was the compassionate tone of Arnie's voice, or the darkness of night, the jukebox playing sad songs or the fact that the secret had been hidden long enough, but suddenly, there it was, "I cheated on Peggy."

Arnie couldn't believe his ears, and his good fortune. This would be, hands down, the best night of his life. If he had to stay until it was morning, he wasn't going anywhere. This was the ammunition he needed to pry lovesick Peggy from her do-gooder husband. Arnie thought fast. He would still have to marry his fiancée tomorrow, but that would be short-lived. She was great in bed, but not the looker he envisioned on his arm at hospital parties. If not for her two best features, he wouldn't have given her a second look. Arnie kept his face compassionate and concerned. "So, how did it happen?"

Rob looked at Arnie with disbelief, aware that he was about to entrust his friend with something that would be devastating if Arnie didn't keep his confidence, but the confession was not to be denied. "Peggy can never find out," Rob said, his eyes welling up with tears, his voice cracking with emotion and the relief of being unburdened.

Arnie moved in closer, his face inches from Rob's, "Of course, she can never find out. That's a given." Arnie's face struggled not to break into a smile, reforming his mouth into concern. Rob picked up his bottle and guzzled the beer. Arnie nodded to the bartender for another round.

"So, you know the nurse on 4 West?" Rob said.

"4 West? Yeah, the blonde with the giant rack?"

Rob picked up a new bottle. "That's her. I don't know how it happened. I've been trying to figure it out. All I do is think about it, until I'm half crazy."

"It will help to talk about it, big guy. Tell me everything, and start from the beginning."

"All I know is that Peggy was home with the children, her time focused on them twenty-four hours a day. I'm working crazy hours and we're not connecting. She's still nursing one of the babies, the other one is barely walking. Peggy had all she could do to put them to sleep and then fall into bed, exhausted night after night, cranky, no time for me, and I'm feeling out of the picture. But, then this nurse, Sheila, comes up to me at work."

Arnie put his beer down. He wasn't about to let any more alcohol impede what was left of his memory. "Sheila, right? I think I know her. The blonde with the giant rack. Her name is Sheila, right?"

"Yup. So, Sheila starts hanging around, chatting me up, sitting with me while I do my charting, bringing me food, home-cooked meals. One night it's Italian, one night it's pot roast, then lamb chops and the next thing you know we're talking on the phone. At my house. In my bedroom. With

Peggy asleep in bed not three feet from me. What the hell was I thinking? But I figured, if Peggy woke up, I'd just say it was the hospital, and she'd never know the difference. But I never had to use that excuse. She was so worn-out, she never even heard me. It was so easy."

Arnie couldn't believe his good luck. He didn't have to pry one word from Rob's mouth. "I know how that happens, buddy. Been there. It's tough. No attention, the wife starts to let herself go, baby fat hanging here and there, and before you know it, wham!"

Rob, in his own guilt-filled world, didn't appear to have heard a word Arnie said, "So one night, I get off early, fully intending to go straight home to help Peggy with the kids, but Sheila wants me to go to her place. I can't focus, because her giant breasts are two inches from my face. Pretty soon, she's got two buttons undone, and we're in the parking garage making out!"

Arnie could barely believe his own ears. Rob's nervous, but still talking, with Arnie's encouragement. "So, you have to go, of course, you do. No one can blame you for that. You're still thinking, it's just a drink, right, Rob?"

Rob's face was flushed from alcohol and embarrassment, but he continued on, "So, I get into her car! Fifteen blocks from the hospital and I don't have the brains to drive myself. That's how messed up I was, like she had me in some kind of a trance."

Arnie was quickly losing his patience, waiting for the good part to come, "No biggie. People get rides with other people every day. Maybe your car didn't start, maybe she wants to ask you something about a case she has."

"Somebody could have seen me. They could have called Peggy, wanting to rat me out. You know how everybody loves Peggy. No way they would have kept their mouths shut to protect me."

Arnie needed the story to move along. The bartender had turned on the lights and pulled out a set of keys, clinking them together loudly. "Ok, Rob, but nobody did see you, right? Now, when was this exactly?"

"A while back, on a Friday night. Then, Saturday all day, and half a day on Sunday. The first half of the day, to be specific, when I climbed out of her bed at noon."

"So, exactly what happened?"

Rob guzzled his beer. "What do you think happened? She had her clothes on the floor before we closed the door. We did it everywhere, the floor, the kitchen counter, the shower, and finally, on the balcony. Outside, where everyone could see us."

"But, nobody did, right?"

"That's not the point. I must have been out of my mind! You know how much I love Peggy. It would kill her if she ever found out. Anyway, it's over. I put an end to it, but here's the thing. Suppose Sheila blabs?"

Arnie smiled. He had everything he needed now, gift wrapped and tied with a bow. "She won't, Rob. I had her myself when my first wife and I were having troubles. Sheila never said a word. She's not that kind. But you don't have to tell me how good she is, like a pro, right Rob?"

"Yeah, great, but if she tells..."

"I just said she won't open her mouth. She never did with me."

"Yes, but that's entirely different. Even if she did tell your wife, or somebody from the hospital, your life wouldn't change. People expect that stuff from you." Arnie cast a disparaging glance Rob's way. "Sorry, Arnie, you know what I mean, people expect you to mess up, and when you do, they don't think anything of it. They don't expect anything more from you, but if I mess up..."

Arnie had to sit on his balled up right hand to keep him from punching Rob in the face. Instead, he grabbed Rob's shoulder with his left hand and said, "Okay, listen to me. You're overthinking this. You've had too much to drink, and it's getting blown out of proportion. Sheila won't say a thing."

Rob, oblivious to Arnie's escalating agitation, continued, "I'll never be able to forgive myself. I don't know why it happened. I think it was the babies, a lack of attention coming my way. I love the kids, don't get me wrong, but I just felt like I was suffocating. I never had the chance to be reckless, growing up. My father made my life so regimented, and once my mother died, there was no one to take my side. It was all studying, working after school, college, medical school, internship, residency, marriage, just pressure after more pressure."

Arnie was exhausted. He had what he needed, and now what he needed was sleep. He was getting married in a few short hours. "Okay, buddy, give yourself a break. You made a mistake, who hasn't? Nobody has to know about it, just put it out of your mind, and pretty soon it will be like it never even happened."

"So, Peggy will never find out, right Arnie?"

"Never! If anyone even thinks of spreading a rumor like that, now or ever, you can count on me. I'm your alibi. You and me, Rob, we're tight, just like brothers. I got your back and you've got mine."

CHAPTER NINE

ARNIE WAS GOOD TO HIS word, protecting Rob's secret, keeping it tucked away, but easily retrievable, when the time was right. Twenty years later, unbeknownst to Arnie, he would have his chance. The day began like any other day in Florida, sunny, warm, ocean breezes, promise of afternoon showers. Peggy Prescott had her routine down, breakfast for her husband, consisting of freshly squeezed orange juice, buttered toast, and bacon. It was Thursday, which meant that it was round-robin day at the clubhouse tennis courts, for all the residents. She knew everyone at the club, but her favorite was her best friend Erica, who moved here five years ago, with her physician husband. She was easygoing and friendly, the type of person who never placed demands on anyone. Round-robin Thursdays were a particular favorite among the group, because anyone could show up or not, without having to be scheduled. Often, Erica and Peggy drove together, unless one or the other had errands to run afterward. Erica usually called the night before to arrange the day, but last night when Erica called, Peggy and Rob were in the midst of battle, so she never picked up the phone or returned the call. It didn't matter, if Erica showed up unannounced, she could ring the bell, or if Peggy was showering, she had a key to the front door.

The smell of coffee perking lured Rob downstairs, always in a hurry, but not so much so that he forgot to kiss me and scarf down breakfast. "So, honey, what's on your schedule today? Oh, never mind," he said chuckling, looking at my outfit, "It's Thursday, round-robin with the girls."

"You're a sharp one," I said laughing, "You don't miss anything!"

His hand reached underneath my skirt, playfully. "I wish I had a few more minutes," he said suggestively. "Maybe later."

"Definitely later. What time will you be home?"

"Usual time. Six, maybe seven. Oh, wait a minute," he said looking at the change of clothes he had just laid across the kitchen chair. "I have a drug rep meeting, some dinner thing, over at the seafood place on Elmont. It might run late, so I don't know."

"I was planning on making lasagna for dinner, but it'll keep until tomorrow. It's always better the next day, anyhow."

"Hmm. That sounds good. If dinner is a bust, I might take a sampling when I get home, but don't worry, I'll have leftovers tomorrow as well. I can never have enough of your cooking. But right now, I gotta go, or I'm going to be late."

I remember giving him a quick kiss goodbye and running upstairs before he walked out of the door. "Okay, let yourself out. Don't forget to lock me in. I'm going to run upstairs and tackle this hair. She cut it too short, don't you think?"

Rob said, "I think it's just perfect. You'd look just as good if you were bald. In fact, that might be a great look. We could both shave our heads this summer, what do you think?" He laughed.

"Try not to be too late."

"I'll get home as soon as I can. Don't wait up, if you're tired. I know where to find you."

The humidity was exceptionally high that day, and my hair refused to lay flat. I went upstairs to give it another try with the straightening iron, when Rob yelled goodbye. "Have fun today," he said. By the time he was halfway down the driveway, he realized he forgot his cell phone on the kitchen counter and opened the door to retrieve it. He noticed a missed call from the hospital, and without thinking, quickly called the surgical unit back, forgetting to lock the door.

I took a long look in the full-length mirror, pleased with the way the personal trainer had managed to slim down my hips and stomach, the look ruined by my untamed hair. If only that was to be my only problem that day. I heard a noise downstairs. "Erica, is that you? Grab some orange juice, and whatever else you find. I'll be down in a minute."

Instead of Erica, a husky male voice called from halfway up the steps. "Erica can't make it today. No need to come down. We're coming up."

I remember screaming when I saw them, two men, their faces covered in ski masks, wearing tee shirts and pants, all black. One said, "If you know what's good for you, you'll shut your mouth right now, you hear me?"

I wanted to keep quiet, but my shrieks were involuntary, coming from a place of disbelief and fear. Then a hand that grabbed my arm, strong and hard. "I said shut up, or you're going to get a bullet right between your eyes, and I'm not playing." I looked down and saw a small caliber handgun, then looked behind him, and saw his partner with another gun, this one aimed at my head. "Do it," he said, and then, closing in on me, added, "He won't think twice about shooting you."

The man coming from behind was taller, and had a smooth, confident voice. His voice commanded business, and I understood that he had no intention of bargaining with me. He flung me onto the bathroom floor. It all happened in seconds. Not knowing what to do, unable to think clearly, all I could say was, "Take whatever you want. I have money. You can have it all, just please don't hurt me. I have two children."

"Yeah, yeah, yeah," said the tall man. "We've heard this story before. How your kids won't survive without you, how your husband needs you, blah, blah, blah. Let me tell you straight up, we don't give a shit about you or your family."

It was then that I knew my attempts at reasoning with them wouldn't help. The newly installed hurricane impact windows and doors made the house nearly soundproofed. I had to think. Rob wouldn't be home till after dark, so he couldn't help me, but if Erica showed up, she could. Maybe she still might come looking for me, I thought. Maybe she'd let herself in, hear the commotion upstairs and call the police. It was all I had to hold onto, and the only hope I had.

The tall one kicked me in the side. "Get up. Get up and give us your money."

"I don't have much in my wallet, but I have money in the safe. I can get it."

"Oh yeah? How much?"

"I'm not sure. Maybe a couple hundred dollars, maybe even a thousand. If you just take it and leave, I promise I won't call the police."

The tall one said, "l think she's lying. What do you think?"

"Yeah, she's probably lying."

Both men laughed. The tall one said, "We don't believe you, lady. Not for a minute. Do you think we're stupid?"

I didn't answer, prompting the tall one to look at his partner, his voice ramped up in anger. "She thinks we're stupid!"

"No, I don't," I said. "l promise, I'll give you everything, and then you can go and I won't say a word."

"You hear that?" the tall one said. "She wants to give us everything. So whaddaya think? You think we should take her up on her offer. She's not bad looking."

The short one said, "Let's take the stuff first, then we can decide."

At the thought that this might not just be a simple robbery, that it might result in rape, or worse, I started screaming again. The tall man said to his partner, "Shut her up, will ya?"

It was becoming clear that the tall man was in charge, and his buddy was eager to do his bidding. "You want I should kill her?" he asked.

"Nah, not now, anyway. Depends on what we get. She'd better be worth our while, or she gets it for sure. Right now, duct tape that miserable, whining mouth of hers, and while you're at it, grab her neckpiece."

The short man did as he was told, tearing at my gold neck chain, snapping my neck forward in the process. Then he picked up my limp body from the floor and tossed me onto the vanity chair. He began duct taping my head to the back of the chair, tearing strands of my hair, and pulling at my scalp. I didn't mean to make a sound, but when he tried to kiss me, I screamed until he taped my mouth shut. I noticed that his gloves had a certain smell to them, like car oil or engine grease, or perhaps, blood, probably from his last victim.

I did my best to try to remain calm, but it was impossible. Instead, deep sobs welled up from inside my chest, constricting my breathing, gagging my throat and nose with thick mucus, until it was nearly impossible to breathe. I don't know how much time had elapsed, but I knew that Erica would not be coming by this late, and neither would anyone else. It was at that exact moment that I believed I didn't have long to live. My heart was pounding in my ears, causing a lack of oxygen to my lungs, and the room started spinning. Then bile began its upward journey, inching toward my throat and mouth.

I knew I had no leverage with the tall man, by the tone of his voice, and the hollow look in his eyes, but I thought I might find sympathy with the short man, who, somehow, I found to be kinder. I stared at the short man, willing my pleas to find a home in his heart, but the tall one intervened. "What the hell are you looking at? You don't get it, do ya, lady? Maybe if ya would've kept your eyes shut like anyone with half a brain woulda done, we wouldn't have to kill ya, but you staring at my partner like this is making me real nervous."

I shut my eyes immediately, prompting the short one to laugh. "I think she's thinking she can't ID us because we got our masks on. I think she wants us to believe she won't tell anybody."

"What are you, a mind reader?" the tall one said. "You inside her head or somethin'? How do you know what she's thinking? For all we know, she might be saying she likes us." His comment gave them both a good laugh, but the taller man studied his partner. "You getting soft?" he asked.

Quickly, the short one said, "If she likes us so much, maybe when we're done here, we'll give her something to remember us by."

"Yeah, maybe I'll screw her first and then kill her." His partner seemed pleased to have his buddy back on track.

"Not before I get a turn." Their laughter echoed off the bathroom walls as they continued duct taping my body and legs to the chair. Immobile, every inch of my muscles ached and cramped but I knew I had to be cooperative if I was to have any chance of living.

The short one spoke, "Thanks for making it so easy for us. It isn't every day that we get an unlocked door, like a special invite to come in."

"Yeah, that was kind of her. We never even had to pick the lock or break the window. Now that's what I call a nice welcome."

So, I thought, that was just like Rob. The younger version of him was much more concerned with my safety, always calling to make sure I didn't need anything on his way home, or asking me how I felt several times a day if I was even slightly under the weather, but this version was all puffed up with hubris, thanks to his patients who practically bowed down to him if they passed him in the street. So, Rob hadn't locked the door when he left this morning. He used to be overly cautious, worrying about the children falling off their bikes, or walking home from school when the sun went down, but no more. Now it is all about Rob, all of the time. No doubt that was one of the selling points when he bought this house in a gated community. The realtor insisted we would all be safe, so I suppose he thought his job of overseeing his family was done. I wonder what he'll think about the realtor's hard sell now.

My mind kept drifting back to earlier times, when it was good, when the relationship endured bumps in the road, but always, I knew two things. Rob loved me, and Rob would never cheat on me. That made everything else worth it. My mind snapped back to the present. I hadn't heard any noise coming from the men for several minutes. I had hoped they decided to take whatever money they found in my purse, or jewelry on the windowsill in the kitchen, and left with enough money to buy some drugs. I assumed that's what all robbers wanted these days, drug money. I had almost convinced myself that the worst was over, when I heard a noise coming from the library adjacent to the master bedroom.

"Neat freaks. Nothing laying around, nothing in the dresser, or the closet. Let's check the safe. A house this big, a Benz in the driveway, you know they got money, and plenty of it. Let's find out where it is."

"Okay, but we need to hurry up. I'm freaking out. What if somebody comes?"

"Nah, nobody's coming, not now. It's not even ten in the morning."

Ten in the morning, I thought. My daughters would be in class by now, unaware that they might be motherless soon. I couldn't bear the thought of them trying to cope without me, and just like that, sobs well up in my throat again, and I desperately try to push them back. They said they were going to kill me, and I believed them. I imagined Rob finding me, calling the police, notifying the colleges, arranging for the airplane flights to brings my daughters back home. It was finals week. Not a good time for them to be upset. No, not upset, devastated. I tried to calm down by taking deep breaths, but all that did was build up carbon monoxide inside the duct tape that was blocking air from my nose and mouth. They certainly had guns to shoot me with, but the sound of the shot would echo through the neighborhood, even with the hurricane glass. Surely, they wouldn't be that foolish. That thought calmed me for a few seconds, but then I tossed another idea back and forth. If they weren't going to shoot me, then they were probably going to beat me. That would make more sense, in light of the noise factor, and with my mouth gagged, they'd have plenty of time to make a getaway, without anyone being the wiser. Suddenly, I was convinced that their plan was to beat me to death.

Despondent, I barely had time to imagine the pain they would cause me, when I heard their footsteps approaching my bedroom, and then sounds of drawers being dumped on the floor. There was only costume jewelry in my dresser, but perhaps they wouldn't be astute enough to know the difference between high-end fakes and the real thing. But suppose they were professionals? Suppose they knew the difference and coming up empty would just heighten their anger? A wave of nausea overcame me, and the poached eggs and toast formed a repulsive concoction that traveled from my stomach to the back of my throat in seconds. I tasted the butter churning inside me, and all of it threatened to make its way to my duct-taped mouth.

I forced myself to breathe, to swallow, and although it was grotesquely unpleasant, it was either swallow or suffocate. I swallowed. I came close to choking, with heaving noises that could not be contained. The small man peeked inside the bathroom, but he said nothing. Then the tall one called him back.

"You got somewhere else to be, or what?" he said angrily. "Pay attention. We're hired to do a job, so let's do it."

Hired to do a job, I thought. That's what he said. Someone hired him to rob the house, how was that possible, and more to the point, who would have done it? I wanted to sort through a list of everyone who might have held a grudge against me or Rob, but I couldn't think of anyone. Sure, we fired the lawn crew several months back, but it was only because they hadn't shown up in weeks. Then there was our housekeeper. She knew the floor plan inside out and backwards, but she said she thought the house was too large for her, that it was causing her back to ache. We didn't offer to raise her wages, we just let her go. But she seemed so sweet, surely, she wouldn't have the money to hire two professional men to rob us. She could have easily stolen our things while she worked for us, and we probably wouldn't have noticed. My mind raced down an imaginary list of everyone we had ever had contact with, until another round of rancid food made it to the back of my throat. This time I couldn't get it back down. Undigested food particles mixed with bile poured out of my nose and blocked what little air passages I had left. The short one glanced inside once again and saw me struggling to breathe. He said, "Hey, she's choking on her own vomit. It's coming out her nose."

The tall one said, "I don't give a damn if it's coming out of her ass, let's go. You coming or what?"

"Yeah, I'll be right there. Just want to check her vanity drawer. Sometimes chicks hide jewelry in crazy places." Rather than looking for jewelry, the short one crept over to me, and I held my breath and shut my eyes, waiting for the beating. Instead of his fist knocking me out, however, his hand reached up and quickly loosened the duct tape from my nostrils, so that I was able to breathe in the air pocket he created. Then he wiped my nose with the arm of his shirt, and whispered, "Not one word, or else."

In the midst of my fear, came incredible gratitude for this man. I could have suffocated right there, but, instead, he took pity on my suffering. At that moment, I felt some type of bond with him. He went from villain to hero in seconds. All I had to do, I thought, was to remain quiet and calm, and maybe this man would save me.

The two moved quickly. They definitely knew what they were doing. Not much talking, but a lot of movement, in the guest room, in the library, in the study, just off the bedroom. Noises of possessions being tossed about filled the air. Then, finally, silence.

I was fairly certain they had come across the safe, hidden inside a library cabinet, bolted to the cement floor. They're going to want the combination, I thought, but reasoned, that if I gave it to them, they'd have no further need to keep me alive. On the other hand, if I didn't give it to them, they very well might torture me until I do.

Their footsteps grew louder, closer, approaching the bathroom. The tall man walked over to the chair to which I was taped, and kicked out the legs, causing the chair to fall over sideways, and my head crashing onto the tile floor. The pain was instant, throbbing, engulfing my entire skull. I could see nothing but darkness. Moments later, my vision returned, but everything was out of focus. Then, I realized the hot breath I felt on my neck was coming from the tall man, leaning over me, just inches away, glaring menacingly. "Give me the combination, lady."

Before I could react, he slapped me hard across my face. He said again, "The combination. I ain't playing. Tap out the first number with your foot. Let's go! First number!"

I managed to twist my ankle around, so that my toe reached the floor, and then, I tapped it once, twice, then three times, pausing for a few seconds. My head hurt, I couldn't think straight, my calf started cramping because of the awkward position of my foot. "Get going lady, if you want to see tomorrow."

I kept tapping with renewed fright, four, five, six and then I had to stop again, to rearrange my thoughts, I honestly couldn't remember what the number was. Rob always opened the safe for me, if I wanted to change rings or bracelets, so I kept imagining the salesman who sold us the safe, telling us to make the numbers memorable, something that would have intimate meaning to us, but no one else. I kept tapping. I stopped at twenty. Twenty years ago, we left Massachusetts, twenty years ago we had two children, and we were happy.

"Is that the number," he asked. "Twenty?"

I tried to nod affirmatively.

"Twenty." He twisted the dial to the right, stopping at the number twenty. "You better be right, lady. Next number, let's go!"

The next number was simple. Four. Rob chose the number four because there were four of us in the family, four parts made the whole, four dates before we slept together, yes, definitely four. I tapped four times, but then I must have passed out. The tall one slapped me awake, and I could taste blood underneath the tape. I ran my tongue over my teeth. They were still there. He turned the dial to the left. "Give me the last number or I'll kill you." His hand was balled up into a fist, and I had no reason to think he was lying. I closed my eyes and waited for the punch that never came. Instead, my foot began tapping as if it wasn't even attached to me. It started, one, two, three, I could almost picture it, the safe that held my twenty-fifth anniversary gift, twenty-five years, twenty-five pearls. When my foot stopped tapping at that number, the short one bolted back into the library and I held my breath, certain about the last two set of numbers, but not the first. Then, relieved, I heard the familiar sound of the metal door opening. In a moment of clarity, my anger at Rob re-emerged, recalling how he said that the installer had promised that the safe would never be stolen from the house, not with those bolts anchoring it into cement floor. "You couldn't move this thing with a Mack truck."

I pictured Rob's face, his confidence, his smugness at the fact that nothing was going to dislodge the safe from its mooring. Too bad, I thought, as bile ran from out of my nose, lodged under the tape and onto my face, that the safe didn't come with a guarantee that I wouldn't be knocked unconscious and probably killed for the combination. Maybe, I thought enraged, maybe those details were located in the fine print.

In and out of consciousness, my mind drifted from one scenario to another, how life was so simple when Rob and I first met, and how I thought, naively, our lives would always stay that way. Our first apartment, filled with thrift store mismatched furniture and chipped dishes was my favorite. It had a certain charm that could not be duplicated with the limited-edition gallery style furnishings we had easily purchased when Rob's bank account matched his professional status. I knew how fortunate I was, and if I ever forgot, Rob was always there to remind me, always ready to brag about our material possessions, which he believed should be all the happiness I need. He could never have understood my longing to go back in time, to when we had nothing but each other, when a meal of Sloppy Joe sandwiches and a cold bottle of off label beer was as much as we could afford. Back then, we lived in the same neighborhood as Rob's peers, all poor, all deserving of riches for the sacrifices they made to care for their patients. I couldn't have known how money would change him. Now, among the glitter of wealth, those days are gone, and so are the dreams that accompanied them.

I distinctly remember the day Rob came home from the conference in Florida. The babies were still in diapers, and I was deliriously happy, greeting him at the door. He barely gave the girls a kiss, before he set his suitcase down and produced a brochure promising blazing sunsets and clouds of crimson pinks, against sparkling ocean waves. His voice quivered with possibility, with the thought of leaving the city I loved so much. "Honey, this place is still under construction, and we can basically choose any lot and any style house, built to our own specifications. We can play tennis, fish, walk the beaches practically from our own backyard. What do you say?"

"I say no, Rob."

I had never expressed an opinion in opposition to his, until that moment. His face tried to hide his anger at my insolence. "It will be for the good of the family. Boston is cold, and unforgiving, traffic, expenses, private schools. Florida is paradise at our fingertips. That's exactly what the realtor said. Look, honey. Look at the pamphlet, these are real photographs, this is what we could wake up to every day."

I knew I was going to lose this battle, but I did the best I could to protest. "But we love it here. It's where we first met, where we got married, where the girls were born. It's all they know."

He was angry. His tone changed when he said, "That's ridiculous and you know it. These kids aren't old enough to remember anything about this place. The realtor said they could swim in the pool twelve months a year, learn boating and surfing, and live in an up-and-coming neighborhood of physicians and other elite professionals."

I let the word sink in. "Elite." Is that what we are now? Elite? Did Rob's job make us better than anyone else? Did he think we were suddenly too good to live in a neighborhood where there were white and blue-collar workers all breaking bread together? I said nothing. What more was there to say?

Rob continued, his adrenalin running amuck. "Look, I know you love the change of seasons," he said, "and playing in the snow with the kids, but I don't have the luxury of staying home like you do. I work. I have to support this family, and when I come home, it would be nice to sit on a warm patio, relaxing with a cold drink and a view of the water."

The way Rob made it sound, raising our children was a sideline hobby of mine, rather than one of enormous responsibility for the lives of actual human beings. I put the girls to bed, and came downstairs, hoping we would be on equal footing, but knowing that this was the defining moment, when only one of us would be making the decisions, and it wouldn't be me. Looking back, I should have dug my feet in, should have demanded an equal say, but I felt powerless. I had two babies under the age of three, and no income. I gave in.

The moving van packed up our lives, and followed us to paradise. It was a two-day trip, with Rob oblivious to my tears, "You'll love it the minute you step foot in the house. Peggy, we made it! We're going to be wealthy, and important. Did you ever think this would happen?"

"No," I said, and I meant it. I never thought the promise of money and prestige would be so important to Rob. I thought he was better than that, deeper than that, but instead, my husband's superficiality stunned me, rendering me mute. This was a battle that could not be won, but it didn't stop there. He was obsessed with the notoriety he received, from former patients, from colleagues, from his friends. Rob had etched himself out a following of admiration because of his talent as a surgeon, and he was admired and sought after. Invitations to dinner parties filled the years, and he wore his successes like a badge of honor. Because of him, I felt on display. "You are so lucky to be married to a man like Rob," people would say often. "How fortunate you are." In a way, I lost my sense of self, smiling and agreeing about my perfect husband, our perfect children, and our perfect life. On our tenth anniversary, Rob surprised me with a five-carat diamond ring, "because that little thing you wear on your finger is embarrassing."

That little thing, as he referred to my engagement ring, was my most valuable possession. It signified our love for each other, our future together, our public display of emotion. I thanked him, but said I didn't want to trade my ring in for a new one, and Rob was outraged. "I thought you'd be grateful that I love you enough to buy you a gorgeous diamond. I could have purchased a boat for the money this ring cost, but instead, you kick me in the teeth." It was then that I realized this was not about me, anymore, this was about Rob and his image. This was about Rob making a statement that he could well-afford to put such an expensive ring on my finger for the world to see. He viewed my hesitation as a sign of my ingratitude and selfishness. I apologized, put it on my finger, and wore it.

The man whose life had humble beginnings, quickly became proficient in the game of greed. There was no end to how much money he could spend and how easily it flew through his hands, insisting on buying me five-thousand-dollar gowns to wear at charity balls, the irony of it passing right over his head. He purchased decorator showcased furniture, designer clothing for me and the girls, and the most expensive makeup and face creams "to keep your skin young and supple." Now, with my head pounding, and my eyes nearly swollen shut, I wondered how my supple skin would look with a bullet between my eyes. My memories distracted me from what was happening, in my own house, to my things, but it wasn't long before the tall man began pulling me by the hair, yanking my head off the floor a few inches high, then letting it drop down hard against the cold marble tile.

I didn't think the pain could become any worse, but I was wrong. "You stink," he screamed. "You stink of vomit and pee. You smell so bad that I can't even do you." He called to the short one, "Hey, you got a bad smeller. You want to do her before we kill her?"

So, I am going to die, I thought, images of my children, knowing they would never get over this loss, with their weeks, months and years spent wondering how awful their mother's final hours were, whether I prayed, or cried, or begged for my life. In a flash I saw their lives without me, and all their future plans altered forever. It was out of my hands, and I prayed for either survival, or a quick death. Then, just when I had surrendered my life to fate, I heard the short man say, "Let her live, she's just a no-good bitch. Why should we go down for murder?"

Again, I thought, he is trying to protect me.

The tall one's voice sounded annoyed. "We're not going down for nothing, because we're not going to get caught. What the hell's wrong with you? You getting soft on me?"

"Nah, not soft. Just smart. We got what we came for. Punch her lights out and let's get the hell out of here."

That was the last thing I remembered.

CHAPTER TEN

WHEN I CAME TO, DARKNESS flooded in the window. I was lying on the floor, cold, bloody, and hurt, but I was alive. There were sounds coming from downstairs, but instead of voices of the two robbers, there was music, women's voices, laughing. It took me a minute to orient myself, when I realized the television set was on in the living room downstairs. I couldn't make out the clock on the bathroom vanity through my half-closed eye, and the other swollen shut, but the moon streaming in the window indicated the hour was late. Rob was home.

I waited anxiously for him to come upstairs, but the minutes passed slowly, until finally I realized he wasn't coming, at least not yet. I smelled food, lasagna. He must be in the kitchen heating up a meal. The meal I cooked, the meal we were supposed to eat together. I heard the bell on the microwave go off. It wouldn't take him long to eat, and then he'd come to untie me, to help me. Finally, the voices on the television were muted, and I heard the sound of his feet plodding up the steps. He was in the bedroom. I heard him whisper, "Peggy, honey, are you awake?" No answer.

In the dark, he must have assumed I was asleep in bed. I heard him take his shoes off and throw them in the closet. Then his clothes would be next. When he turned on the light in the bathroom, he saw me and said, "Oh, my God, Peggy. Peggy, what happened?" I almost felt sorry for him. I'll bet the realtor's brochure didn't have a photograph of this in it. He quickly dialed the police, still shocked at the scene before him, then turned on the light in the bedroom, staring at the empty side of the bed where I usually slept. "Oh my God." His voice was frantic, high-pitched, his feet falling over clothing and jewelry, pillows and comforters strewn about the floor. He raced back into the bathroom, his eyes wildly rolling around in their sockets.

"Oh my God," he said again, standing over me, still, not processing the scene before him. By the horror that lined his face, I must have looked as bad as I imagined, maybe worse. "Peggy, honey, oh my God, what should I do? The police and ambulance are on their way."

He began ripping the tape from my head and mouth. "Stop!" I said as loud as I could, but my voice, dry and raspy, could barely rise above a whisper. "You're hurting me."

Rob, always level-headed in the operating room, was at a loss, his entire body shaking, tears streaming down his face. With my nose and mouth unbound, I started to cry, from deep inside, thankful I was alive, needing something to dull the pain, as well as to erase the images from my mind. "Rob, help me."

Rob was still holding the phone in his hand, the dispatcher yelling for him to answer her questions. "What can you tell me, sir?"

"It looks like a robbery, things everywhere, my wife is strapped to a chair, her head is covered with crusted blood, her nose and mouth were duct-taped and she's barely making sense. I think she might have been raped!"

Raped? I thought to myself. How did he come to that? My clothing covered my body, as far as I could tell, my panties were still intact. I don't recall being raped, or even being touched in a way that made me assume a rape might be imminent. I tried to think, but everything was cloudy, covered in a fog, words that floated above me, disconnected.

"I'll be right back, honey. I have to unlock the front door so they can come in."

"No!" I yelled softly, my voice attempting to return to its normal state. "The robbers might come back," but he was already down the stairs. By the time it took him to return, I continued to process the statement he made to the dispatcher. He sounded convinced that I had been raped. He made assumptions about the crime when he hadn't been here, when I hadn't given him any information.

When he returned, his first question was demanding. "Were you raped?"

"What?"

"Raped. Were you raped before they tied you up?"

They. Rob didn't say he, he said they. I don't think I told him there were two men. Did I? The sirens were ear-piercing, and I could barely think over my pounding headache. But Rob, insistent, stood over me, asked again, demanding an answer.

"I don't think so," I said.

"But if you had been raped you would know, right? Peggy, think hard."

In my confusion, I didn't put everything together, but I did know that a husband's first concern should have been that I was going to live, and his second thought should have been gratitude that he hadn't lost me. Instead, he was worried about a sordid, sexual act. Anger welled inside of me, more rage than I had ever known in my life, rage at a man who promised to love and protect me, who knew me intimately, a man who

I was bound to through marriage vows. Angry words poured from me, my voice, no longer strained, shouted, "If I had been raped, would that disgust you? The thought of another man having his way with me? Then what, Rob? For the rest of our marriage would I be a pretty little bedspread covering soiled sheets?"

"I just need to know," he whispered. "I have to know."

I couldn't believe his insensitivity. Screaming at him, I said, "How could you, Rob?"

These were the exact words that Detective Glen Harvey heard as he rushed up the steps and into the bathroom. Words that hung in the air, over Rob's head, words so powerful they would change the course of our lives. Detective Harvey jerked his head toward Rob, glaring, his hands on his chest, pushing him backwards. "Get out of my way," he said. He knelt down, his face close to mine, paper and pen in hand. "Take it easy, Miss. The ambulance is almost here." Two deputies arrived on his heels, cramming themselves into the bathroom with us. Detective Harvey scowled at Rob, then he said to one of them, nodding in Rob's direction, "Cuff him."

Rob's voice rose, "What? You can't handcuff me. Do you know who I am?" Turning toward him, crossing his arms in front of his chest, his posture a standoff, he said, "Don't be ridiculous. I'm her husband." He turned back to the detective, "You can't possibly believe that I had anything to do with this."

Detective Harvey said, "In my job, I can believe almost anything." Looking back at me, he said, "This wouldn't be too far of a stretch."

My anger quickly dissipated. Rob hadn't done anything to deserve this. All he did was attend a medical meeting and come home late. But now, it seemed Rob was being targeted as a suspect. I had to help him. Rob's face was ashen white, begging me to clear this mistake up. "Tell him, Peggy! Tell him I had nothing to do with this."

It was all so confusing, everyone's tone escalating, my head throbbing, my throat burning, and now this. Rob was yelling, ordering me to say something, while they roughly placed the handcuffs on his wrists. He wanted me to help him, but shouldn't Rob be helping me, I thought? As always, I did as Rob asked. I looked at the detective and said, "No, this is a mistake. Rob only just got home. There were two men wearing ski masks. They did this. I thought they were going to kill me!"

The detective's face remained blank, professional. "Ma'am," he said, his voice even toned. "There's no reason to protect him anymore. You're safe. If your husband had anything to do with this, now's the time to tell me."

Before I could answer, Rob interrupted, yelling, stumbling over his words, drowning out mine. "You're crazy. I would never hurt Peggy. I love her. Do you think I robbed myself? Look around, Detective. You don't have to be a genius to see that they didn't miss much."

Rob's insults did nothing to ingratiate him to the detective, who leaned over to the deputy, speaking to him in a low voice, his head nodding first to me, then to Rob. Whatever that was about, it was interrupted as three paramedics arrived, squeezing themselves and a backboard into the already crowded bathroom. The detective was relentless. "Ma'am, are you saying that your husband did not do this? Are you absolutely positive?"

In the confusion of the moment, I blurted out, "I don't know. I don't know. I don't know anything, anymore."

"Stop it!" Robbed screamed at me. "This is no time to play games."

The detective moved aside so the paramedics could tend to me, but not without one last attempt at getting to the truth. "So, you're saying your husband had nothing to do with this, is that right? He didn't hurt you?"

I stared at Rob, while they cut and removed the duct tape from my head. He couldn't have done this, could he, I wondered? His eyes were menacing, silently threatening. "Yes, that's what I'm saying."

Detective Harvey's thoughts moved quickly. This was a well-respected doctor, and a quick computer search showed no prior reports of domestic violence, nothing substantial to arrest him on, and yet, he had this feeling in his gut that the guy was guilty, very guilty. Still, he couldn't make false accusations, not with his superiors already breathing down his neck. He had to be certain. Giving Rob a stern look, he said, "I'm not finished with you, Prescott, not by a longshot. That's all for now, but don't plan on leaving town." Then he ordered his men to uncuff Rob, but before he turned to leave, he added, "And just for the record, I don't give a damn who you think you are."

The assessment by the medical crew was thorough, kind, and quick. They carefully extracted me from the chair and laid me on a backboard, securing my neck and head with a neck brace before gently lifting the board onto a nearby stretcher. An intravenous bag filled with a normal saline solution was inserted in my vein and was placed beside me on the stretcher. Leads were positioned on my chest that ran to a portable EKG machine. One of the paramedics said, "From the look of this rhythm strip, things are pretty good. You're very fortunate Mrs. Prescott. One more thing, do you have a history of heart disease or high blood pressure?"

Rob immediately inserted himself in front of the paramedic, grabbing the rhythm strip from his hands, checking it quickly, the tone of his voice irritated and loud. "Her heart looks fine. She doesn't have high blood pressure. I'm her husband and a physician. You can address her medical questions to me."

The paramedic backed away two inches and said in a respectful tone, "Her blood pressure is 170 over 110, and with the trauma to her skull, we need to be concerned about a brain bleed or potential stroke." He then followed with, "As you are aware, sir."

Rob frowned, "Her pressure is expectedly high considering what she's been through tonight. I'm not concerned."

I had just enough medical knowledge to worry, even if he wasn't. "I do have a splitting headache from the punch to my head. Could that one punch cause a brain bleed?"

"I doubt it, honey," Rob said. "They shouldn't have worried you with all this." Doubt and medical certainty are two separate issues. Shouldn't my concerned husband be more worried and less casual than he was. His lackadaisical attitude was noted by those in the room, to be addressed at a later date.

The paramedics kept the questions coming, one after another. "Where does it hurt? How is your vision? Are you able to see all right? How many fingers am I holding up? Are you able to hear? Pretty hard blow to the head, hematoma, on the back of her head. Must have hit the floor, head on. A lot of blood loss."

During the questioning, I lost sight of Rob, but once the room began to clear, and I was brought outside on the gurney, I located him across the street standing with Detective Harvey. When he saw me, he ran toward me, only to be stopped by a deputy. "Trying to pull a fast one, huh? Detective Harvey ordered us to keep you away from her."

"I need to be with my wife!" Rob shouted, flailing his arms, causing quite a scene.

Detective Harvey raced over to Rob, and in earshot of the television cameras that had just arrived, said, "Listen Prescott, if you think you're going to have a chance to coach your wife, you can think again. I'm going to stick to you like glue. Where you go, I go, understand?" Then he turned to the paramedics, "I'll follow behind and meet you at the emergency room. If and when she's released, she's not to go home, without my say-so, is that clear? We're going to have a long night ahead of us." Still within earshot of the reporters, the detective gave me one last thing to think about. "Mrs. Prescott, you need to decide whether you want to protect him or not. If he's responsible for this, he won't stop."

Rob chimed in from a few yards away, "You're nuts. I had nothing to do with this, and I resent your insinuations."

Detective Harvey pulled a cigar from his pocket and lit it. Then he walked past Rob, "We'll just have to see how this all plays out, won't we, Dr. Prescott? Maybe your wife will stick to her story, and maybe she won't. My money's on the latter."

Five hours later, and multiple tests and examinations in the emergency room, I was cleared to go home on bed rest. The pale gray sky was yellow-streaked, announcing a perfect sunrise. I was exhausted, but safe. "Where's Rob?" I asked the detective, who stood guard at my hospital room. "Where's my husband?"

"He's around. He's called the front desk every hour asking about your condition, but I delegated him to the parking lot until I can get a handle on what's going on. My guess is that he'll be following us to the station. I know you must be exhausted, and you've been through quite an ordeal, but I'm afraid I'm going to have to take you down to get your official statement, before I can let you go home. That is, if you want to go home. Or I can find you alternate lodging until we are sure that you're safe at home with or without your husband." I didn't bother to argue with him. He was right. I was too exhausted to fight. I just wanted to wake up from this nightmare, but with my head throbbing, my eye bandaged, and my legs weak from sedation, I knew this was no dream.

Detective Harvey escorted me through the side door of the hospital and into the parking lot. Rob was seated in his driver's seat with his eyes on the door. When Rob saw us, he walked quickly to the car, saying to Detective Harvey, "I'm going with her, I have a right to be with her, I have a right to be with my wife."

Detective Harvey sneered. "Back up, Prescott. You don't have any rights. This is an investigation, and I'll let you know when, and if, you get to take your wife home." With that he helped me into his unmarked patrol car, turned the ignition on and drove off with Rob tailing close behind.

When we pulled up to the Sheriff's Office, Rob parked his car quickly, hurrying over to assist me, leaning his body into the car to help me out. "You okay, honey? Don't worry, this will be over soon, and we can go home."

Detective Harvey relit his cigar, "We'll just have to see about that. Now if you'll excuse us." He guided me past Rob and down a hallway.

"I'm coming in with her," Rob insisted.

"You try and I'll have you arrested for tampering with a witness, now get the hell away from us. You're exhausting me, Prescott, and when I get tired, there's no telling what I'm capable of."

Rob stopped in his tracks, glaring at me, as if he thought I should take control of the situation, an expression that was caught by the narrowed, astute eyes of the detective. Once inside his office, he closed the door and turned to me, "I know you've been through a lot, Mrs. Prescott, but I need to see if you can give me a description of the two thugs you said broke into your house so we can get them off the street. Let's take them one at a time. What do you remember?"

I closed my eyes and the entire incident flashed before me, the shock of seeing two masked men coming toward me, the feeling that I was going to die. I began shaking. Then I said, "The short one, he was kinder. He helped me when I couldn't breathe. He loosened the duct tape around my nose."

Detective Harvey wrote copious notes, "Okay, the short one. How tall would you say he is?"

"I don't know. I'm not good with things like that."

"All right, try to think. Was he taller or shorter than say, your husband?"

"About the same height."

"To be clear, you're saying the assailant was approximately the same height as your husband?"

"Yes."

"And how tall is your husband, exactly?"

"Five feet nine."

"What else can you remember? How did he smell, talk, walk?"

"I can't remember anything else about him." But then, suddenly I did remember something else, and added, "I felt love for him."

The detective stopped writing and looked up. "I'm sorry, did you say that you loved him?"

"He was nice to me. He could have killed me, but he didn't." With that, I broke down crying, uncontrollably. "That man allowed me to live, to be a wife to Rob, and a mother to my children." My head was throbbing, and my thoughts were jumbled. "Please, Detective, I need to go to sleep."

"Just a few more questions. The other man. How tall would you say he was?"

"I don't know, maybe six inches taller. Kind of husky, but not fat."

"Anything special about him? The way he walked, the way he spoke? Either of them have an accent?"

"Not that I remember."

"Hair color?"

"They had ski hoods on. I couldn't tell."

"Eyes?"

"I don't know, dark, maybe."

"Has your husband ever hurt you, before? Sorry, strike the word, before."

"Rob? No, of course not."

"Has he ever cheated on you, that you know of? Is there another woman, perhaps?"

"Never! He wouldn't do that. And besides, what would that have to do with it?"

"Well, if he had someone else, and you're in the way, he'd need to dispose of you."

"He would never. We love each other."

"And you, Mrs. Prescott? Are you having an affair, someone who might have caused him to lose his temper and teach you a lesson?"

"Absolutely not. I wouldn't think of doing such a thing."

Detective Harvey was losing ground, and decided to call it a night. "This isn't much to go on. I know you've been through the mill tonight, Mrs. Prescott, but if we don't find these guys, it's likely they'll be back."

"Back? Back for me?" A chill ran through my entire body at the thought of it.

"Hard to say."

"Oh, my God, oh my God!"

"Do you want to go home with your husband tonight? I can arrange for you to stay in a safe space and figure out the rest later, after you've had some sleep."

"I want to go home with Rob."

When the detective was certain I was not going to be of any more help to him, he allowed Rob to bring me home. On the ride home, Rob's entire demeanor seemed agitated, and I didn't know if it was because of me or the detective. When we opened the front door, I refused to go back upstairs. "Let's sleep in the guest room downstairs," he said, "It's been a long night, and I'm exhausted."

Again, my anger resurfaced. He was exhausted? He needed rest? What about me? Once settled in the guest room, Rob didn't close his eyes for a minute, and instead of letting me sleep he continued to obsess about Detective Harvey. "He's nothing but a power-hungry weasel with a badge, hoping to carve a notch in his belt by trying to pin this on me. He probably bullied kids on the playground when he was young, liked the power, got into trouble with the authorities, and then figured out he could become a cop and bully people legally. The very idea that I could have arranged this, and to what end?" Then he glanced at me, my swollen face, the bandages, the bruises, and said, "You could have been a little more helpful, Peggy. Your hesitation when you answered his questions made the detective think I had something to do with this. Remind me to never rely on you to get me out of a mess."

This wasn't the Rob I fell in love with, or the man with whom I shared a bed for twenty-five years. This man was insensitive and self-serving, and at that moment, I felt nothing but contempt for him.

Detective Harvey never left the station that night. He needed a high-profile case and by some miracle, this one dropped right into his lap. He knew what the outcome would be, either solve this case or get demoted.

He couldn't get his mind right with Dr. Prescott. The doctor had a superior air about him that didn't sit well, probably some snotty rich kid who had everything growing up, and by the looks of it, certainly has everything he could ever want now. He imagined Mrs. Prescott was, and would be again, a beautiful woman once her face healed, and with his good looks, it wasn't a stretch that he landed someone like her. But things change. Maybe it was time for his luck to run out.

Harvey knew Rob Prescott's type. Pushing people around, backed by money, just like the kids on the playground that taunted Harvey growing up, mocking his clothing and shoes, his mother working nights to make ends meet, the kids calling his mother a cheap whore. He would put Prescott behind bars, not only for his wife, but for Harvey's deceased mother, who did the best she could to raise him. The morning was already well under way. He had nowhere to be, and no one to go home to, just an empty house and remnants of a failing marriage. He unbuckled his belt, took off his shoes, put his feet on his desk, and leaned back in his chair, going over his notes, making new ones, notes that were both factual and fabricated, detailed and exaggerated. He wasn't going to let that guy go back to his cushy life. Harvey survived on coffee and donuts until long into that night, and the next, with sleep coming in sporadic intervals, overshadowed by the desperate, personal need to solve this case.

CHAPTER ELEVEN

DETECTIVE HARVEY WAS BECOMING AN unannounced, frequent visitor at our home, especially in the evening hours when he assumed Rob would be home from the hospital. His visits coincided with Rob's schedule, always appearing within moments of Rob's arrival for dinner, regardless of the time. Weeknights were consumed with worry, and weekends were delegated to unanswered phone calls and doorbells, attempting to discourage the daily harassment of further questions, always for Rob, and always out of earshot. Infrequently, Detective Harvey would call my phone, asking intrusive questions for which I believed he already had answers, convincing me that Rob was not an innocent party. I began to have reservations as to Rob's innocence, imagining that not only might Rob have had something to do with the home invasion, but that he might have been the mastermind behind the sinister plot. Initially, the idea that my husband would be involved in any way seemed preposterous, but after spending long nights tossing and turning, I began to question things in my own mind, imagining Rob as a criminal hiding behind the guise of the medical profession, rather than a loving husband. I grappled with his motives. In the middle of the night, with outside shadows bouncing off the curtains, my thoughts ran wild. Suddenly, he was not the person who promised to love, cherish and protect me, but rather, a stranger who no longer wanted me around. He could have had me killed, but that would leave him raising our two daughters, a predicament that would burden his daily schedule of being the heroic physician. He could have wanted me to be more dependent upon him, but sometimes I feared he already envisioned me as the noose around his neck. Maybe it was for the insurance money. The jewelry, most of which I never wore, was insured for an outrageous premium. I pictured him dressed like the shorter robber, and at times, even his eyes seemed to mirror the eyes behind the mask. Then in the dark of night, I never thought he would do the job himself, but it would be easy to hire someone, a former patient, maybe an ex-cop he treated in the emergency room.

Again, the motive never made sense. I mean, we did have our disagreements, but what married couple didn't? It was preposterous to think that two people from different backgrounds, with separate dreams, could come together, blended as one agreeable unit all of the time. Most of our arguments lacked substance, nitpicking about nonessential matters because we were exhausted from the day, stressed from events, or just from life in general. Most of our fights were provoked by me, wanting more attention, needing more affection, trying to script every word that came out of his mouth to suit my needs. I needed to talk to someone, but it couldn't be Rob. Not this time. I invited Erica over for lunch, thinking she was a reasonable woman, who would point me back in the right direction. But the conversation didn't go as I thought it would.

She wasn't inside my house more than a minute before she asked, "Do you think that Rob had something to do with the robbery, the home invasion?" Her voice slow and steady, her tone low and measured, she looked at me directly in my eyes, forcing myself to come to terms with her concerns.

"Do you?" I asked.

"Look," she said. "I don't want to start anything here, but when we first met, Rob seemed like the perfect husband. He was attentive, to the point of being ridiculous. I can't tell you how many fights I had with my husband, after we left the two of you. I wanted what you both had. But in the last year or so, he seemed preoccupied. He didn't look at you in the same way, and when you recounted a story, he continually interrupted you with corrections. It was as if you had become an annoyance."

I was stunned. Speechless. She thought Rob had something to do with this. So did the detective. It was too much to process. I trembled, my tears spilling over. "I can't even think about this," I said.

"I shouldn't have said anything, but you're my best friend. I want you to be safe."

"Safe from my own husband?"

"Peggy," she said softly, "You've been under an enormous amount of stress. I don't want to add to it. I'm sorry I brought this up. I've been watching too many mystery movies. I'm nuts. Rob would never hurt you. He loves you." Her words landed easily on my heart, and I needed to believe them. Regardless, the afternoon dragged on, with strained small talk, until she finally left.

I brushed my fears aside. Rob was my entire life, the man, up until this point, I trusted wholeheartedly. Besides, I had become a mere shadow of the strong woman I once was, and I was desperately afraid. It had been weeks past the incident, and I was keeping Rob a prisoner in the house. I didn't know if the enemy was inside, or outside, my husband or a stranger, but the one thing I couldn't bear was to be alone.

I hadn't seen my mother in her nursing home since a few weeks before the home invasion, but now, even though her mind was a hostage to dementia, I needed to talk to her, or at least be in her presence. I couldn't confide in the children, since Rob had convinced me that it would only upset them. They were told nothing of the incident, and at the time I thought Rob was right to exclude them from worry, but now, I am not so sure. My mom was always the one who could get me through anything, and I needed her right now.

Rob was in the living room reading the paper, without a care in the world. "Rob, I was hoping you might take me to see my mom today."

Rob was delighted. Rob had become my personal servant, and he heeded all of my requests. I felt somewhat guilty monopolizing his time, but unconsciously, I believe I might be punishing him for what happened to me. I begged him to take a personal leave from work, and he acquiesced. Suddenly, he had become the chief cook, the grocery shopper, the house-keeper, and now, my chauffeur. "Sure, honey. I think that's a great idea. The nurses at the home will be so excited that you're feeling well enough to visit her."

Anger. There it was again, instant and uncontrollable. "The nurses? What do they know? Why should they care? Don't tell me you've told them about what happened to me."

"Peggy, it was in all the papers, everyone knows what happened. It's not a secret. Everyone wishes you well. They're all pulling for you to feel better."

"I am well. I'm just going through some stuff. Why don't you try being punched in the face, thinking you were going to die, while your husband was downstairs eating homemade lasagna."

"I'm just saying, it will do you good to get out of the house. I'll even go in with you, if you're afraid."

"I'm not afraid. Afraid of what? My own mother? Stop treating me like I'm a child. I don't appreciate it."

Rob couldn't win, and I couldn't stop. "Okay, honey, it's just that you haven't let me out of your sight, except for the few errands I run, and even then, you watch the clock." He seemed genuinely concerned and hurt.

"I'm sorry, Rob. I don't mean to snap at you, I'm just not myself. I'm going to get ready. Do you think we can leave in an hour or so?"

He smiled and gave me a kiss on the cheek. "Absolutely, whatever you say."

When he dropped me off at the front door of the nursing home, it was worse than I expected. I was barraged by well-wishers, from the receptionist to the janitor. "Good to see you, Peggy. God, it must have been awful. How did you ever survive what you've been through? Rob said you're a mess. We've all been praying for you. I know your mother misses you. Now you go on back to see her. You remember the way, don't you dear, or should I walk with you?"

"Of course, I know the way," I snapped. "I don't have brain damage."

"Of course, you don't, sweetie. I'll call back to the nurse's station to let them know you're coming."

The facility, Keys Restorative Nursing Care and Rehabilitation, consisted of five separate wings, connected by long hallways with waxed floors and bulletin boards that boasted inspirational sayings, as if thinking positively could change the outcome of the poor souls who would find this facility their final home. My mother's wing was divided from the main hall by locked doors, protecting wanderers from setting themselves free one last time. Her hallway was dedicated to patients with dementia, still having enough wherewithal to beg anyone in the vicinity to unlock the doors and free them. I had half a mind to do that very thing.

My mother was not categorized as a wanderer. She was content to stay put, lying in bed, or sitting up in a wheelchair, resigned to eat institutional, tasteless food, or watch movies that made no sense to any of the patients, unable to process cognitively.

When it was apparent that my mother could no longer live without assistance with her meals, medications, or hygiene, I knew what had to be done. Rob was supposed to come with me as we both took her to admissions, but I should have known better. At the last minute, Rob had an emergency at the hospital, or so he said, and it was on my shoulders to break my mother's heart. He said he was sorry, but this was not his mother. This was not his heart that he was breaking.

Word of my visit spread quickly, conjuring up staff from all five hallways into my direction, greeting me with hugs, and more well-wishes. I wanted to make them leave me alone, to mind their business, to stop touching me, but most of all, I wanted to scream at Rob, who had breached my confidence and spoke to them without my consent. I'll deal with him later, I thought. Just because I am a doctor's wife, doesn't mean that my life should be on public display.

Mom smelled of ivory soap and baby powder, tucked in for the night, even though it was barely six-thirty. Her face looked peaceful, and sweet, her skin thin and porcelain-like, her cheeks pale pink. She was beautiful, the subject of a Renaissance painter, the mist of an early morning rain, the sweet smell of honeysuckle in the spring. If only she remembered me, if only her illness hadn't ravaged her brain, stealing her dignity, locking her memories away in a box with no key, a woman who was disguised as my mother, but who had become a stranger, even to herself.

I bent down and kissed her forehead softly. In less than an hour I shared everything, the break in, the terror, the detective's theory, and my concerns. Tears streamed down my face, as I willed her to hear me, to open her eyes and give me a sign that I would be alright. "I know you love Rob, Mom," I said, "but I don't know what he's capable of, and I feel alone." It felt good to bare my soul, ashamed that I portrayed my husband in such bad light, especially if he didn't deserve it, but I knew it would go no further. My secret would be safe with her.

It had been more than an hour before I thought about Rob, alone in the parking lot, no doubt making his calls to the hospital, checking his watch, wishing he was anywhere but here. I didn't care. That's the least he can do for me, I thought. Just as I was about to leave, the night nurse peeked in. "I'm sorry, Mrs. Prescott. I hope I didn't startle you. I just wanted to leave her sleeping pill on the nightstand for your mother."

"Leave her sleeping pill? But she's already fast asleep."

"I know, most patients are down for the night before seven, and almost without exception, none of them need this pill, but you know how doctors are." She looked at me and remembered who I was married to. "Sorry, it's nothing personal against your husband, but doctors just hate being called in the middle of the night if a patient can't sleep."

"Yes, I suppose so. But, if she doesn't wake up, then you try again tomorrow night?"

"Something like that, but not with the same pill. That's against the rules. There are strict regulations about that. Every unused pill must be disposed of."

"Thrown away? Now that seems like a waste of money."

"It sure is, but rules are rules. Lots of paperwork, too. That is, if we report that it wasn't administered."

"What do you mean?"

"Can you keep a secret?"

"Of course. As good as all of you have been to me and my family, I'll keep whatever secret you want me to keep."

"Most of us just go ahead and dump them in the toilet, then we record that we gave them out to the patients before they went to sleep. Honestly, since they don't need them, and it eliminates our paperwork, no one's the wiser. You won't tell, will you?"

"No," I laughed, "Your secret is safe with me." Another secret, waiting to be revealed.

CHAPTER TWELVE

I AM EXHAUSTED. SLEEP HAS become almost nonexistent, and when I do sleep, I am jolted awake by the sight, sounds and smells of the two thugs who could have killed me. I hear the words of the detective, ominous and prophetic. It's likely they will return to finish the job. They might come back to kill me, worried that I will identify them. Then, when I tire of worrying about the robbers, I look over at my sleeping husband and wonder if I should be more afraid of him. Still, I need Rob. He is really all I have, but when my hand reaches out to touch him, he recoils slightly, but noticeably, and I sense that he wants to back away. When we speak, we say nothing of value, two people united in a never-ending nightmare. If I ask him, Rob will tell me that he loves me, but I no longer believe anything he says. It seems to me that Rob has turned into quite a liar.

It was the middle of the night, when Rob's phone rang. He automatically answered it, thinking it was the hospital. "Hello?" he said softly, so as not to wake me. He wouldn't have anyway. I was not underneath the pile of blankets on my side of the bed, but instead, I had curled up in the bedroom chair across the room, wide awake.

"Hello?" Rob said into the phone again. "Dr. Prescott here."

The voice on the other end said, "Hey, buddy. What's going on?"

Rob looked at the clock. Three in the morning. "Arnie, is that you? For God's sake, man, it's the middle of the night." Rob again looked over to the messy pile of blankets on my side of the bed. There was no movement.

Arnie sounded drunk. I could hear him through the phone. "Shit, man! You're like a thousand years older now than you were the last time I talked to you, and you were no spring chicken then. Three in the morning? I'd say the party's just getting started."

"What party? Arnie, where are you?"

"Figure of speech. Get it together, man. Wake up! I'm trying to tell you something. First of all, I'm still in Baltimore, still slaving at Parkland General, popping pimples and checking grey heads for skin cancer. How's by you?"

"You're calling to catch up at this hour? Are you drunk?"

"Maybe a little buzzed."

"Go to sleep. We can talk tomorrow."

"No can do. Having a little problem with the wife. She locked me out of the house, so I got a room in a local hotel. I guess I'm being served divorce papers, or so she says."

Rob rubbed his eyes and muttered sarcastically, "So, what else is new?"

Rob checked my blankets for movement. There was none. Then he whispered, "Things aren't so good over here, Arnie. There was an incident, a home invasion, Peggy was beaten. She's okay physically, but..." Rob lowered his voice even further. "She's terrified to be alone. I haven't been able to go to work for months. I can barely leave the house to get groceries. I can't be gone more than ten minutes before she starts calling to check in. I feel like I'm going nuts. I can barely use the bathroom alone."

Arnie's voice reeked of boredom. "Gee, Rob, that's a damn shame. She'll be okay, she's a trooper. In fact, I hope she's better by the fourteenth, because I'm planning a visit to good, old, sunny Florida. A dermatology convention, weekend thing, no biggie. Thought I could hit you up for a room and some of Peggy's famous home cooking."

Rob's voice rose slightly, "Are you deaf? I just told you Peggy's not herself. She's not up to company. Things are really bad here. She's barely able to speak with our girls without finding an excuse to get off the phone. I'm worried about her."

"Yeah, whatever, man. Shit happens. Listen to what happened to me last week. I'm driving on the Beltway, minding my own business, when I get sideswiped by some old guy in a car, so I pull over, thinking he'll be all frazzled, but instead, he pulls a gun on me, aims it right through my window. Now, I'm thinking I'm a dead man. I close my eyes waiting for the bullet to hit, but instead, he gets back in his car and takes off, just like that. I'm shitting through my boxers, but you know what, Rob? I didn't die. I'm still here. So, I buy a new pair, keep driving and go to work."

"What's your point, Arnie?"

"My point is, we all got our troubles, but right now I need to firm up a room for the fourteenth and fifteenth."

I can tell by the sound of Rob's voice that he's about to give in, just like he always does when Arnie manipulates him. "I don't know Arnie, like I said, things are bad. I have a detective breathing down my neck, thinking I'm involved somehow. As if I would ever hurt my wife. I hate to say no, but Peggy's not up for company."

"Well, hey, that's great. I'm hardly what you would consider company. I've stayed with you what, at least eight or ten times over the years? Maybe double that. So, do I qualify as company? No, I don't think so. How's about I call you when I land, or better yet, just ring your doorbell after I rent a car. Since you're handcuffed to Peggy and she's tied to the house, I guess you'll be home. See you in a few weeks, buddy, and thanks a lot."

"So, when is it?"

"Saturday, the fourteenth, leaving the night of the fifteenth."

"All right, I guess so. I'll call you if Peggy says no. Are you bringing your wife? Peggy will want to know the details."

"l just told you, man. No more wife. Unless I get another one between now and then. But the wife and me, nope, splitsville. She tossed most of my stuff on the front lawn. I couldn't blame her though, I put her through cheating hell. Anyway, I'm back in the saddle, so to speak. I figure you and I can hit the town when I get in, and see what might float my way."

"I'll speak with Peggy and let you know. Then I'll give you a call."

"No need. Peggy's not going to say no. She's too polite to make an old friend stay at a hotel. See you in a few weeks. Get ready for a good time, Rob. Give my best to Peggy. In fact, give her a big kiss for me. French kiss, lots of tongue." Arnie laughs out loud.

"You're nothing but a pig, Arnie."

"Ain't that the truth!"

CHAPTER THIRTEEN

I CRAWLED IN BED SOMETIME around five a.m. Rob was still sleeping soundly. My anger continued to escalate. Arnie could make Rob do anything. For the first time in my married life, I tried to imagine what my life would be like without my husband. It felt empty, but good. Then panic ensued, the fear of being alone, and I was right back to needing him. He had taken a leave of absence to be with me, and that was more than most husbands would have done. But when all this was behind us, and I felt more myself, stronger and independent, I was determined to take a stand against Rob's friendship with Arnie. Finally, just as the sun was coming up, I fell asleep.

I was awakened by the sound of a ringing phone, and water running in the shower. Absentmindedly, I picked up the phone, assuming it was the hospital for Rob, or possibly a follow-up phone call from Arnie Stimmel. Perhaps my plan to push him out of our lives would come sooner than I thought.

"Hello?" There was no response. "Arnie, is that you?"

It wasn't Arnie. The voice on the other end was female, and one with an attitude. "Hello? Mrs. Prescott?"

"Yes?"

"Good morning, hope I'm not calling too early."

"Who is this?"

"This is Valerie at Dr. Sherman's office. I'm confirming your appointment tonight at six."

"My six o'clock appointment? No, I'm afraid you must have the wrong number. I don't have an appointment tonight and I'm not familiar with anyone by the name of Dr. Sherman."

By now Valerie was overtly irritated that she had spent more than the allotted few seconds on the phone. She spoke slowly, as if there was a language problem, or I had difficulty with comprehension. "You certainly do have an appointment with Dr. Sherman."

"Who is Dr. Sherman?"

Valerie sighed, "Dr. Sherman is a psychiatrist. You were lucky to get an appointment so quickly."

This had to be a mistake. "I'm sorry, Valerie, but I never made any appointment with a psychiatrist."

Valerie had completely lost her patience with me, speaking loudly and quickly. "You are correct, you didn't make an appointment with Dr. Sherman, your husband did. I spoke with him myself." Her tone was sarcastic and caustic. "Your husband is Dr. Prescott, is he not?"

"Yes, my husband is Dr. Prescott, but he would never make an appointment for me with a psychiatrist."

"Well, Mrs. Prescott, I can assure you he did. If you don't believe me, why don't you ask him?"

"He's in the shower right now."

"Then I suggest when he gets out of the shower, you speak with him, but in any event, Mrs. Prescott, I have other calls to confirm. We'll see you tonight at six."

"But I don't need a psychiatrist!"

Valerie decided it was time to become downright rude. "Apparently your husband begs to differ. So, will you be keeping your appointment for tonight, or not?"

"I most definitely will not. Absolutely not!"

I jumped out of bed and threw on a robe, my anger reaching a crescendo. As soon as the bathroom door opened, I got within inches of Rob's face. "Robert Prescott, who do you think you are, making an appointment for me behind my back, and with a psychiatrist? You are not the boss of me, and I resent that apparently you think that I am unable to make my own decisions. The only crazy person here is you!"

Rob put his arms around me, drops of water dripping from his hair, his posture stooped and his face downtrodden. "Peggy, you need help. We both do. We can't go on like this."

"Don't you tell me what I need, Rob. I went through hell and back, and the least you could do is give me time to get my bearings, without calling in the troops. What I need is some understanding, and a husband who doesn't treat me like I'm some sort of imbecile who can't navigate her own life. If, and when, I think I need to have my head examined, I'll be sure to let you know."

The silence of two people whose lives were quickly unraveling was deafening, neither of us knowing what to do next, both of us holding on by a fragment of what was left of our relationship. Rob spoke first. "I was going to tell you, later, at breakfast. I know this has been a nightmare for you, but it's been months that I haven't been at work, and elective operations are piling up. Some have been given to other surgeons but most people, with this type of surgery, are waiting for me."

"Of course, they are," I said. "You are so important. Everything is all about you, all of the time, isn't it? I don't know how you do it, managing both family and your celebrity status."

"That's not fair, Peggy. Nothing is more important to me than you and the girls, but I'm at my wit's end. You won't leave the house, you barely get dressed, you aren't eating properly, and I don't know how long it's been since either of us has had a good night's sleep. And as for sex..." He knew enough to stop short of finishing that sentence. "Peggy, enough time has passed, and we clearly aren't able to manage this by ourselves."

"I notice how you keep seeing yourself as the victim, as if this happened to both of us, but it didn't, Rob! It happened to me!"

Rob said calmly, "It may have happened to you, but it's affecting both of us. You've pushed your friends away, you barely have an interest in your daughters' phone calls, and you hardly allow me out of the house. As for sleep, take a look at me. I've aged ten years."

"Look at you? Is that what you want me to do, take a good look at you? Okay, I'm looking. You look fine, Rob. I'm sorry you think that my nightmare has aged you ten years and I'm sorry I'm such a burden to you, but how did you decide to insert yourself into this equation? Were you home when they ransacked the house? Did they tie you up and punch you in the face? Or how about this, Rob, did you have to swallow your own vomit while you waited to die? So, if you lost a little sleep, well, that's too damn bad. You took a vow when we got married. You promised for better or worse. Well, this is what they mean when they say worse, Rob, this is worse."

Looking back, my ranting was one of the lowest points in my life. I had no control over my emotions, and I was intentionally hurting the man I loved, the man that stood by me, who dedicated his life to me, who would have done anything to make me happy. Rob said nothing, but the tears welling up in his eyes said it all. Unbelievably, there was no mistaking that he still loved me. I don't know if I could withstand being screamed at and berated the way he has. For the first time since the incident, I actually took a deep breath and did take a good look at Rob. The color in his cheeks paled against the dark circles underneath his eyes, his voice was flat and hopeless, his face was lined with worry. He looked like a broken man. Perhaps he was right. Maybe I did need professional help.

I put my head on his chest and began sobbing. "I'm sorry, honey. I'm so sorry. I don't know what's wrong with me."

"There's nothing wrong with you that talking with a professional won't help. Couldn't you please give Dr. Sherman a chance? If you don't connect with him after the first session, I won't ask you to go back to him. We can try someone else."

"It's not that I'm being obstinate, but I'm afraid, Rob. I don't want to talk about this, I can't relive it, I can't start over with the entire incident, to recount everything."

Rob chose his words carefully. "You won't have to start at the beginning. You'll only have to fill in the blanks. He basically knows the story. I filled him in on everything."

His words stung. Once again, he betrayed what little privacy I had left. My voice, struggling to remain calm, was laced with anger. "You disclosed my personal information to a complete stranger? How dare you! Who gave you permission to spread around my private, personal life to gossip? First it was the nurses at my mother's facility, now this. Is there no stopping you?"

"First of all, honey, the information I gave him is not street gossip, it's factual information that he will need to assess you."

"Assess me? Like I'm a lab rat?"

"That's not fair, Peggy. I'm only trying to help. Dr. Sherman needs to know why you're coming to see him. Besides, he's a colleague of mine, we work in the same hospital, and you and I desperately need his help. Look at us, honey. We never used to argue. We've had the perfect marriage, and now, I don't know who you are anymore, and I don't know where I belong in your life. Things have to change one way or the other."

"Or what, Rob? Are you planning to leave me? Walk out the door and never look back? If that's what you want, be my guest. Don't let me stop you!" I had become so unhinged, that at that moment, I would have gladly thrown him out.

Rob put his arms around me, holding me close. "Peggy, stop this. I will never love another woman, and I'm certainly never going to leave you. I just want to help us end this nightmare. Please, honey. Do this one thing for me."

I felt myself weakening, succumbing to the misery in his voice and the anguish on his face.

"It's too late, I already cancelled the appointment."

"Then I'll call and remake it. Tonight, just this one time, please. For me."

Rob wasn't wrong. I was completely unstable. Often, I'd find myself pulling out the police report, looking at the bare spots on my head where my hair had been yanked out, to prove to myself that the home invasion really happened. Rob was only trying to help me and the least I could do was to try to help myself. "Okay, Rob, I'll go, but I'm scared. Promise you'll stay with me."

"Of course, honey, I promise. I'll never leave your side. We'll do this together. I'll repeat the story for you, if that will help. His office is about a mile from your mother's nursing home. Maybe afterward you can stop in to see her for a few minutes?"

"They get her to bed by six-thirty, but still, I could sit with her. I know she doesn't know I'm there, but I do, and I have to live with myself."

Rob, always eager to throw his weight around, said, "I'll call over there and tell the nurses to keep her up a little longer."

"No, Rob. I don't want you to call anyone about anything, anymore. I just want to slip in and out without any questions. If she's asleep, I'll give her a kiss and leave. It's not like she'd know me anyway."

"Whatever you want, honey. I'm so proud of you for keeping this appointment with Dr. Sherman. Don't worry, you have nothing to be concerned about. I'm with you every step of the way."

Rob dialed Dr. Sherman's number, facing me, mouthing the words, thank you. After the appointment was reset for six that night, Rob came over and gave me a kiss on my cheek. "He's a good man who knows what he's doing. He is going to change our lives. I just know it."

CHAPTER FOURTEEN

DETECTIVE GLEN HARVEY HAD ALREADY spent hundreds of hours on the Prescott case, each time coming up short. His instincts told him there was a connection between the home invasion and Rob Prescott, but he just couldn't connect them with any substantial evidence. Rob's statements held up temporarily, but by Harvey's calculations, from the time the good doctor left the house until he returned, sometime just before midnight, he had more than enough time to ransack his own dwelling with an accomplice, or, more likely, hire two thugs to do his dirty work. If that was the case, all he had to do was find a snitch who could turn these guys in, and once they talked, they'd implicate Rob Prescott. Still, the obstacles piled up, and at the top of the list was Mrs. Prescott's refusal to cooperate. He could see her point. If her husband went to jail, the money wouldn't be rolling in, and even if he got out in a few years, his reputation would be shattered. Or she might feel that she needed to protect him to ensure that her life wouldn't be in danger. If she believed he might be involved, she would do everything in her power not to provoke him. It made sense. He was going over his notes for anything he might have missed, when his supervisor called. "Harvey," he said, "What have you got for me on this damn Prescott fiasco? The paper hasn't been kind to us, and neither has the local news. I need answers, and I need them right now."

Detective Harvey, nervously tapping his coffee cup, stammered, "I'm working on it, boss."

"No, you're not. Not anymore. If you don't have a handle on this, I'm going to put Salinger on it. Someone wanted to hurt that lady and I need to know who that somebody is. As of right now, you're off the case."

"But..."

"That's my final word on the subject. And by the way, isn't your review coming up soon?"

"In a few months. Listen, Captain, I need this job. I'm working hard on it. I'm just waiting for something to break."

"Yeah, well you're waiting on the city's dime."

"I'm not ready to be off the case. I've got a couple of hunches. I just need a little more time."

"No one's stopping you from working on your own time, but not on mine. It's a good thing your uncle, rest his soul, isn't alive to see this. You're a big disappointment to him and the rest of the team."

"Yes sir, I understand."

"I don't think you do. Go ahead and pout if you want, but how do you think I feel? The city can't keep putting money into this case. The thugs are gone, they beat the system, it happens. Plus, I have taxpayer dollars breathing down my neck from the mayor to the commissioners, everybody screaming for answers. The press reports negative shit about us every day, like we're supposed to be miracle workers."

"I can't prove it right now, but it's the husband, I know it. It wouldn't be the first time a homeowner stages his own robbery and hires thugs to beat up his wife. Laying the groundwork, that's what he's doing. Laying the groundwork for what comes next."

The captain was quickly losing his patience, "And just what would that be, Harvey?"

"It might take Prescott a few months, maybe even a few years, but he's preparing for the kill. His home was already targeted, and the wife beaten, so it wouldn't be a stretch to find her wiped out in her garage one day, making it appear that the thugs came to finish the job. It happens. Prescott's not an idiot. He knows the odds. People will jump to the obvious conclusion. Then, he's home free."

"Could be, but we're going for sure things, and the sure thing in this case is that you're officially off it. I'm making a statement to the press today, and I'm assigning you back to light duty. We have files a foot high that have been neglected since you've put all your time into this case."

"I can't shut it down."

"Then do what you have to do on your own time. As of now, you're back on snagging underage sales of cigarettes and liquor. Hit the convenience stores one by one. I've got a seventeen-year-old girl that looks twenty-five with a body that won't quit. I'm giving her a red Porsche convertible and hoping to hell she knows how to drive a stick. If asked, her story will be that she left her wallet with her ID at home. The sale is made, you come behind her and make the arrest. It's a no brainer."

"And, how is that not entrapment?"

"You know, Harvey, you're like a broken record. You ask the same question every time, and here's the same answer. It's just not."

Detective Harvey hung up the phone but not before saying, "Okay, Captain, but mark my words. I'm taking Prescott down. Robert Prescott takes me for a fool, but from here on out, I'm one step ahead of him. If he thinks his wife's file is closed, he's got another thought coming." When he hung up, he put a call into the hospital and had Dr. Prescott paged. He called back immediately.

"This is Dr. Prescott. Can I help you?"

"Yes, I believe you can. Detective Harvey here. I'd like to meet."

"I'm afraid that's not going to be possible. I just made a quick stop at the hospital to pick up my mail, but I have to be back home right away."

"Oh, well, that's a shame, but I'm afraid I'm going to have to insist."

"Sorry, no can do."

"l said, we need to meet. If you aren't going to come to me, I'll be happy to come to you."

"No, not at the hospital."

"Okay, why don't I meet you at home?"

"No, that will just upset Peggy. Can't this be done over the phone?"

"No, it most certainly cannot."

"All right, I'll meet you at the station in twenty minutes, but I have a very important appointment at six tonight, so it has to be quick."

"As long as it takes, Doctor."

"What could you possibly have to talk to me about that we haven't already gone over? Wait, let me save you the trouble. Here's the rundown of my day and night on the date of the home invasion, same as it was last time. I went to work that morning, just like any other. Not much traffic. I arrived ten minutes late because I had breakfast with my lovely wife. I had four surgeries scheduled, all cosmetic, plus one add-on, a drunk whose face plowed through his windshield. That surgery took approximately forty-five minutes, so all in all, I was done around five. Then, I went to dinner with some drug reps, but I got bored, and the food was lousy, so I called a buddy. He was busy, so I bought two pastries from the neighborhood bakery, and did some window shopping while I ate them. They were stale, and didn't do much for my hunger, so when I got home, I microwaved some lasagna. The house was dark when I arrived, so I thought Peggy had gone to bed. I called up to her, but there was no answer. I watched a little television while I ate. When I went upstairs, after midnight, I took off my clothes. The bedroom had stuff tossed all over the floor and Peggy wasn't in bed. I went into the bathroom, and that's when I found Peggy. There was blood everywhere and she was moaning. I called the police and waited for them to arrive. That's it."

Detective Harvey took notes and smiled, "You really have that story down, don't you, Dr. Prescott. Very rehearsed, very proficient. It's exactly like you told it to me last week."

"Yes, funny how that works, how the story never changes. That's because it's exactly what happened."

"A smart, creative man like you, I'd have thought you might change it up a bit, maybe add a detail or two."

"Why would I do that? I don't have to worry about my "story" as you call it, because it's the truth. Maybe you should devote more of your time looking for the real criminals."

"And where should I start looking, Dr. Prescott?"

"How the hell should I know? I don't ask you where I should make my incisions when I'm operating. I do my job, you do yours. Are we done, or do you still want me at the station?"

"You're in quite a hurry, aren't you?"

"I told you, I have to get home to my wife. Yes, as a matter of fact I am in a hurry. I'm up to my eyeballs in owing people favors, and right now my wife is waiting."

"You sound frustrated, Doc. Guess you didn't think your little plan through. Guess you thought this would be an open and shut case. Well, you can think again."

"I don't appreciate your inferences and attempts at intimidation. They won't work. Now, if you're done playing Detective 101, it's been a pleasure talking with you, but I believe class is dismissed. I'm going to hang up the phone."

"No one is stopping you, Prescott, at least not for now, but keep your calendar open. I believe we'll be speaking again very soon." Detective Harvey ended the call and poured himself his seventh cup of coffee for the day. He had nothing, no leads, no similar crimes, no copycat robberies. He searched through his notes again. Still nothing. Regardless, he refused to give up. He smelled murder on the horizon, and as far as he was concerned, he had just spoken to the potential murderer. There was only one problem. Mrs. Prescott was still very much alive.

CHAPTER FIFTEEN

Dr. Sherman's building was located just south of the busy downtown district, on the third floor of a red brick building in what is commonly known as Physician's Row. The building had already been emptied of people at this late hour, allowing the elevator to arrive with no interruption. Rob's hand was cool underneath my sweaty palm, and I felt panic rising within. His smile was meant to reassure me, but it didn't help.

If the exterior of the building had been modernized, Dr. Sherman's office had not, as far as I could tell, when we opened the waiting room door. Inside, were mismatched pieces of worn furniture, in various shades of brown. Outdated magazines were tossed carelessly about, with the labels torn from the front cover. The secretary's desk was located underneath the window facing the street, neatly organized, and vacant. Rob chose a low, pillowed couch that sunk underneath the weight of him, and although he patted an adjacent cushion for me to sit, I preferred to stand. Actually, I preferred not to be there at all, and unscripted, random excuses raced through my brain, all of them closing in, pushing me toward the exit.

Before I was able to make my escape, the interior office door opened, and an older man appeared, who, under any other circumstance, would have caused me to laugh out loud. As if in costume, he portrayed the exact image of Sigmund Freud himself. From the look of him, he was in his early seventies, wiry, with gray, thinning hair and a mustache in need of trimming. He had a full beard of matching color, and unlike his hair, it was thick and coiffed. The color of his clothing blended in with his waiting room décor, ranging from tan to dark brown, complete with a wool vest and corduroy pants. His brown shoes were old and scuffed and looked as if they were in need of polishing. His eyes, steel blue and piercing, cast the only noticeable color.

Dr. Sherman was short in stature, and slightly stooped, with an air of arrogance that lengthened him. He looked directly at me, his eyes boring a hole, while he spoke to Rob sitting a few yards to my left. "So," he said to Rob, "this must be your wife." Rob stood up to shake hands, but Dr. Sherman did not extend his. "And, this must be my patient," he said.

Rob put his hand in his pocket, nervously, "Yes, this is my wife, Peggy," he said, coming closer to me. "'Peggy, I am pleased to introduce you to Dr. Sherman."

I had an urgent need to use the bathroom, but I dared not ask. There were no niceties exchanged, and he quickly dismissed Rob, saying, "Sorry the waiting room is a bit of a mess. My secretary left early today. Help yourself to coffee, although it's probably stale by now. Your wife and I shall return in precisely fifty minutes." He beckoned me with his fingers, "Come, please, we must begin." With that he began the few steps toward his inner office.

I didn't follow him. Rob protectively came to my side, putting his arm around my shoulders. "I'd like to come in with my wife, if that's alright with you."

Dr. Sherman turned, gave a slight grin, then wiped it clean. "I'm afraid that won't be possible, Dr. Prescott. This session is for Mrs.

Prescott, alone." Then, with a slight bend of the waist, he added, formally, "My apologies."

I looked at Rob, assuming he would straighten this out, but he just stood there, in obeyance. I blurted out, "My husband needs to be here with me. He promised. I can't do this without him."

Dr. Sherman eyed me sharply, and said, without hesitation, "Well, now, that is a bit of a shame. We've only just met and already we are faced with a dilemma. It seems you have put your husband in a rather precarious position, Mrs. Prescott." He turned his head to Rob, then back to me. "Inadvertently, I'm sure, but nonetheless, now he'll be forced to choose."

Rob shuffled his weight nervously from one foot to the other. His face wore a confused expression, as if he had no idea where his loyalties lie, and to the contrary, Dr. Sherman appeared to be in complete control. "Yes, Mrs. Prescott, you see, he will either have to choose you, his wife, with whom he owes his allegiance, or choose me, the psychiatrist, with whom he has placed great trust. However, since this is my office, I believe, as a member of the medical profession, that he understands the protocol of respecting the therapeutic setting."

Rob continued to shuffle his weight, a habit he often did in awkward situations. Dr. Sherman seemed quite pleased with Rob's inability to defend me. Finally, Rob gave in. "You go ahead, honey. You'll be okay. I'll be waiting right here for you."

"No," I said, fighting back tears. "That wasn't the deal. I can't do it."

"Peggy, please."

Not wanting to cause trouble, or make a scene, I tentatively followed Dr. Sherman into his inner sanctum. He waited until he had closed the door, before he turned to me, his voice low, and threatening, "Therapy is a private endeavor, Mrs. Prescott. Alone, you and I will have the opportunity to become acquainted without having a third person, an intruder, in the room. I'm quite sure you'll agree."

"I just don't think I can talk to you without Rob here," I said, my voice shaking back tears. "He can explain everything."

"You are asking your husband to explain an event that happened not to him, but to you? As well, you expect him to either go against your wishes or go against mine. I suggest he go against yours, so we can get started. After all, time is money, is it not?" His voice was mocking, and insinuating, as if I had no value for money. As usual, when facing confrontation, I reluctantly agreed, but I also decided at that moment, that once the session was over, I would never return.

Dr. Sherman pointed to several leather office chairs in varying shades of brown. "Please select whichever chair pleases you." Then, he sat down behind a large, walnut desk, settling into a well-worn, dark brown leather high-back swivel chair.

I stood motionless, unable to decide which chair to choose. "Which one do you suggest, Dr. Sherman?"

My indecision apparently immediately triggered a negative transference, which I only now understand was a painful reminder of his former wife, whose only decision in their entire forty-year marriage was to have an affair with his colleague, thereby making him the laughingstock of the hospital. He wanted to punish her, and if truth be told, he had nightly images of slitting her throat, but instead, he stood helplessly watching, as most of their furniture and belongings were loaded into a moving van and relocated to a house owned by her lover.

It was apparent that Dr. Sherman immediately disliked me. "Mrs. Prescott, I am neither your husband nor your caretaker. It matters not to me where you sit, or if you sit at all. Let me be clear. Quite simply stated, I am not about to make your decisions for you. This is not brain surgery. Your decision is not life or death. Choose an area where you either sit, or stand, but commit to something, I implore you." At that, he shifted his unlit pipe from one side of his mouth to the other, and began studying his fingernails, while he waited.

I chose an armchair, the seat of which was so deep, that my feet dangled inches above the floor. His eyes shifted to my shoes and back to my eyes, amused, and looking at his watch, said, "Now, let us begin. Would you prefer that I call you Mrs. Prescott or Peggy?"

For fear of delivering the wrong answer, I offered none. "I don't care," I said.

"I see," Dr. Sherman said, picking up his pen and paper, jotting down the beginning of what was later to become copious notes. Then he looked up at me and said, "I don't care is a standard statement made by people who have no idea of the actual meaning of the phrase. I will interpret it for you. It means, literally, that you have no reason to care, that it is that unimportant to you, and therefore, I am unimportant to you. As well, it leads me to believe that you are not taking me or my profession seriously."

"No, Dr. Sherman, that's not it at all. I just have a habit of saying I don't care. It doesn't mean anything."

"My dear Mrs. Prescott, all words matter. Furthermore, it seems by your actions that you are not at all interested in taking an active part in your therapy, or perhaps there is something about me that makes you such a misguided and miserable creature."

His remark landed in the pit of my stomach, and I became physically ill with indigestion. "I don't understand. I'm doing the best that I can." Tears began running down my cheeks, but to Dr. Sherman, this was similar to his former wife's ploys to manipulate him. He had a negative transference of his own and he wasn't going to fall for it, the way he once did with her.

He stood up, attempting in vain to brush away the deep creases from his trousers, and pushed his chair away from his desk saying, "Well, you've managed to successfully break the record of the shortest amount of time any patient has spent in this office under the guise of wanting to get well. Perhaps you might be better suited with someone else, and I'll be more than happy to refer you." He pulled open his desk drawer and pulled out what appeared to be a leatherbound phone book.

I was well aware that if I left my appointment after only a few minutes, Rob would be full of questions, none of which I wanted to answer. I regret making the promise to him that I would go to therapy, but now I felt compelled to uphold that promise. "Wait, Dr. Sherman," I said. "I'm sorry. I'll try to do better." Dr. Sherman smiled, pleased with his assessment of my weak character and his victorious control.

Dr. Sherman was a man of few words, but his mind worked on multiple levels. Just as I suspected, he mused to himself, she crumbles easily, and will be an easy target for intimidation. If she thought she was going to be in control in my office, the way my former wife controlled my entire married life, she has another thought coming. No woman will ever make a fool out of me again. He turned and said with feigned patience, "All right, I suppose I shall have to take you at your word, but know this, Mrs. Prescott, if you really want to get well, you are going to have to follow my directions, without question, and put in more effort than you have ever exerted in your entire life. You will have to trust me in a way you have trusted no other person before, and that includes your husband. Is that clear?"

Gripping the armrest of my chair, I shook my head in the affirmative. This is going to be very entertaining, Dr. Sherman thought, as he explained, "I am a blank slate, someone with whom you can share your secrets, someone with whom you will not withhold any information, no matter how miniscule, either by lie or omission. It is only then, when your feelings and emotions are laid bare, when every secret you have ever repressed is revealed, only then will you be well, and therapy can be concluded. Do I make myself clear?"

I said nothing, afraid that whatever I said would be misconstrued. Dr. Sherman walked toward my chair, towering over me, "Do we have an agreement, or not?"

I stared at his feet, small, by men's standards, and narrow. Captivated by his size and the possible ramifications of his other body parts, I forced myself to focus, but a nervous laugh barely hid itself inside my throat. "Yes, I want to trust you, but it's not easy. I'm afraid to talk about the, you know, the problem."

"You mean the home invasion, don't you, Mrs. Prescott? Surely, we're mature enough to use our words. Rest assured, the therapy that goes on in this room is patient-centered. That means, you will be in charge of the discussion topics. You will decide what you do or do not want to talk about, and to what degree you want to delve into details, but know this, eventually, everything, and I do mean everything, will have to be discussed."

"So, what you're saying is that I don't have to talk about the, you know, right now?" I paused until I was able to say the words, "home invasion?"

"That is precisely what I just said. Tell me, do you have any difficulty with your hearing, Mrs. Prescott?"

"No."

"Good, then I suppose you will be one of those resistant patients that I have to coddle along, but I should tell you, I am not a man who enjoys coddling."

Again, I found myself apologizing, "Yes, I'm sorry."

"As I was saying, if you do not wish to reveal a particular topic right away, that's fine, but the topics you do or do not bring up for discussion will determine the length of time that your treatment will take. To summarize, if you are cooperative, we will be able to allay your anxieties within a few months, however, if you are not compliant, it may take years. That, of course, is strictly up to you. Do I make myself clear?" Dr. Sherman waited patiently for a response that wasn't forthcoming. He became increasingly impatient, and his impatience always enhanced his sadistic streak.

Finally, when I could no longer stand the silence, I said, "I shouldn't think this will take too long. My childhood was great, my family is great, my husband is the love of my life, my mother is in a nursing home, but not suffering, and my only problem, really, is what happened recently."

"I see. Suppose you let me be the judge of that." Dr. Sherman adjusted his pipe and reclined his chair back slightly. "Tell me, Mrs. Prescott, are you always this controlling?"

I felt like he was purposefully making it difficult for me, but I was also trapped. "I don't think of myself as controlling. No one has ever accused me of that before. In fact, I prefer it when Rob makes the decisions, because he knows me so well, so whatever decision he makes is with me in mind."

Dr. Sherman continued taking notes, without looking up. "Your comments are extremely defensive, Mrs. Prescott. Why is that?"

"I'm not trying to be defensive but you're accusing me of something that I don't believe I am. I'm easy going, I hate confrontation, and I go out of my way to avoid arguments."

"And yet, here you are, arguing with me. You might want to give this some thought, my dear, and perhaps come to the conclusion that you don't know yourself as well as you think. You've wasted precious time tonight, debating much of everything I've said."

"Maybe you're right," I said in defeat, tears streaming down my face. "Maybe I don't know who I am anymore."

Dr. Sherman was on a sadistic streak, and rather liked the one-sided banter. He was alone in his own thoughts. She is pretty, I'll give her that. Then he quickly reminded himself that every pretty woman he has ever known has been unfaithful and unscrupulous, beginning with his former wife. He learned from her that women who appear sweet and demure, are only passive because they are planning their strategy, their manipulation, calculating their moves to get to the goal. He wished in vain that he could punish them all, but at least he could take on as many as possible, one at a time. "We have a few minutes left, Mrs. Prescott. What would you like to talk about?"

I had nothing to say. I wanted to get out of the confines of the room, but just when I thought our session was coming to a close, it suddenly felt as if he had only just begun. "Is there a clock somewhere?" I asked.

"Do you have somewhere you must be?" he asked.

"No, I'm just worried that it's getting late, and I should let you go."

"You should let me go. That's quite humorous. Controlling," he said, and wrote that down on his note paper along with all the other comments I made during the hour. "A classic example, for which I thank you."

"I'm just trying to be honest with you."

"And yet, so far, you've told me nothing."

I took a deep breath and began speaking more freely, hoping if I exchanged my concerns, the hour would end that much sooner. "I feel worried and anxious all of the time. I can't sleep, and when I do fall asleep, I have nightmares. I'm worried that I'll never feel safe again, that I can never be alone, that I can't be the wife and mother I used to be."

"Ah, finally, a bit of information. Congratulations on your decision to speak about something important. How do you get along during the day when your husband is at work?"

"Rob hasn't been back to work since the...you know."

"No, I'm afraid I don't know."

"Since the incident."

"Which incident?"

I knew what he wanted me to say, and I also knew he was relentless in forcing me to say it. "Since the home invasion."

"Oh, and why is that?"

"I'm terrified those men will come back, and if not them, then maybe somebody else. I can't watch television or listen to the news without imagining that I will be the next target of whatever I hear, that anything can happen to me at any time."

"So, you have kept your husband hostage, by not allowing him to go to work?"

"Rob doesn't need to work," I explained. "Financially, we're fine. We have both girls' colleges paid off, we don't have a mortgage on the house, and we have money in the bank. Lots of money. Those years when we could barely make ends meet, thankfully, are long behind us. We could live to be one hundred and still not go through the money. My husband has made very wise investments."

Dr. Sherman was suddenly very attentive, always interested in the topic of money, and specifically, how much of it he could swindle from her pocket into his. If what she said was accurate, he could string her therapy along for years. Still, he thought, he couldn't rush it. He'd have to pace himself, give her enough praise to keep her coming back, but insert enough psychological maneuvers to keep her off balance. One thing was for certain, he could not allow his professional ego to get in the way. This was not a woman he had any desire to cure.

I continued. "I don't know why Rob can't be happy staying home with me. He's worked hard for the past twenty-five years, and now I think he should retire."

Dr. Sherman had stopped listening to my dribble ten minutes earlier. He was still formulating his plan, thinking, if he played this right, perhaps he could make a bundle of money and leave this thankless profession behind. Then who'd have the last laugh? Certainly not his former wife. "Mrs. Prescott, your husband may not need to work to pay your bills like the rest of us, but I don't believe that money has ever been his motivation. Your husband's reputation is spotless. He is held in high esteem for his work ethic, as well as his compassionate nature. I do not want to seem maudlin, but I believe that he works out of his sheer desire to benefit mankind, and yet, selfishly, you want to rob him of that pleasure."

My tears started falling again at his backhanded accusation of my selfishness, and I wondered if he was correct in his assessment. After all, Dr. Sherman seemed to recognize my character faults, traits that I wasn't aware of, until he began laying them out. First, defensive, then controlling, now selfish.

"Yes, I know you're right. He never cared about the money, whether we had it or not. Even when we couldn't pay our own bills, half the time he didn't charge those patients who couldn't afford to pay, and rarely collected from those who could. He'd just let them slide. He's such a wonderful man, I don't deserve him."

My emotional outburst might have tugged at Dr. Sherman's heartstrings years ago, back when he was an idealist, a man who hadn't uncovered what he now believed was the evilness that resided in the hearts of all women, but since his divorce, tears falling from the eyes of any female patient didn't upset him in the least. He looked at me and felt absolutely nothing. "Dr. Sherman, tell me the truth. Do you think you can help me? I'm so afraid of losing Rob."

His radar was immediately on high alert. Losing Rob, now that was an angle he hadn't thought of. He should thank her for the tip. "I'm particularly interested in your concern about "losing" your husband. What makes you say such a thing? We should be discussing how one day you might be well enough to stop sabotaging your husband's career."

"I'm not doing that! I've always put my husband and children first."

Dr. Sherman had filled up several pages in his notebook. "Ah, finally, your anger emerges. Exactly what is it that you want, Mrs. Prescott?"

"I want to be well, and I don't want to spend years in therapy to get there."

"I see, in other words, if I understand correctly, you are not here because you want to be, but rather because you feel that you might lose your husband if you don't agree to therapy, is that right?"

"Yes. I don't know what he might do. I don't trust him."

"Please, go on."

"I think he might want to leave me. I think he made me come here so that you could tell him that you believe I'm crazy, and then he'd have a legitimate reason to divorce me. No one would expect him to live out his years with a wife who is crazy."

"So, it is your belief that your husband has decided to pay me to be in collusion with him, the goal being that he will then be granted a divorce?"

Dr. Sherman was twisting my words, until I had no idea what I meant at all. Finally, all I could think of to say was, "Trickery! Yes, I think it's possible that you and Rob schemed to get me here through deception and trickery."

Dr. Sherman attempted to hide his laughter with his handkerchief covering his mouth, pretending to stifle a cough. When he had composed himself properly, he laid his pen down and took a good look at Peggy Prescott. He disliked her more by the minute, and similar to his former wife, he depicted Mrs. Prescott as a whining, sniveling, self-centered bitch of a woman whose husband didn't see the trap coming.

Dr. Sherman certainly had no thoughts of marriage when his wife trounced into his life years ago, using her sexuality as a tool to win over his heart. It wasn't long after their wedding vows that her good nature shifted toward being a chronic complainer, pointing out his shortcomings at every turn. When he finally rebelled against his wife's antics, well into the marriage, she became defiant, and that defiance propelled her into the next phase of torturous mental castration. He felt the sweat beading just under his collar, every time he thought about it. He took a long drink of water, carefully placing his glass back onto the monogramed coaster before saying calmly, "And just how did we do that, Mrs. Prescott? The very idea that you believe you are the victim of trickery must be very troubling for you. I know I certainly wouldn't want anyone to deceive me, and I very much appreciate that you shouldn't want that either."

I was sobbing now, unable to control my emotions at all. "I don't want to be deceived!" But even as I said the words, I knew they weren't true. I was simply afraid, afraid of the process of making me remember. "I'm so confused," I said, and I was. It seemed that Dr. Sherman was actually siding with me, rather than defending himself. Trying to explain, I said, "For years Rob's best friend, Arnie Stimmel, tricked me. I dislike him intensely, so much so, that Rob and I used to have arguments about him, but Rob always defended him. Their friendship goes all the way back to medical school, and we haven't gotten rid of him since."

"Hmm. Arnie Stimmel, huh? What specifically causes you to dislike him?"

"I feel like he always has something up his sleeve, something that's not on the up and up, something that always involves me."

"Involves you? My, how everything in your world seems to revolve around you. Doesn't your husband deserve to have a best friend, or do you think he should only devote himself to you?"

"Arnie just gives me the creeps, that's all."

"How often do you see him?"

"Not that often. He lives in Baltimore, but he does spend weekends at least once or twice a year."

"Once or twice a year, hmm." Dr. Sherman was feverishly writing. "Do you now have the benefit of seeing, firsthand, your controlling nature? Did it ever occur to you that perhaps Rob needs an outlet that doesn't involve you, or maybe even needs an outlet away from you?"

"Away from me? No, I don't think he wants to get away from me."

"Every man needs to get away from his wife at some point, and that is a fact." Dr. Sherman watched coldly as my tears smeared my eye makeup, causing it to run down my face in long black streaks. He considered handing me a box of tissues, but quickly thought better of it. He wasn't going to rescue me, and he wasn't going to fall for what he considered to be a helpless act. It was amazing how much I reminded him of his former wife, he thought. She was forever starting fights, only to crumble into tears, so that she could be rescued. He didn't know much about women back then, with a controlling older mother and no female siblings, but after clawing his way through puberty and the excruciating rejection of women throughout his dating years, he learned from the best. Cheryl, his former wife, was a master of manipulation, cunning, calculating, stealing his power from right under his nose. Those days are over, he thought.

"I'm just so disappointed," I said.

"It seems to me, that it is I who should be disappointed. You have come to therapy under false pretenses. You don't want therapy at all. You simply are securing your marriage by giving your husband the false impression that you are going to apply yourself in here, when quite clearly, you are not. That position is self-serving and, quite frankly, deceitful in and of itself."

I had to get away from the emotional pain he was inflicting. I had to make this better. I had to make him like me. "Dr. Sherman, I want to get better, I really do. I don't know why I said all those things. I will trust you."

Dr. Sherman, himself, was well-versed in the art of manipulation, and quite masterful at spinning patient's words around until they found themselves in a mental quandary, more often than not. This was going to be no challenge at all, he thought sadly, the challenge becoming less fun, acknowledging her frailty and vulnerability, but he was not about to let her win. "Yet, you, yourself, said that you believed I was involved in some sort of trickery with your husband, against you. Those were your words. That doesn't sound much like trust to me."

I wiped my eyes, took some deep breaths and stammered my reply. "I'm sorry. I didn't mean what I said. The truth is, that I didn't want to come here at first, but now I do. I'll do whatever you say, Dr. Sherman."

Really, you bitch, thought Dr. Sherman. Well, let's put that to the test right now. Rob had confided in him on the telephone when he booked the appointment, that Peggy was a purist, one of those women who didn't believe in medication, no smoking, no drinking, no chemicals of any kind. He was amused to see just how far he would be able to push her. "All right, I'll keep you on as a patient, but this will be your one and only chance, let's call it a sort of probationary period. Believe me, I have plenty of people who would love to fill your slot in my appointment book, and yet, I have allotted this time to you, unappreciated, I might add. Your thinking is confused, and your communication skills lack clarity, logic and reasoning, therefore, for now, I will be forced to do your thinking for you. As this extremely trying session comes to an end, I am going to suggest to you that what you need, first and foremost, is sleep. It is impossible to work with anyone who is as confused and sleep-deprived as you."

Dr. Sherman opened his center desk drawer and took out his prescription pad. "I am ordering sleeping pills for you, one every night before bed, beginning tonight. I am going to start you with a moderate dose, and as you improve, I will decrease the dosage. Is that agreeable to you?" He almost couldn't contain his laughter, watching me squirm, knowing that I vehemently wanted to object, but didn't dare. Not if I was afraid of being thrown out of therapy and losing my marriage. Fear. A very powerful emotion.

"All right, Dr. Sherman, I'll get it filled tomorrow."

"No, you'll get it filled tonight. There is a 24-hour pharmacy just two blocks from here. Any objections?"

"No," I said complicitly, eager to be free of this interrogation.

With the session concluded, Dr. Sherman opened the door to the waiting room, only to find Rob nervously pacing. Codependent, he thought, without respect. Rob raced over to Peggy, throwing his arms around her, noticing her disheveled makeup. "Are you okay?" he asked with concern.

Dr. Sherman could barely tolerate his childlike whimpering. "I can assure you she will be fine, as long as she follows my instructions." Handing the script to Rob, he said, "Please have this filled immediately at the pharmacy around the corner, and see that your wife takes one before bed, beginning tonight. It's crucial for her to get some much-needed rest if any therapy is to be successful."

Rob nodded, anxious for more information. "Yes, certainly, Dr. Sherman, but can you tell me, did the session go well?"

"As well as can be expected with someone who is torn between what she wants and what she needs. She will soon learn she cannot serve two masters."

Rob shook Dr. Sherman's hand, pumping it up and down with exuberance. "I can't thank you enough! In one session you have gotten her to agree to take medication. Now that's progress!"

"Your exuberance is somewhat premature, Dr. Prescott. Why don't we re-evaluate her progress, or lack thereof, in a few months. Only then will you be able to decide on the amount of gratitude you wish to bestow upon me."

CHAPTER SIXTEEN

IT TOOK LESS THAN FIVE minutes to make it to the drive-through window at the pharmacy, but in that short amount of time, I had already lodged several concerns to my husband, attempting to make them less of resistance, and more of an intellectual conversation, to no avail. "I know you don't want to take sleeping pills, honey," he said, as if he was talking to a three-year-old, "but it is in your best interest. Dr. Sherman has been doing this for a long time and has a stellar reputation for turning people's lives around." When I attempted another rebuttal, he spoke in medical terms, quoting statistics, telling me about the neuro-functioning of my brain, of posttraumatic stress disorder, of the inability to pretend I can cure myself by time. He won, of course, as he always did.

After we paid for the pills, I opened the package, gazing at the poison Dr. Sherman prescribed, toxins, as far as I was concerned, that would interfere with my daily functioning, and disturb the natural order of things. They were pink, round, and small, their color obviously trying to lure people into believing they were not the enemy. I was not going to be fooled. Rob parked in front of the nursing home, offering to walk me inside, but I declined. It was almost eight o'clock. Mom was sound asleep, her sleeping pills next to her bed on the bedside table. I noticed they were the same color and shape as mine. Her nurse stopped in to say hello. "Are you going to stay awhile, or is this just a quick peek in to see how your mom's doing?"

"I thought I'd stay for a little bit, just to watch her sleep. She seems so peaceful. Is she doing okay during the day?"

"Oh, yes, she's doing just fine. She eats her meals like she hasn't seen food in years, but that's because our staff just loves to feed her. She can't eat by herself, of course, but you don't have a thing to worry about. She gets lots of love here. I wish all our residents were as sweet as your mother."

"Yes, she is sweet. I used to think I inherited some of her good nature, but now, I'm not so sure."

"You'll get back to normal, Peggy. After the ordeal you've been through, no one could blame you if you're a little on edge." Then, she thought better of what she said, trying to correct any offense she might have caused. "What I mean is, we all think you're just as wonderful as you've always been."

"Thank you. I'm doing the best I can, but some days, it's not easy."

"I know, honey. Don't you fret. Everything will be just fine. By the way, my shift ends in less than an hour. Before you go, would you mind tossing her sleeping pill into the toilet. I know you've already been well versed in how we dispose of pills we don't use. Now, flush it good or we'll all be looking for another job."

"Of course, you don't have to worry about me," and she didn't. I did as I said, and threw away the pill, without a second thought. "Well, Mom," I said, "It's official. I've now become you."

By the time we arrived home, it was nearly ten o'clock. I lingered as much as I could, taking off my makeup, washing my face, massaging body butter onto my arms and legs, but regardless of how late the hour was becoming, Rob lay in bed reading. "Peggy," he finally said. "I know what you're doing. You're waiting for me to go to sleep, so you don't have to take your sleeping pill. I hate to interfere in your plans, honey, but I'll stay awake all night if I have to."

"Rob," I said, my voice shaking, "Please let me try one more night without the medication. I promise I'll take it tomorrow night if I don't fall asleep by myself tonight. Just give me one more chance."

Rob was sweet, but firm. "Peggy, we made a deal. We agreed that you would see Dr. Sherman and comply with his treatment."

"I never agreed to medication. You know how I feel about ingesting any chemicals. This goes against everything I stand for."

Rob was exhausted, and almost too tired to argue, but his pleas sounded pathetic. "Please, Peggy, I'm begging you to listen to Dr. Sherman. He knows what's best. If I were in your shoes, I'd give up the fight and just do what he says. The way I feel right now, if I slept for a year, I still wouldn't be rested."

There it was again, Rob's insistence on inserting himself as a victim, as if his health and wellbeing depended on my cooperation

"You're going back to see Dr. Sherman tomorrow night. He will want to know how you did. Surely, you're not going to lie to him."

"Maybe I could say that you and I discussed it, and it was your idea to hold off for another night or two, and see what happens. He respects your opinion. He might feel that you two are a team."

"Peggy, I'm tired. This is not a game. You promised you would listen to him, and I'm not going to cover for you. I want you to swallow this pill, and, for the love of God, please, just close your eyes and go to sleep."

"I don't want to take medicine, Rob. He bullied me into it, somehow," I shrieked. "He's making me do things against my will, and you're in on it!"

"Did you say that I'm "in on it" with Dr. Sherman? What exactly am I being accused of now?"

"Everything, making me go to Dr. Sherman, telling everyone at the nursing home my private information, letting them think I'm insane."

"I can't believe we're going through this again. I did what I thought was best for you. The nursing home staff heard all about the home invasion on the news. For crying out loud, you'd have thought I concocted the story myself, just to embarrass you. I hate to tell you, Peggy, but the entire town knows what's happened. Do you think I want to have to face people? No, I don't. It's somewhat embarrassing to be the center of attention, but I deal with it."

"Now, there's a first. You not wanting to be the center of attention. That's all you've ever been since we moved to this place. This feeds your ego. The celebrity doctor having to care for his insane wife. I'll bet everyone's having quite the gossip-fest, sitting around judging me."

"That's not true," Rob answered. "If anything, people are judging me. After all, I'm the one who left the door unlocked." And just like that, there it was, the missing puzzle piece, the admission of his carelessness. "I was going to lock it when I went back for my phone, but then the hospital called, and I got wrapped up in a patient's case, and I completely forgot about you."

"You forgot about me? That's special, Rob. Really great."

"I don't mean that I didn't think of you, I meant, well, I don't know what I meant. It was a complicated case, they were giving me the details, I got distracted, and I just pulled out of the driveway."

"You left me alone in this big house with the door unlocked? You might as well have left the door wide open, in fact, you should have just put a sign on the front lawn inviting the muggers inside."

"I'm so sorry. You have no idea how this has been haunting me. I mean it could have happened anyway, they might have had to jimmy the lock or break a window, but then you might have heard them, run for cover, and called the police before they had time to get to you." Rob was shaking, his voice trembling. My anger was spewed in every direction, at Dr. Sherman for belittling me, and at Rob for spilling my personal story to everyone.

It wasn't fair. I knew that. It wasn't anyone's fault. I needed to get a grip. "I'm sorry, Rob. I'm not angry at you." To highlight my apology, I climbed in bed next to him, and I swallowed the pill. Rob lay next to me, my head on his chest, the sound of his heart beating rhythmically in my ear. My eyes were getting heavy, and no matter how much I tried, I was unable to stay awake.

CHAPTER SEVENTEEN

DREAMS HAVE BEEN THE SUBJECT of study since the beginning of time, covert images to keep away the truth, people and places from everyday life coded in symbols, emotions repressed. The interpretation of dreams is speculative, at best, but every so often, when the content is blatant, when even the dreamer themself understands the meaning clearly, the signifi cance of the unconscious can no longer be denied.

Within minutes after drifting off, I found myself in a town, unfamil iar, but not unsettling. It was winter. Snow dusted the sidewalks, sparkling underneath streetlights, landing cold upon my eyelashes. I wanted to be a part of this place, where it felt like cares were a million miles away. I was dressed in a warm parka and fur-lined boots, that reminded me of a pair leftover from my teenage years, boots that I continued to wear in Boston, finally discarding them after the move to Florida. But suddenly, here I was, a stranger in a small town, not knowing if I lived here, or I was just visiting. I tried to remember, but all I could concentrate on was the crispness of the cold air filled with possibilities. The sound of laughter brought my awareness to children, running past me, and couples walking arm in arm, making their way to the town center, where a Christmas tree stood, surrounded by carolers, as well as town folk carrying bags filled with festively wrapped packages. Suddenly, there was a burst of color, and what seemed like the entire town applauding the lighting of the tree. I stood in awe, as the crowd began to disperse. A woman walked up to me and said, "We've been expecting you." Others looking my way, smiled and nodded in agreement, as if they knew something that I didn't.

Then, just like that, the scene before me vanished, and I found myself walking on a cobblestone path. Shop lights fell behind me, and cabins appeared, lights pouring from their windows as night arrived. Neighbors waved to me from their porches, and although I didn't know them, I had the distinct feeling that they knew me. Soon, the cobblestones gave way to a worn-out dirt road ahead. The snow was falling heavily now, and ice formed at my feet. Slipping, and cautious, I felt as if I would never arrive at a yet unknown destination, and urgency hastened my steps.

The town was far away now, and soon I became lost in thickets of evergreen trees, hiding whatever destination lurked behind them. It was dark. My mind urged me to turn back, but my heart propelled me forward, to what, I didn't know. The dog spotted me first, his tail wagging with excitement, his owner, still unaware of my impending presence. The light from the overhead porch lamp that sculpted his posture, the crook of his neck, and the curls of his hair cascading over his coat collar, stirred familiar feelings in me that had been hidden so long ago. This was a man that I recognized, that I had traveled so far to meet, and yet, I couldn't quite place him. His dog raced down the porch steps, leaping through the snow, to get to me. The man called after him, but the moment he saw me, his eyes never left mine, beckoning me toward him. Suddenly, I fell into his arms, against his chest, my body fitting easily into his, the way it always did. His long hair brushed my face, the smell of him so familiar it caused me to weep. He cupped my face with his hand, calloused, strong, purposeful. His tears matched my own, as he leaned down to kiss me. Then, without notice, the image of him faded, and sunlight streamed through my bedroom window, forcing my eyes open.

Rob looked at me, pleased. "You were in such a deep sleep, but it's been nine hours. I knew Dr. Sherman was going to make everything all right. Can you imagine that one sleeping pill has completely changed our lives in just one night?"

I closed my eyes to block Rob's image, but when I opened them again, he was still there, smiling, grateful. He shouldn't have been. He was right about one thing, our lives were about to change, but neither of us could have imagined what was to come.

CHAPTER EIGHTEEN

ERICA WAS THRILLED WHEN I invited her to come over to the house for lunch. I hadn't seen or talked to her for a while, and I wanted to confide in her about my dream. She sat at the kitchen table, and it felt just like old times. We made small talk, she told me what was going on with the tennis group, and how they missed me, and then I told her about going to my session with Dr. Sherman. "It was crazy. I mean you should have seen him. It was like he walked right out of a movie set, in full costume, pretending to be Sigmund Freud, reincarnated."

Erica laughed, pouring another glass of iced tea, and said, "Was it weird, talking about personal things, stuff from your past, or you know, what happened to you?"

"He called it patient-centered therapy, meaning, I only have to talk about what I want to talk about. Rob really wanted me to go. Personally, I think the guy is a quack, and really rude. Plus, he hates me."

"I doubt he hates you. Nobody could hate you. Especially after what you've been through, and it didn't ruin your good looks, that's for sure.

You've never looked better, actually. What happened since I've been gone? You and Rob making lots of nookie in the bedroom?"

"What? Oh, no," I lied. "Not really since, the, you know. Dr. Sherman says my vocabulary is lacking nouns, but I just can't put what happened to me in words."

"Isn't that just like a man, criticizing you for something that is so irrelevant, and missing the bigger picture?"

"Yes, I suppose so. But that's not what I wanted to talk to you about. I had this dream…" I paused to construct my words carefully. "I dreamt I was in a small town in the dead of winter and even though I don't think I had ever been there before, people seemed to know me, and be happy to see me. I felt like I was propelled by some unknown force to see him. Destiny."

"Him, who?"

"That's just it. I can't remember his face right now, but in the dream, it seemed so real. I fell into his arms. It was a feeling. I had an overwhelming need to be with him."

"Wow, that's some kind of dream. I'd like to have a dream where I was with another man."

"It wasn't like that. It was beyond my control. It wasn't like I was cheating on Rob. In the dream, Rob didn't exist."

Erica immediately came to Rob's defense, and I realized I had gone too far. "I know it was just a dream, Peggy, but you seem to be almost infatuated with this dream guy. Rob doesn't deserve this. In fact, I wish I was married to Rob."

I felt betrayed, and it was ridiculous. Rob was real, and the man was imaginary. "Of course, I would never have kissed anyone else," I said. I should have known better than to trust my confidences with Erica. The only person sworn to secrecy was Dr. Sherman, and much as I hated to admit it, he's the man I should be talking to.

It was nearly dark by the time Rob and I reached Dr. Sherman's office. My appointment was pushed back to eight o'clock because of an emergency, and Dr. Sherman said he didn't mind the late hour. I did. I wanted to go home and fall into a drug-induced sleep. Valerie, his secretary, had long gone, but the routine was the same. Rob skimmed the magazine rack, poured himself some coffee, and settled in, watching me as I followed Dr. Sherman into his office.

Dr. Sherman immediately took note of my posture, more relaxed, happier, and I sensed that he was not happy with my overnight progress.

"Good evening, Mrs. Prescott. How are you feeling tonight?"

"Actually, I felt pretty good earlier, although I decided not to have anything more to do with my friend Erica. Actually, I'm pleased to be here. I have things to talk about."

"Is that so, Mrs. Prescott?" Dr. Sherman was not at all pleased by this turn of events. He sized me up, recognizing quickly that I carried a sense of confidence, not at all the dribbling fool I was yesterday. My voice was strong, my shoulders no longer stooped, and most upsetting to him, was the manner in which I made eye contact when I spoke, seemingly unafraid of making wrong statements. If I was capable of progressing this quickly, he thought, then he was afraid I'd be cured in no time, and he certainly couldn't have that, not at all. That would be unacceptable, and more importantly, unprofitable.

He began writing in his notebook. Patient appears happy, almost euphoric, despite a slight meltdown (her words) this afternoon with a friend. I will keep in the forefront of my mind, the diagnosis of mania, in the event that her mood doesn't stabilize. Bipolar depression could have been nesting in the recesses of her mind for years, only to be triggered by the home invasion. He stopped writing and looked up, and I began speaking, as if on cue. "What are you writing about me?"

"General observations."

"Can I see what you've written?"

"No, that would be like me looking in your lingerie drawer. How would you feel about that?" That comment was immediately off-putting.

"l don't know what you mean?"

"l beg your pardon? You don't understand that your lingerie drawer is private to yourself, just as my notes are private to myself? It's an abstraction, Mrs. Prescott. Something akin to a rolling stone gathers no moss." He looked at me, noting my silence. He cleared his throat loudly, "Nothing? Never mind, let's move on, shall we?"

"I feel as though I'm saying or doing something wrong when I'm here. That I'm not smart enough or that I'm not trying hard enough."

Dr. Sherman began writing as he spoke, "Wrong? That's interesting. Very interesting, indeed. There is no right or wrong in therapy, there are only feelings and perceptions, and I've yet to hear about yours. Whatever is on your mind is to be shared, Mrs. Prescott. I believe I made that clear the last time I saw you, but it bears repeating. I am excellent at what I do, but unfortunately, I have yet to master the art of mindreading. On that note, I'd appreciate if you would please begin."

I took a sip of water from the side table, swallowed, took a deep breath and collected myself. Then I said, "l woke up feeling great. I had a dream. I can't remember too much, except there was this man." I stopped, measuring whether I could trust him not to mention this to Rob.

"Go on, please, Mrs. Prescott. What has you in such a good mood? Almost happy."

"Yes, and also Rob and I were intimate."

"Intimate? What is that, the broad stroke of leaving out the details? Are you saying you had sex?"

"Yes, we did, this morning. I had just awakened. I initiated it, something I never did before, and even before the incident, I used to always follow Rob's lead, but this time it was different. I felt desire, I wanted to, you know, have sex."

From my vantage point, I was aware that Dr. Sherman was writing numbers in the side columns of his notes, and it looked like he was planning the amount of money I would pay him for sessions three times each week for one year. "Excuse me, Dr. Sherman. May I ask what you are doing?"

"More to the point, my dear Mrs. Prescott, may I ask what you are doing, sitting in my office and offering me nothing that is on your mind, except your sex life."

I hesitated. I wanted to stay in his good graces. "I just wanted to say that for the first time in months, I had a good night's sleep, and I awakened feeling happy."

"I see, and to what do you attribute this good feeling is from, having been a sniveling mess just one day earlier?"

I blurted out, "I think it's the sleeping pill. It worked really well. I never used the bathroom all night."

"And you would consider that a major feat, would you? Not having to use the bathroom in the middle of the night is your barometer for feeling better?"

"Dr. Sherman, you're not a woman, but if you were, you wouldn't even have to ask that question, especially if you were approaching menopause. Then, you'd understand that one night of uninterrupted sleep is a godsend."

Dr. Sherman was making all sorts of notes, many in the margins, half of his usually legible handwriting reduced to scribble, partly from rushing, mostly from anger. This bitch was ruining everything, he thought. He would have to lower my sense of inflated self-confidence, right here and now. "So, I see you are quite a hypocrite. You say you advocate for a pure body, free of chemicals and preservatives, but at the first chance you get, you are suddenly touting a love affair with sleeping pills."

"I know. I can't believe it either, but somehow, they jam all that magic into one pink pill. I mean it's so tiny, and yet, it works wonders. Just not long enough."

"That comment is short-sighted and narrow-minded, something I'd expect from someone with a lesser education than you claim to possess. As well, you seem to be giving no credit whatsoever to our session. Apparently, we are both wasting our time. Perhaps, I should set you up with a pill mill doctor and you can be on your way toward certain addiction."

"Oh, no, Dr. Sherman," I said, "that's not what I meant. Of course, I value my therapy, but I'm also agreeing with you, that there is nothing like a good night's sleep to put things into perspective. Isn't that what you said?"

Dr. Sherman began shifting in his chair, his balled-up hand sat in his lap underneath his desk. At that moment, he wanted to actually do me physical harm. "I find that I am most disappointed in your simplistic view of the therapeutic process. As I understand it, according to your rendition of your story, your so-called "drug fix" has you high as a kite, and unless you are planning a career as an addict, I don't think that is the direction for which we are striving. We haven't yet broached the subject of unraveling your psyche, although I'm getting a glimpse into your lack of understanding and appreciation of the process. You are not here on a lark, Mrs. Prescott. Therapy is a total commitment, a desire to understand what makes you "tick" if I may use layman's terms, simple enough for even you to understand. Pills are a temporary fix, a band-aid that covers a weeping wound, whereas the therapy I am attempting to offer you, is a permanent resolution of your problems. Surely, you must see that?"

I wanted out. I wanted to get up and leave, wishing for the hour to be over. I needed to turn this around. "I am committed. You may have misunderstood me. I will put in the effort, I promise. All I am trying to say, is that I feel better."

"Yes, so you say. Since, you are so obsessed with your newfound and delightful sleep, let's discuss that topic for a moment, if that's all right with you?"

"Whatever you say."

"No, my dear woman, whatever you say. As I explained before, this is patient-centered therapy. You will decide what you are comfortable talking about. May I ask, do you have difficulty retaining information, Mrs. Prescott?"

"What? No, at least I don't think so. I'm just agreeing with you. I am happy to discuss my sleep last night."

"All right. What time did you go to bed?"

"Right after the ten o'clock news."

"I didn't ask you what you watched on the television, did I? Rather, I asked a specific question. I'll repeat it. What time did you go to bed last night?"

"Eleven."

"You took your sleeping pill?"

"Yes"

"How quickly would you say that you began feeling drowsy?"

"I fell asleep immediately. I don't remember anything other than lying down."

"What time did you awaken?"

"Usually I'm up by seven, after tossing and turning all night, but this morning I slept past nine, with Rob bringing me coffee."

"Did you dream last night?"

"Yes, but that's the problem. I didn't sleep long enough to remember my dream, and as hard as I try, it has nearly faded."

"Yes, that is the very nature of dreams, Mrs. Prescott." Dr. Sherman began writing again, filling at least five or six more pages. "I must say, I'm surprised. Usually, this type of medication gives rise to quite memorable dreams, either bad or good, or no dreams at all. I just want to make certain that it is not giving you nightmares."

"No. Quite the contrary. My dream was fantastic. I remembered my dream vividly in the first few seconds of being awake, but now the images are gone. I'm going to write my dream down next time. That's what my mother used to do. In fact, we used to sit around the breakfast table growing up, everyone talking about their dreams and when it came to my turn--"

"Yes, I'm sure that's all very nostalgic, but we're not here to reminisce about your childhood habits. I am simply trying to establish whether the sleeping pill has caused you adverse effects, but I can see that apparently it hasn't. Now, let's make sure the dosage is right for you. Did you feel unusually groggy when you awakened this morning?"

"Groggy? No. I felt extremely satisfied."

"I beg your pardon?"

"You asked me how I felt. I said that I felt satisfied."

"Yes, I do not suffer from auditory difficulties, it's just that I do not comprehend your use of the word."

"Really? Why is that?"

Dr. Sherman sighed heavily, and weighed his words carefully, speaking slowly as though he once again thought I had cognitive impairment. "In case you hadn't noticed, I am quite a stickler for semantics, Mrs. Prescott. Most people are careless with their words, giving little thought when they butcher the language, and I cannot tolerate inserting an incorrect word, when it costs nothing to use the appropriate one. The word "satisfied" is analogous to some type of sexual feelings, eroticism, sexual activities. You mentioned having sex?"

"Yes, but not in the middle of the night."

"Do you think you had a dream of a sexual nature?"

"No."

"Ah, that response came very quickly. Are you embarrassed talking about this subject?"

"I am a little uncomfortable. Rob and I don't talk about sex openly."

"Never? In twenty-five years of marriage, the two of you have never spoken to each other about your fantasies?"

"Rob and I don't have fantasies."

"Mrs. Prescott, I cannot speak as a woman, but I can speak from the point of view of a man, and I can assure you that all men have fantasies."

I took another sip of water. Beads of perspiration were forming on my forehead. Dr. Sherman was out of line, I thought. It was the manner in which he stared at me, the same type of look that Arnie Stimmel has given me on multiple occasions, sexual in nature, but then I decided I must be mistaken. He's a professional, after all. "Men have fantasies about their wives?" I asked, innocently.

He smiled patiently, "Almost never about their wives."

"Oh." Could Rob be fantasizing about someone else when he is in bed with me? Did he this morning, I wondered?

"Do you believe that your husband is happily married?"

"Yes, of course. Rob and I are very happily married. Dr. Sherman, to be clear, I have loved my husband and no other man, ever. I have never felt the need to imagine, or fantasize, about being with anyone else, nor would ever consider being with anyone else. Rob feels the same way. If you are insinuating that Rob has to think of other women to be satisfied in bed, you're wrong."

"I'm quite impressed, Mrs. Prescott. You've used the word satisfied correctly in a sentence, allowing me to believe that you do have a basic understanding of the meaning of the word. Yet, you've used the word earlier to describe how you felt when you awakened this morning. Do you believe that your husband was having his way with you while you were under the influence of the sleeping pill, without your knowledge, or, I might add, consent?"

"No. That's impossible. I don't want to talk about this anymore." Dr. Sherman sat quietly, writing, until I made another attempt to clear the air. "I just want to emphasize that I very much appreciate you, and the fact that through your therapy, and with the help of the sleeping pill, I am beginning to feel better. I know I have a long way to go, and I intend to keep my commitment to therapy."

Dr. Sherman was pleased. He had Peggy squirming in her chair, he thought, but he dared not push her too much further. Just enough to cut that air of confidence to the quick, so that she was once again a sniveling shell of the woman who initially walked through his door the previous evening. He had her right where he wanted her. "I appreciate the back-handed compliment, Mrs. Prescott, but you do know that I had nothing to do with the discovery of the chemical ingredients that became the pharmaceutical wonder, under the umbrella name of sleeping pills, neither do I manufacture them. My only interest is to delve into the inner workings of your psyche, interpret your thoughts, and guide you on your journey back to mental health. The goal of the sleeping pill is simply to knock you out. Which of these shall we give credence to?"

I was quickly tiring of this game, if, in fact, that's what it was. "You, of course. You're always more important."

Dr. Sherman did not appreciate the undertone in my voice, and he was not about to let me think that I could speak to him that way, without being called out. "Are you always that condescending, Mrs. Prescott, when you are asked to make a choice?"

I was fighting back tears. "No, it's just that you bring out the worst in me, and I don't understand why."

"Perhaps the worst already resides inside you, and you have managed all these years to keep the worst at bay, but now, under stress, you can no longer keep up the facade of being the sweet woman that everyone thinks you are. Is that possible, do you think?"

"I'm sorry. I'm just exhausted. I really want to leave now."

"No need for apologies. You do not have to hide your true feelings, or shall we say, hostilities, from me. Your secrets are safe inside the confines of this office."

I was now fully engulfed in tears. I couldn't bear the way I felt, only emphasizing my need for further, extensive therapy. Suddenly, thanks to Dr. Sherman, I believed that Rob had to think of other women in order to have sex with me, that I wasn't as nice as I had always held myself out to be, and that Dr. Sherman was the only one who could truly help me by exposing my shortcomings in order to rearrange me. I suddenly found myself feeling entirely dependent upon him, needy, and vulnerable.

"I think what is really bothering me is that Arnie, Rob's friend, is coming to visit soon."

"Ah, yes, the friend you spoke of before. What is his full name?"

"Arnie Stimmel, Rob's friend from medical school. I hate him."

"Go on, please."

"Rob was on the phone with him in the middle of the night. He thought I was asleep in bed, but I was really in the chair on the far side of the bedroom. He was whispering, but I could hear him clearly. It sounded, from Rob's end of the conversation, that Arnie needed a place to stay for an upcoming weekend, because he was coming to Florida for a convention. He's a dermatologist."

"Did you agree to allow him to stay at your house?"

"Not exactly. Rob never mentioned it to me. I just overheard them."

"Why do you think he didn't bring it up to you?"

"I guess he doesn't want to put pressure on me. He doesn't know I overheard them."

"But you did hear the conversation."

"Yes, but he doesn't know that."

"That's quite deceptive, isn't it? To know something and pretend that you don't?"

"Rob's the one being deceptive."

"Perhaps, but he must want to see his friend very badly."

"I don't want him to come. He makes advances toward me. Rob doesn't need to know about that. He would be crushed to know what Arnie is really like, after all he did for him and his career."

"Have you and Arnie had sex?"

"Of course not!"

"Do you plan on having sex with him while he is in town?"

"No, never. The thought of that is repulsive."

"Then there is no harm in Rob's friend coming for a visit, as long as you continue to thwart his advances. Men have desires, Mrs. Prescott. They desire beautiful women. They desire what they don't have. Men are competitive, and they don't give up easily. In this case, it appears that Mr. Stimmel is coveting his best friend's wife."

"So, knowing this, do you still think I should let him come?"

"I think you're playing a game you can't win. You are selfish and controlling. You have little understanding about men, and you are puritanical regarding sexual matters, repressed, one might say. You have mood swings and a suspicious nature. It seems that you have quite a few more problems than we first thought, Mrs. Prescott."

"Maybe you're right. I feel like I'm never going to be well. Am I a hopeless case?"

Dr. Sherman couldn't have planned this session better if he had scripted it himself. "I know one thing, if you are going to work hard in here, then you will succeed." He looked at his watch. "Oh, my, we have again exceeded our time here. It is well past nine-thirty. I will see you next time. However, I want you to double up on your sleeping pills. I believe you are not going into REM sleep. Do you have your list of our appointment days and times?"

"Yes, thank you." I rose from my chair and started toward the door, attempting to pass by Dr. Sherman, who stood in my way.

"One more thing, Mrs. Prescott. Do you think you might try to drive here by yourself next time, without your husband?"

"Rob likes to bring me. He said so."

"Really? What were his exact words?"

"He said he didn't mind."

"Ah, I see. But that's not exactly the same thing, is it? When you "want" to do something, that's one thing, but when you "don't mind", well, that's quite another. One is a genuinely positive statement of fact, while the other is polite acceptance of a situation for which there is no other answer, if there is peace to be kept. Semantics, my dear Mrs. Prescott, semantics."

CHAPTER NINETEEN

A FEW NIGHTS LATER, AFTER dinner, Rob and I took a long walk in the neighborhood. I was jumpy, petrified that someone would leap out from the bushes, or a car might target us, but Rob held his arm around me securely as we strolled. "I'd never let anything happen to you, Peggy. You have to trust me."

I desperately wanted to, and as the days became weeks, I did. It was almost time for my biweekly appointment with Dr. Sherman. I begged Rob, "I just don't want to go to my appointment, Rob," I said. "I'm feeling so much better, less anxious, and a little more like my old self."

Rob, of course, was ecstatic, singing Dr. Sherman's praises. "The man is a genius," he said. "Our entire lives are changing before our eyes, wouldn't you say, darling? You can't stop your treatment now, honey."

But, as we headed home, I began sinking back into my depression. "Dr. Sherman doesn't like me," I said unexpectedly.

"What do you mean, sweetheart? He doesn't like or dislike you. He's a shrink. He's like a blank piece of paper that you transfer your feelings to, without any repercussions. You're just overly sensitive right now, and rightly so, but believe me, Dr. Sherman is a good man."

His faith in Dr. Sherman ignited my anger. Why didn't he have that kind of faith in me? It was all I could do not to grab hold of Rob's shoulders and shake him. The man he thinks is so great, and his prescription pad, is leading me right out of my marriage.

"Rob, do you hate me?" I asked.

"Hate you, what are you talking about? I have loved you every day, since the first day I laid eyes on you. You are my life, Peggy."

"Dr. Sherman thinks I'm being selfish, keeping you from going back to work full time. Do you think I'm selfish?"

Rob hesitated for just a second too long before he answered, but his pregnant pause was enough to send me into a rage, which he quickly tried to dispel. "I think you're not yourself, that's all. But the hospital does need me back at work as soon as possible. There's only so much I can do over the telephone. Suppose I called Erica, and she could stay with you while I go to work? Would you like that?"

He didn't know that I had given up on my friendship with Erica, and if I couldn't trust being with her, my best friend, I certainly didn't want to make small talk with any of the other friends I had. By now, I was yelling at the top of my lungs. "I didn't marry my friends, Rob, I married you! I'm your responsibility. That's what you promised me at the altar, and that's what I expect, not a husband who can't wait to get away from me."

Rob lowered his voice to a whisper, hoping none of the neighbors could hear me. "I'm just trying to help you, honey."

"How are you trying to help me, by pawning me off on other peo-ple? Stop acting like you know what's best for me. You and that quack, Dr. Sherman, putting so much stock in those damn sleeping pills, hoping that I can sleep my misery away. You don't know what they're doing to me. I haven't been the same since I started taking them."

I knew I was making no sense. Rob's voice was soft, but firm. "You promised you would do this for me, and Dr. Sherman is the best psychiatrist in his field, at least in these parts. I know this is traumatic for you, and I don't know if I'd be as strong as you are, but I'm so proud of you. We're going to beat this thing, and Dr. Sherman is the one who is going to help us do that."

I didn't want to argue anymore. Deep down, I knew Rob was right. I didn't recognize myself, yelling at Rob, accusing my psychiatrist of being in collusion with my own husband, not to mention, spending hours wishing I was with another man. I was exhausted and truth be told, I felt crazy. The past few nights, after I swallowed the pills, I went back to the same dream, the same man, but I was unable to move forward to be with him. I desperately wanted to know what might happen next.

Then it came to me. It was the dosage. The dosage, though increased, was still not sufficient to keep me in my dream long enough. I needed more. A lot more. As it was, I was almost out of the pills from my prescription. If I had more, if I took more, perhaps I could go to the man, and stay longer. The problem was getting them. If Dr. Sherman had an inkling that I was going to increase my dosage without his permission, he'd likely stop prescribing them altogether. But, if I began visiting my mother every night, if I pocketed her pill instead of disposing it, I'd have enough to try my experiment. That would mean, of course, that I'd have to be brave enough to drive myself, and I didn't know if I was ready to do that. The alternative, of course, was that if I didn't, my desire to stay with the man longer would never come to fruition. I had made my decision. I began leaving the nursing home each night, with her pill inside my pocket. That and a new prescription was all I needed.

CHAPTER TWENTY

I FELL ASLEEP IMMEDIATELY, AND took the dirt path leading to the man, but for some reason, I couldn't make it up the hill, my feet taking steps that led nowhere. An old woman, whose cabin was directly next door, greeted me, her broom in hand. "Hello," she said. "Will you be staying longer this time, dear?"

I needed confirmation to what I already suspected. "I've been here before, haven't I?"

"Yes, nearly every day for a week or so, but your stays have been short. He's been waiting a long time for you, but you'll have to go to him. He isn't allowed to come to you."

"Who is he?" I asked.

"In this town, everyone knows everyone, and all their stories, even yours."

"My story?"

She smiled as she nodded, "Yes, your story is one of the oldest ones here. You've come to reconnect with the man. He's been waiting for you, to see if it's possible to have a second chance."

"But I'm married. I have a husband and children, and I love them very much."

"At one time, you loved the man very much as well. You were going to marry him, but circumstances took that chance away."

"You don't understand. I would never betray my husband."

"Your husband lives a world apart from this one. You have an opportunity to choose. You will have to decide for yourself." She quickly covered her mouth with her hand. "Oh, no," she cried. "Now I've said too much. I'm just an old woman who can't keep her mouth closed." She went back to her sweeping.

"I'm trying to climb the hill, but my feet aren't getting me there."

"Ask your heart. It knows the way."

She was right. One thought of the man, and a force led me straight to his porch, where he and the dog stood waiting for me. He held out his arms, and I fell right into them. He held me tight, and I nestled into his flannel shirt, his skin warm, his unshaven face brushing against my cheek. He was no stranger. I have never felt such a feeling of intense love pouring from my being. I don't know how long we remained that way, tethered to each other, needing nothing more than what we had at that moment. He bent down to kiss me, and it was at that moment when I looked deep into the blue of his eyes, that I really knew him, knew us.

Our story unfolded as memories flipping quickly past, as if they were a movie screen, snippets of our lives together, whizzing by, fragments of ourselves when we were young, and very much in love. Waves breaking on the shoreline, walking the boardwalk hand in hand. Lying near the dunes under a moonlit sky, kissing the salt left behind from his lips. I was wildly happy and free. Clouds came and went, and summer changed to fall. A chill was in the air, and we huddled together for warmth. Apples in orchards as far as the eye could see, filling our baskets, sneaking bites of the ripe sweetness, juice covering our chins. Long rides into the hills, the top down on his sports car, my hair blowing in the wind. He reached over and took my hand. The touch of his skin on mine was all that I needed for heat. The sky was laced with threatening snow, leaves descending to their final resting place, as we continued our journey together.

Thermos bottles of coffee, blankets over our legs, camping in front of a fire, still searching the horizon. When the sky gave way, and snow fell, we tossed fistfuls of snowballs, and finally, lay down together, flush with emotion, and promises of a future to come. Winter welcomed a spring thaw, and waterlilies floated across Buzzards Bay. In the warming sun, I looked at him, thinking how each day I loved him more than the day before. But when he looked back, his eyes held a premonition of the future. So many plans, so many innocent promises, laced with obstacles that starry-eyed lovers could not have envisioned.

This was a man I knew well, in a different time and place, a man whose every word was truth, whose love of the ocean became mine, whose desire for nature was my desire, whose every love, I loved. I was connected to him in a way that could not be denied. His kiss was as passionate now as it was then, unmistakable in its fervor, this time the awkwardness of his youth making way for the needs of a grown man.

"Is it really you?" I asked.

"Yes," he answered, his arms holding me tightly.

"How is this possible?"

"I never left you. I knew your heart, and knew you had never forgotten me. That is why I came here. I never gave up hope that we might be together again one day."

"Am I dreaming?" I asked.

"I wish it could be that simple, but for now, just know that we are together. Destiny has intervened and granted my greatest wish."

He began to loosen his hold on me, and as his image soon faded, I heard myself begging him not to go. The sun poured in the window as it always did on a Florida morning, jolting me awake. This was the lengthiest encounter I had with the man, and my sleeping pill theory had proven successful. There was so much to talk about, with no one to talk to, except for Dr. Sherman. I decided not to mention the pills to Dr. Sherman, but I did need to talk to him about the man. After all, he was bound to secrecy, and I needed guidance, even if it was from an unempathetic doctor such as himself. Yet, for the next several sessions, Dr. Sherman was so hateful, that I kept the man's encounter to myself, at least, temporarily, as I nearly finished the second bottle of sleeping pills.

CHAPTER TWENTY-ONE

I DISCOVERED THAT IF I put all my efforts into taking care of my husband and daughters, the man didn't take precedence, didn't cause my obsession with him to run amuck. I focused on daily tasks, the laundry, gardening, ironing, and not so much on how many more hours it would be until my next meeting with the man. As of yet, I hadn't spoken to Dr. Sherman at length about him, but I had made progress in driving alone, much to Rob's delight. Of course, my underlying motive was to pocket my mother's sleep medicine, and I was becoming quite proficient at being the devoted daughter and consummate thief.

Rob was working now, at least half days, sometimes more, and we were getting along just fine. He was in the shower when the phone rang, and I picked it up, assuming it was the hospital for him. Instead, it was Arnie Stimmel.

"Hello?" I said, sitting at the edge of the bed.

"Hey, baby doll, how's it going?"

"Arnie? How are you?"

"Good I guess. How ya doin?"

"Okay, I guess, all things considered." I instantly felt my anxiety mounting, hoping that Rob was nearly finished with his morning routine, but I still heard the shower running through the closed bathroom door. My heart pounded inside my chest.

"Yeah, I heard you had a little problem a while back. Tough break."

"Yes, I'm really not comfortable talking about it." I tried to keep my tone even, but my anger, quick to surface, was near the boiling point. He had no right to talk to me in such a cavalier manner. He had no idea what I had been through.

"Yeah, that's good, 'cause I don't need to hear you rehash it. Shit happens." I considered hanging up the phone, and came close, but in the end, my manners kept me hanging on. "Doll face, you still there?"

"Yes, I'm still here, Arnie."

"Okay, so like I was saying, I'll be coming to stay with you for a few days. I'm sure Rob told you, right?"

I wanted to yell into the phone, that he certainly did not tell me, that my spineless husband was afraid to confront him, to deny him anything. I wanted to add, "by the way, you'd be proud of him, that Rob had turned into quite a deceitful person, keeping secrets from me," but instead, I said, "Yes, he told me." Then, there was silence.

Finally, Arnie said, "Listen doll, if you're gonna keep zoning out, can you just put Rob on the phone?"

"Rob can't come to the phone right now. I know you're coming. I'll have the guest room set up for you." Then, I added, mostly to prove Dr. Sherman's opinion of me wrong, "I'm glad to have you."

Now, I thought, I can confirm that "liar" should officially be added to Dr. Sherman's list of my character flaws. I'm sure he'll be pleased. I had to lie, because that is what a wife is supposed to do for her coward of a husband. If I didn't cover for Rob, Arnie might think that our marriage was on the rocks, and Rob was the only buffer I had against Arnie's unwanted advances. When the conversation ended, I was furious.

When the bathroom door opened, with Rob still toweling his wet hair, and all smiles, I was quick to verbally attack him, "How could you, Rob?"

"How could I what?"

"Your friend, Arnie, that's what. He's a permanent fixture, isn't he, Rob. Good old Arnie, bossing around poor, pathetic Rob. How could you make me lie for you? Just when, exactly, were you going to tell me I'm going to have to entertain him, on top of everything else I've been through?"

Rob hung his pajamas behind the door, stalling for time. "I was planning on telling you tonight," he said. "And you don't have to fix dinners or anything like that. I'll get carry out, and even clean up afterward. Besides, he's not coming in until after seven, and I'll be home way before then."

"Home from where?" I yelled. I still trembled at the thought of Rob not being home with me.

"Peggy, we talked about this."

"No, you and Dr. Sherman talked about it on the phone. I never agreed."

"Yes, you did. I'm going to work as little as possible, and I'll be home by five, I promise. I had to get back, before they fired me. You know all this. Surgery is backed up, and they need me. I can call Erica to stay with you. You two can have a girl's day."

I was coming unglued. "You've checked off all the boxes, haven't you? Food, check. Clean clothes, check. On call companion for my needy wife, check. Well, here's something you might want to add to your list. I hate Erica, I hate Florida, and right now, I hate you. You've dragged me away from Boston, with all its culture, brimming with the arts, pried me away from my friends and dumped me into a beach town where people walk around half naked, sand between their toes, and nothing in their minds. But did I put up a fuss when we moved? No, I did not. I was the dutiful little woman following behind you. Well, guess what? Now it's my turn. I want out of this town and out of this life. I want us to move back where we belong."

"Wait a second, Peggy. How did we get started on this topic? I thought we were talking about work and Arnie."

"We were, but right now, I'm talking about leaving this swamp, permanently."

Rob continued dressing and said, "Peggy, you know the reason we moved here, and we both agreed. I was offered a good opportunity to work and live in a wonderful place, where there is beautiful weather nearly twelve months each year, where the crime rate is low, and there were lots of activities for the girls. Look around. We moved to a great neighborhood, a gated community, upscale. I did this all for you."

"You did this for me? Please don't do me any more favors, because this one nearly got me killed. These guys break into our house, tie me up, punch me in the face, leave me bleeding on the floor, so thanks a lot. So much for your position on low crime rate. Why didn't they pick someone else? How about that bitch who lives in the pink house down the street? She deserves to die with that snotty attitude of hers, or the lady with the bad breath and her three obnoxious dogs that bark morning, noon and night. Maybe she needs to be put out of her misery, but not me. I didn't deserve this."

"Peggy, it wasn't as though you were targeted. It was random. Besides, you wouldn't want to wish what happened to you on anybody."

"Why not? Does that mar your perfect image of me? Sweet little Peggy, once again taking the hit for the team, is that it?"

While I screamed, I noticed that Mrs. Monroe, our neighbor down the street, walked past our house for the third time, with her eyes aimed straight at the open bedroom window. I couldn't have cared less. I kept at it, louder, to make sure she wouldn't have to strain her ears. "If you want to know what's wrong with you, Rob, it's that pious attitude of yours, your need to let everybody know how caring you are. Sacrifice me, save the neighbors, that's your motto."

"You're talking nonsense, honey. I always put you first."

"Really? Look around. Did I ever ask for any of this, the big house, the expensive cars, no, I did not. None of this was for me. It was for you, trying to make up for the fact that you could never amount to anything in your father's eyes, and your guilt for not being the son your father wanted you to be. You're pathetic, still trying to prove your value to a man who's six feet under." I knew I had crossed a line, and I was ashamed, but it didn't deter my rage from continuing to bubble over. He should have hauled off and slapped me, and I might have respected him for doing it, but Rob didn't have it in him. Not a mean bone in his body, or at least I didn't think so. He tried to put his arms around me, but I couldn't stand the touch of him against my skin. "I'm not finished. Your good-for-nothing leech of a friend is arriving in two days. I want him gone by the end of the weekend, and I don't give a damn what Dr. Sherman says."

"Dr. Sherman? How did he get into this?"

"It's a secret, Rob. You have your secrets and I have mine. How does it feel? Oh, and by the way, this is not your house, so you don't get to decide who comes and goes, without running it by me, but since you didn't have enough respect for me to ask, he can stay in your half of the house."

Rob was finally fed up, but he attempted to keep his voice low and calm. "You're being ridiculous. I'm doing the best that I can. What more do you want from me?"

"I want you to understand what I'm going through, and I want you to stop trying to impress everyone. I didn't come from money, and I don't need it like you do."

Rob walked over to the window, shutting the blinds. "Really?" he said. "Because your clothes and vacations say differently."

It was all I could do not to slap him. "You know something? Sometimes I really can't stand you."

Rob sat in the bedroom chair, defeated. I took a couple of deep breaths to calm my nerves. Time passed, then he said, "Sweetheart, come here, please. Let's not fight. Look at us. We're not these people. We can't let those thugs make victims of us twice. We've given them too much power already. Can't you see how much I love you?"

I fell into his arms, sobbing. My emotions were all over the place, and now, spent, I say, "I'm so sorry, I'm a mess. I just feel like everything is ruined."

"Ruined, how?"

"That's just it. I don't know, but it's not your fault. I can't believe you don't just divorce me after all I've put you through."

"Divorce you? Are you kidding? I am thankful every day that I have you, that you weren't killed. This is just a phase, a blip on the screen of our otherwise happy marriage. You're the reason why I wake up every morning, and the reason I go to work, to make money for you. I want you to have everything, but if you want me to retire, I will. I'll stay home with you until we're old and gray. Whatever it takes, whatever you want."

I backtracked, "I don't really want you to quit your job, I just need to get myself together. Dr. Sherman is right. I can't stop seeing him anytime soon. He's pointed out a lot of problems I didn't know I had, but I think with his help there's no telling what changes are in store. I'm going to be better. He said it's going to take a while. Will you wait for me?"

Rob kissed my tears away, "I promise I will wait for you until the end of time."

Finally, exhausted, I said, "I promise I will never leave you."

I was beginning to understand Dr. Sherman's obsession with semantics. Sometimes, the spoken word is impossible to live up to, coming from
a place that hasn't yet been discovered, even by the liar. Semantics. Now
there is a word that is almost always underestimated.

CHAPTER TWENTY-TWO

ROB HAS A NEW MORNING routine, one that doesn't involve me. He grabs a quick cup of coffee at home, then a second cup at the donut shop in town before heading to the hospital. His promise of only working half days has quickly morphed into full days, which often run late into the evening. In other words, he has moved on from the home invasion and my fragile state, leaving me to pick up the pieces. I don't want to play tennis, I don't want to have lunch with the girls, and I certainly don't want to jeopardize my relationship by complaining, so most days I sit in the kitchen, holding vigil at the kitchen window, on alert for any unrecognizable car that happens by. I want to beg Rob to stay home with me, but I am heeding Dr. Sherman's advice, his words convincing me that if I don't give Rob some space, our marriage will be headed for disaster.

This morning seemed like any other, kissing Rob goodbye at the door, watching the car pull out of the driveway, pouring a second cup of coffee, then going into the living room to turn on the television. No sooner had I left my post at the kitchen window, when the doorbell rang. "Oh,

God," I thought, "they're back!" I dropped to the floor out of view of the window and dialed 911. The dispatcher answered immediately.

"Operator. Police, fire or ambulance?"

I screamed into the phone, lightheaded, feeling like my voice was coming from inside a tunnel. "Police! I need the police. My name is Peggy Prescott. I need the police right away! Please hurry! I'm home alone."

It was all I could do to remember my address, then more screaming, my words garbled, even to me. The dispatcher assured me that the police were on their way and attempted to calm me down. "It's okay, honey. Don't hang up the phone. Stay with me and tell me what's going on."

The doorbell rang a second time. I was out of breath, barely able to think. "There's an intruder!"

The dispatcher asked, "Are you saying there is an intruder inside your house?"

"No, at the front door. Someone rang the doorbell. I can't see who it is. I'm on the floor. I don't want to get close to the window. They might see me."

"Who might see you, ma'am?"

"The people who rang my bell. I'm a victim of a home invasion."

"You say you're having a home invasion, right now?"

"No! I had a home invasion a few months ago. You must have it in your records. Peggy Prescott. Detective Harvey said these guys are still on the loose, and they might come back for me, and I'm afraid that now they have!" I said, sobbing.

"Calm down, ma'am. I doubt that home invaders would ring your doorbell and expect you to let them in. Just take a peek out the window," the dispatcher said, calmly.

"I know how this sounds, but don't you see, ringing the bell is exactly what they would do. Earlier, I got a phone call from some life insurance salesman, and now to throw me off guard, they send the thugs to ring my bell. They want me to think they wouldn't be foolish enough to ring the bell, so I'd open the door, expecting it to be someone I know, and then they pounce on me, slit my throat, and it's all over." By now I am hyperventilating. "Why aren't the police here?"

"They're on the way, just a few more minutes."

The doorbell rang a third time, and a man's voice said, "Peggy, open up. I know you're in there, I can hear you talking."

"Oh, my God! A man is ordering me to open the door. He knows my name!"

"Ma'am, can you recognize his voice?"

"I don't know."

"Can you please take a peek out the window and see if you can recognize him. Give me a description."

I crouch down underneath the window on all fours and pull the curtain aside, ever so slightly, with barely a sliver of daylight coming through the windowpane. I can't see much. Just the back of the man's head. "Are you still there?" I ask the dispatcher.

"Yes, ma'am, still right here. What is he wearing?"

"He's wearing a Hawaiian-style shirt and carrying a suitcase."

"The thug has a suitcase?" The dispatcher puts me on hold momentarily and notifies the police to drag their feet.

"Yes, a Louis Vuitton."

"Ma'am, is this some kind of joke?"

The man turned around so that I could see his face. "Oh my God, it's Arnie!" I wiped away my tears and pulled open the door, threw my arms around him, burying my face in his neck. My relief was overwhelming. For the first time since I met Arnie Stimmel years ago, I was ecstatic to see him.

"Ma'am, do you still need the police, or not?" The dispatcher didn't bother to wait for an answer, as she cancelled the call.

"What? No, sorry to bother you, it's my husband's friend, here for a visit from out of town. I know him."

"So, then, you're safe?"

"Yes, thank you so much for your help."

"Yes ma'am, have a nice day." The dispatcher picked up the newspaper and turned to the classified section. There had to be a better job than this, she thought.

Arnie walked into my house like he owned the place, setting his suitcase near the stairs.

"Hey, doll, how's my number one girl? And by the way, what in God's name are you wearing?"

I looked down at my old housecoat, stained from too many coffee spills and yellowed from too many washings. Arnie, on the other hand, looked like he just stepped off the cover of a travel magazine from the Chamber of Commerce, the face of tourism promotion. He was decked out in a loud, purple and yellow tropical flowered-print shirt, and perfectly creased beige pants, with a wide gold belt buckle that spelled out his initials. On his head sat a wide brimmed Panama hat complete with a hot pink band. His outfit would have been perfect for Florida except for the shiny, pointed black alligator shoes that screamed Prada.

"Arnie, what are you doing here?"

"Well, that's a fine how-do-you-do! You do remember we spoke not long ago? On the telephone? My plans for the weekend?"

"Yes, I remember, but I thought that you were arriving tonight."

"Hmm. Must have gotten the time mixed up. Anyhow, here I am." He whirled me around and planted a kiss smack on my lips, his body pushing my breasts into his chest. Then he said, "God, you look delicious, despite your wardrobe faux pas! Better than you did last time, and last time you looked good enough to eat!" Arnie eyed the room. "Your old man gone?"

"Yes, Rob went to work a little while ago. We didn't expect you until after the conference."

"Yeah, funny story. I kind of ditched the conference. Truth be told, there never really was a conference. I just wanted to see you. Got some new cologne. Come here and smell me."

I backed away toward the hall phone. "I'll just give Rob a call and let him know you arrived. Maybe he can free up his schedule and come home early."

"No need, little lady. I called him myself on the way here. He's tied up. You know how important he thinks he is. Got a drink for an old friend?"

"I have orange juice or water. Sorry, but no soda. Maybe coffee?"

"Yeah, I was hoping for something a little stronger. Something to get my blood flowing. Down there, if you know what I mean." He laughs. "Screwdriver sounds good. I'll make it. Liquor cabinet still in the den?" He walked into the next room, "How about you, doll face?"

"No, nothing for me. I'm afraid I'm not going to be much company. I know Rob told you about what happened."

Arnie walked back, glass in one hand, liquor in the other. He opened the refrigerator and pulled out the orange juice. "Okay, about that, listen babe, you're going to have to get past all that. It's over, finished, just like a couple of my marriages. They were bad, and now they're history."

I began to calm down and get my senses back. "I hardly think you can compare a couple of your bad marriages to my almost being killed."

"Oh, glad to see you still have a little feistiness left in you. Very sexy. It may not be the same as my marital woes, but how's dwelling on it going to solve anything? What's done is done. And speaking of solving anything, did they ever catch the guys who roughed you up?"

"No," I said quietly.

"Do you think Rob did it?" he asked. Arnie was fishing, but by the look on my face, he must have decided that he hit a nerve.

"Rob? Don't be ridiculous! He would never do anything like that, and I resent you saying so. You're just like the detective, trying to make Rob into a guilty man."

"The detective? What does he have to say?"

"Oh, something about that Rob might have hired the men to make it look like a robbery, or even kill me. Some nonsense like that."

"So, the detective thinks Rob had something to do with it, huh? Smart man. Rob always did have that vindictive side to him."

I was becoming increasingly uncomfortable, but I took the bait. "What vindictive side? I've never seen anything of the sort. He's never even raised his voice to me or the girls."

"Really?" he said. "I seem to recall the past a little differently. Rob might not have said anything to your face, but behind your back, he said plenty."

I was stunned into silence for a few moments, but he continued on. "To be clear, he voiced plenty of complaints about you, to me." Arnie was on a roll, always at his best when he had the opponent off balance. Game on, he thought.

I couldn't believe what I was hearing, "He complained about me? When? About what?"

If Arnie was capable of compassion, he would have stopped right there, but instead, his story escalated. "All was well, until the two of you moved in together. After that, he blew up my phone, telling me how you used to nitpick everything he did, and that he was sick and tired of it." Arnie winked at me and said, "You don't still do that, do you, babe?"

"I never 'nitpicked' anything, at least not that I'm aware of. We were so happy, still are."

"Then, I guess whatever problems you two were having must have gotten worked out."

"Problems? What problems?"

"Okay, Peggy, I've come this far, so I suppose it's only fair that I come clean about the rest of it. Just between you and me, there were more than a handful of times over the years that Rob would call me and discuss wanting a separation."

"Separation?"

"He contemplated divorcing you. He only stayed because of the kids."

I started to cry, angry that I let my emotions take over, devastated, but thankful that Arnie turned out to be a good enough friend to confide in me. "It's just that he never told me he was unhappy, never! I can't believe it!"

Arnie's face showed supreme satisfaction with his fabrication, but he was enormously convincing, and he seemed genuinely interested in comforting me, "Now, now, Peggy, he didn't go through with it. You're still married, aren't you? But at one point he wanted to serve you divorce papers, and actually consulted with an attorney. I just assumed, since he didn't go through with it, that there might be the possibility that he chickened out, thinking a divorce would put a blemish on his image in the community. Nobody likes a guy who tosses his wife away. But getting rid of you permanently, I got to hand it to him, would kill two birds with one stone. You'd be gone, and he'd get plenty of sympathy. As an added plus, he wouldn't have to share his money, if you know what I mean. Money that he always believed was his, since you didn't do anything to contribute to the pot."

I couldn't contain myself, sobbing openly, wiping my nose on my sleeve. "He never wanted me to work. He wanted me to raise the children. It was his idea for me to stay home!"

"And was it his idea that you have a maid once a week? Because I remember him telling me how resentful he was that his wife hobnobbed at the club while he busted his keyster."

"He's the one who hired the maid. He said he didn't want me to be the only doctor's wife in town mopping her own floors."

Arnie paused, stroking his chin. "That so?" He looked into my eyes, and said quietly, "We both know that's not true."

I didn't know what the truth was, anymore. I tried to think back, when we moved to this big house, when he said he hired a housekeeper. I never asked for one. But maybe I made a comment suggesting I was overwhelmed with the enormity of the house, as well as raising two young children. I couldn't get my thoughts together. "I just can't believe that Rob ever thought of divorcing me!"

Arnie went over and sat on the living room couch. He said, "Look, it's water under the bridge now, and by the way, he'd be furious with me if he knew I was ratting him out. I mean it would completely end my relationship with him, since he trusts me like a brother. You're not going to mention this to him, are you, Peggy? You have to promise that you won't."

"I need to confront him."

"No, you can't. Don't you see, if he's not on to me, I can continue to spy on him and report back to you. That way, he doesn't blindside you. We have to team up against him."

"I don't know, I've never lied to Rob."

"Never? Well, let me say this. He's certainly lied about a lot of things to you, none that I'm going to go into right now, but think Sheila, the operating room nurse. Trust me, there are things you don't know about Rob. Let's just say you're going to need me in your life."

Arnie's voice was laced with sympathy, which quickly shifted my loyalty from Rob to him. "Okay, I won't say anything, but I don't know what to do. I don't want to be married to someone who doesn't want me, and who might have even thought about doing away with me, but I also don't want to lose him. I can't make it on my own. I can't be alone, especially after what happened, I just can't be."

"You'll never be alone. I'll always be here to take care of you."

"What do you mean?"

"Isn't it obvious, Peggy? The way I feel about you? I've done my best to hide it over the years, but from the moment Rob brought you home, I fell in love with you. You had to feel it, my sadness that you never looked at me in that way, the heartbreak of witnessing you marry Rob, instead of me. All that I had to endure while Rob talked badly about you, the way he disrespected you, it made me sick to my stomach, but he is my best friend, so I kept his secrets. But no more, Peggy, not when he resorts to hurting you, to hiring a couple of thugs to kill you. It's only by the grace of God that they botched the job. But I'm here now, and believe me, I'll figure something out, some way of making Rob talk. If Rob is ever dumb enough to actually file for divorce, I'm only a phone call away."

"Do you honestly believe that Rob had something to do with the home invasion?"

"Yes, I honestly do. I'm sorry, Peggy. But now that you're telling me the detective feels the same way, well, he's trained to trust his gut. I think the detective very much believes Rob wants you dead. I hate to say it, Peggy, but it looks like Rob's a very disturbed man."

"But he's trying to help me get better. He arranged for me to see a friend of his, a psychiatrist."

"A psychiatrist that he knows. Someone he can pay to collude with him. Be careful, Peggy. Shrinks are trained to twist your mind, and make you believe you're crazy, until you actually go crazy."

I collapsed in a heap on the sofa, my legs buckling under the weight of Arnie's shared secrets. "I don't know what to think. I'm so mixed up.

If not for you having to travel for the convention this weekend, I might never have known."

Arnie put his arm around me, and said, "Okay, again, full disclosure, as I believe I explained earlier, there never was a convention this weekend. I made that entire story up, because I had a bad feeling about things, once I heard about the danger you were in. I put two and two together, knowing how much Rob despised you, and I had to come check them out. I can see now that my worry of you being in danger was accurate."

"So, you think I'm in danger now?"

"I believe that you are, yes."

"In danger because of Rob?" I began to feel lightheaded, like I was going to faint. I got up to get a glass of water, but my knees buckled again, and I fell back into the couch.

"You are not looking well, Peggy. I know this is a shock to you, but you're going to have to keep this to yourself. I'll size up the situation tonight when Rob and I go out drinking. He never could hold his liquor. After a few shots, he'll start talking, he always does. Then I'll see exactly what he has up his sleeve."

"I'm sorry, Arnie, but I have to lie down. This whole thing has taken a toll on me. I don't mean to be rude, but..."

"I got you, babe. I'll take myself around to see the sights, and I'll be back by dinnertime. Just play it cool, and we'll make believe I was never here. I'm going to stick to my story about the convention, so Rob won't get suspicious." He began heading toward the door, then turned back for a last look, picking up his suitcase to put back in the car. "Maybe I'll pick you up a few tight skirts, so you can remember what you used to look like. Would you like that, doll?"

"No. Not at all. I don't like lying to Rob, and I can't take much more of this. I mean it, Arnie, don't you dare buy me anything."

"You're a bit testy, aren't you? I like it. Just stick to our story and I'll dig up some dirt later on tonight. Go get some rest, and I'll let myself out. Better yet, you let me out so you can lock up, tight. Make sure to put the chain on the door."

As he walked out the door, he said, "Leave your car unlocked, and I'll leave some boxes in your trunk that you can sneak inside later."

"What? No! I have nice clothes. Rob always buys me the best, whatever I want."

"Okay, okay, don't get your panties in a wad. Just stick to the plan. I'll come to your door around six, you see me for the first time, and that's it."

"I'll be telling Rob a lie."

"A necessary lie, unless you want to wind up dead. I need to see what he's up to. Besides, God knows, Rob's the biggest liar I know."

"Please go, Arnie. I have a headache. I need to take an aspirin." I locked the door behind him, went upstairs and reached into the medicine cabinet. Next to the bottle of aspirin, I spotted the bottle of sleeping pills. I spilled three pink pills into my hand, and without hesitation, swallowed them.

CHAPTER TWENTY-THREE

THIS TIME, I WALKED WITH certainty, to whatever lay before me, to whatever my destiny might be. Snow drifts piled high, much greater than the last time I was here, until the house, the man and the dog were within sight. The dog raced down the steps to greet me, nearly knocking me over. The man stood back, allowing us to have our time together, until finally, the dog tired of me and went back to the man. His smile told me all I needed to know, his arms open wide, his eyes never leaving mine. A feeling came over me, and I felt trepidation, because no matter what, I was going to lose something. I looked to the man for comfort, as I put words to the question going around in my head. "Where am I?"

He looked at me with such love, that I was at once at ease. "Home," he said. "Where you belong." The man opened the door to his cabin, leading me inside.

It was manly, furnished with heavy oversized furniture, dark wood, and handmade quilts hanging on the walls. His surfboard and snow skis leaned against the closet door. Suddenly, it was another man that I thought of. Rob was a good husband, and my selfishness, though he would be none the wiser, was unfair to my family. "I have questions," I said.

"Yes, I suspect that you do."

"I am married. I have children."

"I know." He held out his hand, and mine caught it with such intent, that I surprised myself. He sat me on the bed next to him. "Let me explain. I live in a town called Hope, a place where I have lived for many lifetimes, waiting for you. It is an in-between space that I have chosen to come to. Everyone who lives here has lost someone they love very much, so much that they are willing to devote the rest of eternity, hoping that person will find a way back to them. Most of us are not as lucky, not the first time or even the hundredth time, but we continue to return for as long as we are willing to wait. I always believed that you would find another way, and thankfully, here you are."

I was confused, as he knew I would be. "Are you doomed to live out your life this way?"

"Not at all. Many of us do not chose to come back to Hope, but rather, to continue our journey in the spirit world. I have never considered moving on, without the chance to reconcile."

"What do you mean, keep coming back?"

"All of us here have one year to find a loved one, until we die. It is the anniversary of the year of our earthly death. For me, I was thirty-three when I died. That is not a long time to live, but it is long enough to have tasted love, to have known heartache, and to have wished for another chance."

"So, somehow you lost me?"

"We were young, teenagers. I was a few years older than you, but not by much. No one thought our love was real, but we knew it was. You gave in to the notion that you shouldn't tie yourself down to your first love, that you needed to see what the world had to offer. You weren't ready to move on, but you thought you would always find a way back to me, after college, after other boyfriends, when your days of irresponsibility were over, but when you tried to come back, you couldn't find me. I had already moved on."

"Moved on?"

"I was injured in an accident. By the time you found out, I had already died. You cried for me, and begged me not to leave you, so I didn't. I couldn't deny anything you ever asked for, including for me to come back to you. I had a choice, as we all do, and my choice was to hope that we could someday be reunited. I have loved you for thousands of years, but not in the way you might think. Our paths have crossed before, and each time we were very much in love. Unfortunately, there are rules to be followed, and circumstances did not allow us to remain together." The man stared into space, a tear running down his cheek. "If I could, I would stay with you forever, but time is short. You only came to me very late this time around, and because of that, I am desperate to make every moment we have together count."

"How did I come to you now?"

"There are certain things I am not allowed to know. If I knew how you managed to pass through the portal this time, I would tell you to remember for the next time, but I don't know, and neither do you."

"I think I do know." Suddenly, I felt as if I had the answer, as if in my other dimension, there was an explanation which I solved, a channel through the portal, but I couldn't form my mind around the details. All I knew, is that I could not bear to lose him again. "I will stay with you forever. I am making that promise to you right now."

"It is not that easy. I am destined to die at the same age as I did on earth. I know when that day will come, by my age, but not the exact date or time. Each lifetime varies, each lifetime the circumstances are different. I do not know the manner in which it will end, until the time comes. The only way we can be together for eternity, would be if we died together, me when it is my time, and you, purely by accident, perishing at the exact same moment."

"Suppose I take my life at the same time? Then we will die together."

"Yes, but not by natural causes. It is written in my contract, that if either of us take our own life, or plan any such event, that all future meetings will not be honored."

"l wish I never left you when we were both on earth." Memories flooded back, but they were clouded by an unfair fate, taking a turn. He was right, I was young. I had found my first and only true love, and yet, somehow, even with the diamond engagement ring on my finger, I began to have doubts. My friends were immediately infatuated with his personality and sense of humor, the way I was, but when they stripped him of his outer layers, they believed him to be too controlling, his life with me pushing them out. It wasn't his fault. I wanted to be with only him, happily morphing into whatever he wanted me to become. My parents were concerned, projecting my potential unhappiness, a wife too immature, trapped by small-town aspirations. Their opinions held weight, I was too young to stand up for my needs, if I even understood what those needs were. I ended it, and just like that, the trajectory of my life took a permanent detour. I loved him even as I left him. I looked at the man, so hopeful, so happy with what little time we had left. I kissed his lips, and whispered, "This time I will never leave you."

The man turned away, whispering under his breath, "But you will."

CHAPTER TWENTY-FOUR

AWAY FROM THE SCRUTINY OF his superiors, Detective Harvey was free to pursue the Prescott case at home, away from any gossip, and the embarrassing, humiliating stares of his buddies at the station house. Nailing Rob Prescott would put an end to all the whispers at the water cooler about his incompetence. Yup, he thought, Prescott behind bars would breathe new life into his credibility, and he would see to it that he gets him there.

His home office was piled high with various notes, legible and illegible, including reports, hospital notes, surveillance, witness statements and photographs, all of which had so far led to a dead end. He despised Prescott, and all that he stood for, his money, his notoriety, his smug attitude and his assumption that he was smarter than anyone else, but Detective Harvey had dealt with being the dunce in the room all his life, and he was about to put that to a halt. He especially despised the fact that Prescott's wife seemed more than willing to cover for her husband and protect him, and whatever flimsy alibi he'd come up with. Unfortunately, Harvey's case was filled with holes, and he was hard-pressed to find a single person who would utter a bad word about the larger-than-life doctor. But if Harvey learned anything in his unfortunate life thus far, it was that he would not be sidetracked, doing whatever he had to do to take a potential killer off the streets, and in his opinion, the day would come when Dr. Rob Prescott would eventually attempt to murder his wife. He might even kill the two thugs he hired, as a safety measure. If they can't talk, he's in the clear. If Harvey's hunch was correct, it would only be a matter of time before Prescott would have to find someone new, someone skirting just below the radar, to finish the job, and free him from the constraints of his needy wife.

Truth be told, he, himself, couldn't be married to Peggy Prescott for even one day, one hour, with all her neurotic demands. That poor bastard is barely able to loosen the leash long enough to leave the house, and only then, to go to work, but that's par for the course with women, he thought. You marry them and they own you, it's just that simple. It happens every time. What he couldn't figure out, however, was why Rob Prescott would resort to attempted murder, when divorce is a piece of cake in Florida. All anyone has to say is that they're sick of their spouse, and that's good enough for the judge. Then again, money is always the number one motive for murder. Maybe watching Peggy Prescott walk away with half the money, only to marry another man on the rebound was too hard to take. Harvey never made more than 56,000 dollars a year in his entire career and Prescott can make that money in half a day. He didn't have to kill for it. If anything, it would make more sense if his wife wanted him dead for the insurance money. Nope, he's more valuable alive, the money manufactured faster than he could count it, every patient a potential windfall. Harvey made a mental note. The ease at which Prescott makes big money was another reason to hate him.

The private investigator that Detective Harvey hired, with his own personal funds, came up cold. He reported that the good doctor spent most of his time going to the grocery store, the gas station and work. That's it. Oh, and one more thing, he wrote in his report back to Harvey, the poor schlep, until recently, had to drive his needy wife everywhere she had to go, a dependent woman who is afraid of her own shadow. Her now twice-weekly chaperoned trip to her psychiatrist, Dr. Sherman, had come to an end and she began driving herself. He heard that the psychiatrist's reputation was less than stellar and was in need of a little therapy himself. Rumor had it he was a once brilliant, but now questionable doctor, with a shady past.

Photographs depicted nothing. Harvey dumped the photographs into the shredder. Useless, he muttered under his breath. Two thousand dollars for nothing. Irritated with his lack of progress, Harvey put a call to the hospital and had Prescott paged. When Rob answered, Harvey was ready for him.

"Hello?" Rob said.

"Prescott? This is Detective Harvey. We need to meet again."

"No can do, Detective. I'm on my way home. The wife and I have plans."

Harvey hated his cockiness. "Oh? That's a shame, but this won't take long. I'll decide what your night holds."

"I think not. We're having company, and I have things to do before he arrives. Maybe some other time."

"Maybe right now. The hospital or the station, your choice."

"I already told you, I'm busy."

"Okay, why don't I come by the house, in say, one hour?"

"The house? No. Definitely not. Did you hear me say I have company coming?"

"That so? Who is it?"

"Not that it's any of your business, but an old friend, Arnie Stimmel. I don't want my wife to have to be alone with him."

"Why not?"

"Because she's in a fragile state, or did you forget she was the victim of a home invasion?"

"Okay, Prescott. Go home to your lovely wife, and company. We're done for now, but not for long."

Rob arrived home just after five, his arms laden with a bouquet of red, long-stemmed roses and two bottles of wine. He yelled upstairs, "Peggy, I'm home. Hope you're almost ready. Arnie should be here soon." There was no response.

To Rob, the seemingly empty house felt like deja vu, coming home, his wife nowhere to be found. He took the stairs, two at a time, his heart racing, running into the bedroom, only to find his wife asleep under a mound of covers. "Peggy," he said softly, tapping her on the shoulder, "Honey, wake up. We're about to have company. Arnie will be here any minute. Are you not feeling well?"

I jolted awake, wiping the sleep from my eyes, trying to get my bearings, trying to go back to my dream, to the man. It took me a few seconds to focus. Arnie. Arnie was coming. Arnie had already been here, but I wasn't supposed to tell Rob. Rob might kill me. Arnie thinks Rob is capable of killing me. I recoiled from Rob's hand on my shoulder. "Peggy, what's wrong. You look as if you've seen a ghost."

I collected myself on the way into the bathroom, leaving the door open for Rob to follow me in. The coldness of water splashing on my face put things into perspective. Rob was my husband. He wouldn't hurt me. He loves me.

Rob turned on the lights, staring into my face. "Are you sick?" he asked.

"No, sorry, I'm okay. I was suddenly just so tired, so I took a nap. What time is it?"

Rob checked his watch. "Nearly six. Arnie should be pulling in momentarily."

I was supposed to have a nice dinner prepared, but instead, I slept most of the day away. How could that have happened? Then I remembered the sleeping pills, which accounted for my groggy state of mind. "I didn't make dinner," I said.

"Don't worry about it. Arnie's so classless he would just as soon have fast food take-out. I'll order a couple of pizzas and we'll be just fine."

"Arnie's a pig, Rob. Really."

"I know, but he still has to eat."

"No, I mean it, literally, he's a pig, and he's not your friend."

"Why? Did something happen?"

I wanted to tell him. I didn't want to lie, but I couldn't take the chance on telling him the truth. If Rob was hiding something, Arnie was the only person he would confide in, and if I keep this secret, Arnie will trust me. "Not exactly."

Rob stopped in his tracks. "What do you mean, not exactly? Did something happen, or not?"

Rob's mouth was twisted, his entire face contorted in anger, a rage that rose inside of him in seconds. He made me afraid. "No, nothing happened. I just don't like him, that's all. You know that. I don't want him around me."

Rob relaxed. "I know he's a bit much, and he can be crude, no doubt about that, but he is my best friend."

"You tell him everything, don't you?"

"Yeah, I suppose I do. More so, in the old days, before I had you to talk to. I know you're angry that I told him about the home invasion, but I had to, otherwise he'd crack all kinds of insensitive jokes about who knows what? Besides, knowing about the incident is no big deal to Arnie. He's so self-absorbed, he probably wouldn't give it much thought. If it's not about him, he's not interested."

"Rob, I really wish I could trust you."

"Trust me? Of course, you can trust me. What kind of thing is that to say? I'm your husband, if you can't trust me with your life, who can you trust?"

"Why did you say, with my life?"

"What?"

"Your words were, I should trust you with my life. What does my life have to do with anything?"

"It's just an expression, but now that I think about it, it doesn't make much sense, does it? Now, you go take a quick shower, then come down when you're ready."

"Rob, can I ask you something else?"

"Anything, honey, but I'm begging you to hurry. Arnie's going to be pulling in any second."

"Do you ever think about divorcing me?"

"Divorcing you? Are we going to talk about this again? The answer is no!" But instead of Rob's words sounding sympathetic to my concerns, his tone held an edge of irritation, either, because he couldn't believe I was accusing him of something so offensive, or because I was on to something, and he was infuriated that he had been found out. "Listen, Peggy," he said, his voice now patient and reserved, "We are having a guest, any minute. I don't know what has gotten into you, but it seems that every time Arnie comes to visit, you lose your grip. Can you please just hold it together for the next two days? Arnie doesn't deserve to get dragged into your little drama."

I hadn't glossed over his words. He said, "my little drama." It's pretty clear that's what I've been to Rob all along, a dramatic housewife, an albatross around his neck, a roadblock in the middle of his future happiness. It only stands to reason that he would want me gone.

CHAPTER TWENTY-FIVE

I BARELY LOOKED AT ARNIE when he strolled arrogantly into the foyer, carrying his suitcase and a large clothing box. His mouth smirked, as if he had something on me, a look that made me certain he knew that I hadn't told Rob about our early morning visit. Cleverly, he made me an unwitting accomplice to his grand charade, while my poor husband welcomed him into our home, offered him a drink, and spoke congenially about their good old days. It's difficult to imagine what twist of fate could have possibly paired these two men together for the past thirty or so years, and it was impossible to foresee any disruption in their so-called friendship. "Here, babe," he said, handing me the package, wrapped in red satin ribbon, "Just a little surprise, as a way of saying thanks for your hospitality. A little outfit from your favorite store. You're surprised, right?" His eyes twinkled with mischief and deceit. He knew very well that he had backed me into yet another corner of lies.

"Arnie, what a nice thing to do," Rob said. "You know how much Peggy loves clothing."

"Yes," Arnie responded, "I'll bet she looks good even when she's not expecting company." His eyes darted quickly from Rob to me, and back to Rob. "She's always been quite the looker."

I set the gift, unopened, on the couch in the living room. Rob poured Arnie a scotch and soda, a Vodka Collins for himself, and a glass of red wine for me. "Cheers," he toasted, looking at Arnie, "to my oldest friend."

Arnie clinked glasses, his eyes taking it all in, raising his glass to me, as if we were in cahoots, making Rob look like a fool. He delighted in humiliating him, and although I wanted to expose him for who he really was, I didn't want to hurt Rob, so once again, I kept silent. The weight of the lies I carried, caused my knees to buckle. "Let's all sit down for a few minutes before dinner."

"Sure thing, babe," Arnie said following me into the living room. "What's cooking?"

"I didn't really..."

Rob cut me off, coming to my rescue. "Peggy wanted to make your favorite prime rib dinner, but I insisted that you'd be just as happy with pizza. It should arrive any minute. Hope you're hungry."

"You know it, man," Arnie said. "Besides roast beef, pizza is my all-time favorite. After we eat, how about we hit the bar, have a little man time, you know, to catch up."

Rob stood a little closer to me, instinctively protective. "I thought we could catch up right here. Peggy shouldn't be alone at night, she's not ready for that yet."

Arnie's mouth had a slight twitch, the way it used to, when he tried to hide his irritation. "Man, you are really whipped. The little woman won't even allow you to go to the corner bar on such a short leash?"

Rob shuffled from one foot to the other, wanting to please his friend, but needing to keep his promise to stay by my side. Without thinking, I said, "That's okay, boys. After dessert, go have some fun. I'll be fine with the dog for company."

Both men stared at me with the same mixture of confusion and astonishment. Instantly, I realized what I'd said without meaning to. "Honey," Rob said, "We don't have a dog."

Two worlds blending, lines blurred, temporarily uncertain of which world I was in. "Of course, we don't," I laughed. "Just checking to see if you two were paying attention."

While they devoured slices of pizza and more than a few beers, I checked myself. Rob was my reality. The man was a dream, and nothing more.

After dinner, Rob and Arnie headed toward the bar, leaving me to deal with kitchen duties. I checked the locks on both doors and all the windows, but still, I had the sense that something sinister was about to happen.

CHAPTER TWENTY-SIX

THE CORNER BAR WAS OLD and dank, once popular, but now, only partially attended. The worn leather bar seats were a testament to the lack of remodeling and ambiance, but this was exactly the type of place where Arnie did his best work. Beer was selling at happy hour prices all night, and as far as they could remember, it didn't close its doors until the last customer packed it in. Rob and Arnie slugged down their fair share of drinks as the night wore on. The clock was heading toward two in the morning, and after ordering one last round, Rob rubbed his eyes and stretched. He was ready to go home. The bartender stacked glasses from the dishwasher, wiping any smudges with a clean rag. Rob pushed his glass away and excused himself, stumbling toward the men's room. "Have to drain the dragon," he said in slurred speech. Looking back at Arnie, he said, "No more for me. I've had it."

Arnie, on the other hand, was having a good time, and had no intention of leaving. "Come on, Rob. It's still early."

Rob nearly missed his seat on his way back from the bathroom, as he tried motioning the bartender to tally the bill. Arnie laughed silently, just about ready to pounce. "You okay, buddy? I forgot what a lightweight I'm dealing with."

Rob held his head in his hands. "I can't imagine what your liver looks like. It must be pickled. I'm really beat. Let's get out of here. Tonight's on me."

"Go home and do what? The night's still young. The sun hasn't even come up yet." Looking at his watch, Arnie said, "I know kids in grammar school that stay up later than this on a Friday night."

"I just need to check on Peggy. I'd feel better if I went home to make sure she's alright. This is the first time I've gone out this late since the home invasion."

"Peggy's fine. She's a big girl, Rob. Besides, if there's a problem, she can always call me."

"I think you mean she can always call me. You do remember that I'm her husband."

The timing was impeccable. Arnie smirked, "I know what I said, man. I think she'd call me if she has any problems, same as she always does."

Rob sobered up quickly. "Why in the hell would she call you? When has she ever called you?"

"I gave her my number back a few months ago, because she specifically asked for it. Every so often, she gives me a call, you know, just to be friendly and catch up."

"You're a liar! Peggy would never call you. She can't stand you."

It was on, now, for Arnie. "Don't be too sure about that, buddy. Peggy and I had quite a little visit this morning, while you were gone. At your house. Face to face. She's quite hospitable. Never says no."

Rob's voice escalated, causing the bartender to eye the two guys at table nine. They were both clearly drunk. "Face to face? Exactly what does that mean?"

"It means, you don't know your wife as well as you think you do. She was quite the little hostess. I called to let her know my plane had arrived, and she asked me to come over, both of us knowing full well that you wouldn't be home anytime soon. I tried to say no, but she begged me. Said she needed company. She said no one would notice if I attended the conference a little bit late, so what could I do? I mean she is the wife of my best friend. Should I have declined her invitation? She needed company and I gave it to her. And then I gave it to her again. By the time I left, she was still in bed, tuckered out. She closed her eyes and fell asleep before I left the room."

"In your dreams, Arnie," but, Rob thought back, Peggy was in a deep sleep when he came home from work, so tired that she forgot to make dinner. He reflected back, was she naked? He never paid attention to what she might or might not have been wearing, now wishing he had.

"Actually, it wasn't in my dreams, Rob. It was in reality. We had a nice little chat, your missus and me, about the home invasion, about how terrified she is of you, about how she feels protected when I'm with her. She actually believes that you had something to do with it. She nearly had me convinced. I guess she's working with the detective, trying to give him something that he can use against you. So, did you, Rob? Did you hire the thugs to rob your own house and beat your wife?"

Rob was on his feet now. The bartender edged closer, ready to step in. "You're crazy! And drunk! My wife would never confide in you, or talk about me behind my back."

"So, like I was saying, one thing led to another, and before I knew it, we were doing a lot more than talking, if you know what I mean. She came on to me, pretty strong. I didn't know she had it in her."

"Shut up!"

"Honestly, I'm thinking I'm coming over for a cup of coffee, maybe some eggs, if I'm lucky, but then she gets to talking, her hand resting on my thigh, crawling up my leg, and the next thing I know she's taking me upstairs. I wasn't going to turn her down, Rob. Just like you didn't turn down Sheila twenty-something years ago. I guess what goes around, comes around, huh, Robbie-Boy?"

"I don't believe you. You're jealous! You've always been jealous of what I have. My sister pegged you from day one, but I didn't want to listen. Let me tell you how it really is, Arnie. You've always walked in my shadow, and that is where you'll stay. Peggy wouldn't have you, even if I was dead and buried."

"Hey, now, that's an idea. Once you're out of the way, I slide in to comfort the little widow. I like the house, not my taste in furniture, but we can buy new stuff with the life insurance money. You do have life insurance, right? This might just work. You die, everyone is in mourning, tears all around. Of course, as your best friend, I'd give the eulogy, you know, touch the highlights, best friends, awful shame, terrible thing, no amount of sorrow is enough, blah, blah, blah. Then, on the very night they shovel dirt on your casket, I carry her to what is now our bed. She'll shed a few tears, at first, of course, but by the time I'm finished, she'll be gasping for air."

Rob's hands were balled up in a fist. "I mean it Arnie, shut up!"

"Who's gonna make me? You, Dr. Famous Plastic Surgeon? Your precious hands can't get wounded, otherwise how you gonna keep pulling in the big bucks? You always thought you were better than me, didn't you, Rob, but you can move over, cause there's a new man in town."

The bartender stood between them, his full, six-foot three frame poised to handle business.

Rob said, "Don't bother. I'm leaving." He threw a credit card on the table, and turned to Arnie. "Get yourself a cab, and get the hell out of here. You won't be staying with me and Peggy, not now, not ever. We're done."

Arnie started for the door, "Peggy will be so disappointed. I know she was hoping for another round with me. Give her my best."

Rob left his car and walked the three miles home, barely enough time to digest what he could remember of the night. The one thing he did take away, was that Arnie was a disgusting liar with a great imagination. Still, he couldn't shake the thought that it might be true. That Arnie might have actually been in his house this morning, while Rob was at the hospital. That he might have revealed his secret about cheating with Sheila so long ago. He had to think quickly. He got home just after three a.m. He opened the door to a quiet, dark house. Arnie's overnight bag was still in the hallway, and the gift he gave to Peggy, still on the couch, unopened. He threw both out into the night, and then locked the door.

When Rob stumbled upstairs, he was already yelling, accusingly, "Was Arnie here this morning, while I was at work? I want the truth!"

His voice was so loud, so angry, that I began to cry. "Yes," I said, "But it's not like you think. All he did was come in for a few minutes, get a drink, and left. He gave me a headache, so I went upstairs and took some sleeping pills. That's why I overslept. The pills made me drowsy."

"You increased your dosage?"

"No, Dr. Sherman told me I could increase the dose if I needed to, so I did."

"How long has this been going on?"

"A couple of weeks. I just forgot to tell you."

Rob looked at me in a way no husband should ever have to look at his wife. He was suspicious of my withholding information from him, but all of this was his fault to begin with. If he hadn't made me go to Dr. Sherman in the first place, if he hadn't pushed the sleeping pills down my throat, if he hadn't gone back to work, none of this would have happened, and I wouldn't have ended up in the arms of another man.

I didn't dare tell Rob that night that Arnie confided Rob's intentions to divorce me or that he believed Rob was behind the home invasion. I didn't know who to believe, but I didn't want to make an enemy of Arnie, not if I needed his protection. I couldn't decide if Rob was a devoted husband or a potential cold-blooded murderer, like Detective Harvey said. I had to speak with Dr. Sherman. He was on vacation for one week, but I didn't tell my husband about his absence, leading Rob to assume that I was going for my twice-weekly sessions as usual. Leaving the house, I drove straight to the nursing home, and this time my mother was awake. My eyes scanned the table. There was no sleeping pill left on the nightstand. "Hi, Mom," I said. "How are you tonight?"

She looked straight at me, without any sign of recognition. "I'm fine. Just fine."

"You look so pretty. They must have just washed your hair. Do you want me to brush it for you?"

"You seem like a nice girl," she said. "Do I know you?"

"I'm your daughter, Peggy." I said, holding back tears. The thought that she didn't know me was unbearable, the anguish repeating itself over and over again.

The night nurse made her rounds, introducing herself when she entered my mother's room. She was a new hire. "I'll be back in a short while, and if your mother is not asleep, I'll give her a sleeping pill."

I needed that sleeping pill. I had to get back to the man. The nurse continued, "I'm also the new night supervisor, and I've made some changes. Some of my assistants have been lax about keeping medication under lock and key, so medication will no longer be dispensed unless needed." I did some quick calculations. Dr. Sherman wouldn't be back for a few more days. I need him to refill my prescription, but just in case, I would have to forego ingesting my pills until he returned.

I arrived back at the house slightly earlier than expected. Rob and I hadn't spoken about Arnie for several days, but neither of us slept well since his departure, me, hoarding my pills until Dr. Sherman's return, and Rob, furious after Arnie's visit. His anger percolating near the tipping point. Not long after he threw Arnie out of the house, while I was attempting to sleep, he went downstairs and picked up our landline. He dialed Arnie's phone, but Arnie didn't answer.

Instead, the answering machine asked the caller to leave a message. Rob made the assumption that Arnie was screening his calls, which finally pushed him to the boiling point, leaving this message, "Arnie, this is good old Robbie-Boy, as you like to say, but this time you can address me by my full title, Dr. Robert Prescott. I think I earned it. Unlike you, who stole everything I ever had, there's something you're never going to steal, and that's my wife. By the way, you were correct all along, I'm a better man than you'll ever be. At least I am a plastic surgeon, while all you are is a lowly dermatologist, going nowhere fast. There's no way I believe my wife would ever cheat on me with you, so I'm going to say this one last time. You better think twice the next time you boast about sleeping with her. In fact, if I were you, I'd watch my back."

When Rob hung up the phone, he poured himself a tall glass of Cabernet, savoring both the wine and the moment. Then he crawled in bed and enjoyed the best sleep he'd had in months.

CHAPTER TWENTY-SEVEN

FINALLY, DR. SHERMAN WAS BACK in town, and I had rehearsed my strategy all day. I wanted him to prescribe a large quantity of pills, now that I was unable to pilfer them at the nursing home. I didn't want to seem too needy, and I had to make sure I stroked his narcissistic ego. Ever since Rob had stopped accompanying me to my sessions, Dr. Sherman was free to unleash his full fury, so I had to be careful.

"Good evening, Mrs. Prescott. How are you doing this fine evening?"

"Actually, I'm doing quite well. Really well, in fact," I said. Dr. Sherman quickly jotted down notes, scribing that his patient had made an unusually rapid recovery from depression, which, in and of itself, was suspect. My body language continued to support my suggestion that I was coming out of my anxiety, although we had yet to discuss the crux of why I was there in the first place. "If I continue like this, I might not need to come much longer, but I would like to have some refills of my sleeping pill, you know, in the case of emergencies down the road."

That was not anything that Dr. Sherman was eager to hear. He wrote another note, remarking that he believed I had no respect for the study of human behavior. "So, my dear Mrs. Prescott, you think with the blink of an eye, you are cured?"

"I've been coming for months. I'm sleeping great, I am happy with my progress and with my relationship with my husband. I can drive myself to my sessions without Rob, and when he goes to work during the day, I am quite fine."

"And to what do you attribute this turn of events? Certainly, I hope you're not going to bore me with your theory that sleeping pills are more valuable than therapy. If you recall, we've been over all that, before. Further, you are aware, are you not, that we haven't yet broached the subject of your home invasion, isn't that correct, Mrs. Prescott?"

"Yes, yes. I do know that, but I have something more important to discuss today."

"More important than a home invasion, more important than the battering of your body by thugs who left you to die? Well, I can barely wait to hear what that might be. Do tell."

"I'm going to tell you this as clearly as possible, so you will understand."

"Well, that certainly would be a pleasure. To actually have intelligent, substantive conversation with you would be not only novel, but hopefully, informative."

His sarcasm was not missed by me, but I had more important things to think about. "You know how I'm supposed to tell you whatever is on my mind, and you're not supposed to judge?"

Dr. Sherman was amused, "Yes, I believe that is the way therapy is supposed to work, but thank you for refreshing me on the particulars."

"Okay, but if I tell you something that is super-confidential, do you have to write it in your notes? I mean what I'm about to tell you can never be divulged."

"My dear woman, you are not going to single-handedly change the course of my entire profession because you do not want your notes written. The notes are confidential. No one refers to them, with the exception of me. I do my own filing, so not even my secretary has access to them. They are kept in my office under lock and key. Now, please go on, if you must."

"So, do you remember I tried to tell you about my dreams?"

"Ah, yes. Something about a man, one who seemed familiar. Do you suddenly know who he reminds you of?"

"It's better than that! I've had the same dream over and over, but with the help of the sleeping pills, when I double up the dose, I can go back to him every night. He loves me, and I love him. I never knew I could love two men at the same time, but I do."

Dr. Sherman sighed, his pen never leaving his notebook, "Are you insinuating that you are being cured by dream therapy, with you starring as both the therapist and the patient? Perhaps I can submit this extraordinary model to the American Psychological Association, and you can make a name for yourself. It would really be something, that without any formal training, you have become the leading expert on dream therapy."

"I know it sounds impossible, but it's true."

"I don't doubt that you believe it's true, by your misplaced enthusiasm, but I'm curious about something you just said. Did you comment that you are having the same dream every night, with the same man, with whom you are now having a relationship?"

"Yes, the first couple of times that I dreamt about him, I didn't connect that it would be an ongoing theme, but after a while, I realized that we're together every night, and we've become inseparable. The problem is that I can't travel to him without the sleeping pills, but I've experimented and realized that by exceeding the prescribed dosage, not only do I arrive in Hope, but I can stay longer and longer."

For the first time in this session, Dr. Sherman felt relieved. Mrs. Prescott, he believed, was clearly stark raving mad, so crazy that it would be obvious his bank account would not have to suffer in the least, regardless of her desire to terminate her sessions. Once he confided this story to her husband, he would force her to continue. It was more imperative than ever, he thought, to take detailed, copious notes, in the event the length of her sessions should ever be in question. With any luck, he thought, she may be suffering from hallucinations or delusions. He made a notation, consider schizophrenia. "This is very interesting, Mrs. Prescott. Please elaborate."

"Well, I can tell you that I am intimate with this man."

Dr. Sherman perked up, "Are you saying your dreams are of a sexual nature?"

"When you say it like that, you make it sound cheap, and this is anything but cheap. This is a man who loves me, and I love him. I go to him as often as I can, we walk, we talk, we look up at the stars, and then we make love."

"And this takes place, where?"

"In his cabin, in Hope, where he lives along with his dog."

"I'm sorry, did you say that you and this man are in love?"

"Yes, we dated in another life, but we parted. He never got over me, so he asked permission to live in a town called Hope, where people can wait, hoping their loved ones will one day return."

Dr. Sherman quoted her statements verbatim in his notes. When he had sufficiently duplicated her sentences, he looked up and said, "I'm sure they are exciting dreams, but you do understand that in your life, your actual life, the place in which you and I reside, on the planet earth, that there is no man with whom you meet. What I'm saying, Mrs. Prescott, is that he may, in fact seem real to you, but he is most definitely, imaginary."

I suppose I didn't think this through, expecting that although astonishing, Dr. Sherman would believe me. "Maybe I'm not telling this in a way you are able to understand."

"Oh, I understand, all right. I understand that you can't possibly be in love with your husband, if all you can think about is abusing sleeping pills to get back to your unidentified man every night." It was just as he suspected, he thought, she was a run-of-the-mill gold digger who took a perfectly decent man and somehow manipulated him into marrying her. Now, he thought, she was bored with him, so she fantasized about a man who didn't exist, throwing me and my reputation in the mix. He lit his pipe, and smoked it in front of his patient, tossing all rules out the window. "Mrs. Prescott, the way I see it, there are two possible explanations for your dreams. The first is, that you are having sex with your husband under the influence of your sleeping pills, which distorts the actual events as they are occurring. The second is that you have a very vivid imagination, perhaps because of side effects to your medication, giving you intense dreams that are so believable it is difficult for you to differentiate between reality and fantasy."

"I can assure you, Dr. Sherman, the sex is real. I wake up breathing hard and sweating, drenched but satisfied."

"You're having a sexual dream, that's all it is. It is unusual for women to have them, but men have them all the time. Exactly how old are you, Mrs. Prescott?"

"Forty-five."

"That could certainly explain the night sweats. The scientific answer would be perimenopause."

"Perimenopause?" I asked.

"Mrs. Prescott, please feel free to research the topic, on your own time. I find the limitations that you have on your vocabulary quite amazing."

I had finally had enough of his criticism, and voiced my irritation. "I know the stages of menopause, I believe better than you, Dr. Sherman, and in the case of my dream, a scientific explanation misses the point. This is a matter of the heart. If you are going to continue minimizing my feelings about this man, then I am no longer going to speak about him. But, if we don't talk about what is on my mind, then what is the point of my being here, in this so-called, patient-centered therapy?"

Dr. Sherman had to admit, she had a point. He would either have to entertain her delusions, or lose her as a patient. He did some quick thinking, as well as mathematical calculations, while she continued speaking, "I know how this must sound to you, but he does exist. He knows about my husband and my children, and while he doesn't want to influence me away from them, he has told me he loves me, that he has always loved me, and I'm sorry to have to say this, Dr. Sherman, but I love him, too."

Dr. Sherman changed his tone from shocked and annoyed to caring and compassionate. "So, am I to understand that you visit him every night, at his home?"

"Yes."

"While you're in bed with your husband?"

"Don't get me wrong. I love my husband, but he doesn't know anything about this and it isn't hurting anyone. I take my sleeping pills, climb in bed, and I'm transported to the man."

"How long do you think you can keep this up, this sham of loving two men, sleeping with both of them at the same time, one fictitious and one real? Forever?"

"No. He can't stay forever. He told me he will die each lifetime, on the anniversary year of when he actually died on earth."

"And when will that be?"

"I can't remember."

"Yes, I'm not surprised." Dr. Sherman looked at the clock. Thankfully, her session was nearing conclusion. He couldn't have stood much more of this nonsense. "Let me be clear, once again. There is no other life, Mrs. Prescott. This is your only life, the one in which you are married to Dr. Prescott, and you are now sitting with me right here in my office, located in the Florida Keys. Your lines are becoming blurred, somehow, and you're mixing up your facts. But one thing is for sure, there is no other man, other than your husband. Unless you're cheating with someone that you haven't told me about in 'this life' as you would say."

"Of course, I'm not cheating! I understand that you don't believe me, but I am begging you to never breathe a word of this to Rob. It would break his heart if he knew I was in love with someone else."

"Yes, I'm sure it would. May I remind you, my dear, confused woman, that I am obligated to keep your confidentiality by law, so, no, I won't be mentioning this to your husband, or anyone else. In the second place, well, there is no second place. Our time is up, let's pick this up on our next visit."

"But, what about another prescription for sleeping pills? I'm nearly out."

Dr. Sherman walked me to the door, his aggravation beading down his neck. "I have decided to cut you off, as of now. Have a safe ride home."

Dr. Sherman couldn't wait for her to leave. If ever there was an area of disgust that hadn't already seeped into every pore of his being, he felt it tonight. Women are never satisfied, he thought. It wasn't enough that she probably derailed her husband's life by inserting herself into what should have been dedication to his professional life without distraction, but now she fantasizes about a man that isn't real. I know her type, he ruminated, hell I was married to one, jetting off to New York, leaving me to mind the house and my practice, and then, when she tired of me, she found a new love interest. The next thing I know, I'm sleeping on a blow-up mattress on the floor of what used to be my beautifully furnished residence. He opened the bottom drawer of his desk and pulled out a half-filled bottle of

Kentucky Bourbon. He poured himself a glass, sipping it slowly, until the whiskey replaced his anger. When the bottle was empty, he went back to his notes, rereading them to ensure nothing had been left out. He ended with this, scribbled in the margins, God, I despise this woman.

CHAPTER TWENTY-EIGHT

WHEN THE PHONE RINGS AFTER five o'clock, at Detective Harvey's desk, it is never a good sign. Most cops and personnel are gone by four, sometimes earlier than that. Detective Harvey looked over at the ringing phone, trying to decide whether to pick it up or let it go to answering machine, but in the end, his curiosity kicked in. "18th Precinct, Detective Harvey speaking."

"Ah, yes, Harvey did you say? This is Sergeant Barney Bristol, on a recorded line, from the Baltimore Police Department. I think I may have some information that you may find useful."

"That so?" Harvey replied, as he moaned silently, wishing he had gone home earlier. This guy was dragging out his words as if enunciating every syllable was the missing link to conveying his message. "Yes, sir, what do you have?"

"Well, Detective, I'm sorry, what did you say your name is?"

"Harvey."

"Yes, Detective Harvey. Let me just jot that down, not good with names, never have been, really. Same thing happened to my old man. He used to look at me and my brothers and just start slinging names into the air, hoping one would stick."

Detective Harvey was quickly losing patience. "Good story, please go on. You said you're calling to give me information?"

"We had a murder here yesterday. Home invasion. Nothing missing, but someone thought it was a good idea to pop a bullet between the victim's eyes."

"And that's of interest to me, how?" Harvey checked the clock. Five fifteen.

"Well, sir, that's what I'm getting to. We found his identification, driver's license and such, registered to a man by the name of Dr. Arnie Stimmel. Does that name ring a bell?"

"Arnie Stimmel? Nope, sorry, can't say that I remember hearing that name," but even as he uttered those words, the name did have a slightly familiar ring to it.

Sergeant Bristol's voice flipped into drama-mode. "I was afraid of that, sure was. Makes my job a helluva lot more difficult. Thought for sure that name might have crossed your desk."

"No, sorry. Like I said, never heard of him." The clock moaned on. "How about we table this discussion until tomorrow? It's past closing time and I've got some things I have to take care of."

"Yup, the pile just keeps getting higher and higher on the plate of life. I hear you. This will be quick. We made a thorough search of Mr. Stimmel's house, and it seems that we found a message from one of your citizens. We got the phone records and traced it to a Dr. Robert Prescott. Apparently, he hails from your neck of the woods."

Detective Harvey sat up straight, and adjusted the phone. "Dr. Prescott! Yes, I know him. The plastic surgeon." Harvey wasn't going anywhere now. "Go on."

"It appears that the victim and Dr. Prescott had some sort of falling out, and Prescott made some threats on the answering machine. When Stimmel didn't show up for work, the police made a welfare check, and found the guy murdered in his house. Looks like a home invasion."

"Did you say it was a home invasion?"

"Yup. Whoever broke into the front door, went straight up to his bedroom where he was asleep, and put a bullet in his head. Nothing of value seems to be missing, but you never know. Looks like Stimmel was targeted. His former wife was located, but she wasn't any help. She said the bastard had it coming, said if we find out who did it, to tell her, so she can pin a medal on his chest. No leads, other than Dr. Prescott."

"What kind of threatening message?"

"Well, I have it written down word for word, but the gist of it was, that he told Stimmel to stay away from his wife, or he'd be sorry. Sounds like Stimmel might have been having an affair with Prescott's wife."

Harvey couldn't believe his ears. Mrs. Prescott having an affair? "Are you sure about the affair?"

Bristol said, "Just a guess."

"Educated?"

"Yes sir, I went to the Baltimore Police Academy and worked my way up from road patrol to desk cop and finally, here I am, a full-fledged Sergeant."

"Not your education, Bristol. I'm asking if you're making an educated guess or just a hunch."

"Oh, I get you. That's a good one."

"Yes, very funny."

"I guess you'd call it gut instinct. That and the fact that Mr. Stimmel had just come back from a trip to Florida according to the return plane ticket on his desk. No hotel record, though. He came through the Miami

International Airport. Maybe he drove to the Prescott house and stayed with them. Maybe he got caught in bed with Dr. Prescott's wife. Isn't that always the way? No good deed goes unpunished, as the saying goes."

Detective Harvey's mind was racing. "Anything else?"

"Not right now, but if they did have a thing going, you know, a romantic affair, the husband is always the last to know, as they say. Probably didn't know while he was in Florida, or he'd have killed him on the spot. Maybe the wife blabbed, guilty conscience and all that. You might want to check his records, see if Prescott took a plane to Baltimore in the past few days."

Now this guy was trying to tell Harvey how to do his job. He desperately wanted to end the call. "Yeah, thanks, I'll do that. I'll check out Prescott's alibi, then call you tomorrow and let you know what I found. Is this the number where I can reach you, the one on the caller ID?"

"Yes, sir."

"You gonna be available tomorrow?"

"Sure thing, crime never sleeps, that's my motto."

"You got that right." Detective Harvey ended the call, lit a cigar and pondered his next move. He had a feeling that the good doctor's character wasn't as squeaky clean as his reputation made him out to be, but he didn't make the wife for a cheater. It's just too similar, two home invasions, both linked to Prescott. He made a notation to check the airline schedule flights from Florida to Maryland, but even without that, it's not a stretch to think Prescott hired a hit man and paid him for a good day's work. He turned out the lights, locked his door, and took the elevator to the parking garage. The next day he'd go after Prescott, unannounced.

CHAPTER TWENTY-NINE

PRESCOTT'S CAR WAS STILL IN his parking space in the underground garage. Showy car, Detective Harvey thought, as he looked inside the windows of the Mercedes 350 E Class. It's not enough the guy is making an easy six figures, but he has to ram his wealth down bystander's throats everywhere he goes. Harvey looked at his watch. He figured he still had about an hour or so to kill, so he popped into the hospital gift shop, bought a book of crossword puzzles, sat down in the lobby, got stuck on the first puzzle, and tossed it into a nearby trash can. The less effort he had to put into anything, the better he liked it. With fifteen minutes to spare, he walked down the service steps, and waited just across from the parking garage elevator. He didn't have to wait long. The elevator door opened, and Rob Prescott was in such a hurry, he never saw the detective standing nearby until he reached his car door. "Long time, no see, Prescott," Harvey said standing behind him.

Rob was visibly shaken, but quickly regrouped, his voice measured and calm. "Detective, always a pleasure. What do you want?"

Harvey waited a few extra seconds before answering, just to heighten the suspense. "What do you think? I want to ask you a few questions."

Rob's voice could no longer hide his irritation. "Listen, Detective, as much fun as it is to play twenty questions, I really don't have the time for this. I'm already running late, and I don't want Peggy to be alone for much longer." Rob pushed past the detective, and unlocked the car door. Then, looking over his shoulder he said, "If you'll excuse me."

Harvey threw his body between Rob and the opened door. "Not so fast. We have a little business to attend to."

"I'm not going to be detained by you. I have every intention of leaving here and going home, so, if you don't mind, get the hell out of my way."

Detective Harvey stood frozen in place. "Dr. Prescott, the way I see it, we can do this down at the station, or I can follow you to your house. Maybe your wife made enough dinner for unexpected company. As it is, I'm starving. I don't mind saying, that camping out here for half the evening gave me quite an appetite."

"I don't want you anywhere near my house. It will upset my wife, not to mention, stir up gossip in the neighborhood. I'm sure we can do this some other time and place."

"Sure thing. I can get a warrant for your arrest, and we can do this behind bars."

"You can't arrest me. For what?"

"You don't get to ask the questions. Now, we can do this my way or my way. Which is it?" The look on Rob's face was one that few people have ever seen. It was sinister, threatening, and evil. Harvey was all the more certain he had the right guy.

Rob drove to the police station with Detective Harvey following close behind. He was going to call Peggy to say he'd be late because of an add-on surgical case, but then thought better of it. This lying thing was getting out of hand, he thought. Instead, he called Peggy and told her the truth. "This damn detective is harassing me again. I'm calling my lawyer first thing in the morning, but for now, he wants me back to the station for questioning. I doubt this will take long, because I'm not giving him anything." Then he added, "Not that there's anything to hide."

When they were back at the station, the detective squinted his eyes, stared right at Rob, and said, "You know anybody by the name of Arnie Stimmel?"

Just hearing his name made Rob's blood pressure shoot up. The veins in his neck began pulsating, and his face turned four shades of red. "Stimmel, yeah, I know him. What about him?"

"Friend of yours?" he asked.

"I wouldn't say that. He was, but not anymore."

"Do you mind telling me when you saw him last?"

"About a week ago, why? What's this all about?" Rob assumed Arnie was scheming as usual, trying to find a way to pin something on Rob, always trying to get the last word.

"So, you say you're not friends, anymore?"

"I just told you, no."

"Why not?"

"Because he's a pig. Just ask my wife."

"I intend to." Harvey found his opening, a hole just large enough for Rob to fall into. "So, then I suppose that you know about the affair your wife was having with your friend, Arnie?"

Rob was rendered speechless, his mind flailing in every direction. It couldn't be true, he thought, but Arnie said it was. He didn't know what to believe. "An affair? Look, everything that comes out of Arnie's mouth is a damn lie. He's a serial liar. I don't care what he said, or how it looks, she wouldn't cheat on me, especially not with him."

Harvey stood up, and began clapping loudly. "I commend you. Great acting job, Prescott. You deserve an Oscar for your performance. But sorry, I can't give you a good review. I never root for the bad guy."

"I don't know what you're talking about, Detective, and frankly, I don't care. I have no use for Arnie, not anymore."

"Yes, that's obvious."

"I'm smarter than he is, more successful than he is, and I'm married."

"And, you're alive."

"What's that supposed to mean?"

"In case it slipped your mind, Prescott, you had Stimmel killed the other night."

"Killed?" Rob's face went white, his legs weak. "Arnie's dead?"

"I have to say, your acting is suburb. If I didn't know better, I'd believe you. But your face tells another story. You look a bit rattled."

"Of course, I'm rattled. You're telling me that my best friend is dead. How would you expect me to react?"

"You just told me that your former best friend is a pig who slept with your wife."

Rob was shaken to the core. "No, you said that."

"Look, Prescott, I'm not getting into a pissing match with you. Why don't you just tell me what happened."

"Why don't you tell me what happened?"

"I'll try to refresh your memory. Does home invasion ring a bell? Sound familiar? Same type of thing that happened to your wife just six months earlier, except she's still alive."

"Why would anyone kill Arnie?"

"Guess he had an enemy. You know anyone who might want him dead?"

"No, of course not."

"Funny thing. When the police went to clean up the mess, they took a look at his answering machine. Your call was on there. It didn't sound like you left him a very friendly message. You want to tell me about that?"

"Okay, it was no big deal. We had a disagreement. It was nothing. He was planning to stay at our house for the weekend, but he left early. After that, I don't know anything. I didn't have anything to do with this. I can account for my whereabouts practically down to the minute."

"That's certainly convenient, isn't it? Except murder is still murder, even if you aren't the one pulling the trigger. Your message makes you our number one suspect. Here, let me play it back for you." Detective Harvey pushes the play button on his tape recorder. "Arnie, this is good old Robbie-Boy, as you like to say, but this time you can address me by my full title, Dr. Robert Prescott..." When the message ended, Rob was sweating and breathing fast. Harvey didn't let up. "You wanted to off your wife, but the thugs you hired messed up the job. Looks like they got smarter with Stimmel. You must have coached them well, maybe drove up the money pot. They took care of your wife's boyfriend permanently. Well played, Doctor. He knew more than you wanted him to know, what with your wife confiding in him, that she suspects you were involved. You couldn't take the chance that he'd go to the cops and spill the beans. But it's almost over for you. Just a few more loose ends to tie up, and you'll be living in a six by eight cell."

"I haven't hired anyone to do anything, also, my wife and I are happily married. She doesn't have a boyfriend, and even if she did, it certainly wouldn't be Arnie. She hates him."

"So, she says," Detective Harvey replied.

Rob stood up shakily, "I've had enough of this conversation, and I've had enough of you. From here on, you can deal with my attorney. If you're so sure that I killed Arnie, then prove it. Until then, get off my back!"

"I intend to prove it, Doctor. That is precisely my intention."

Rob slammed the office door behind him when he left, as Harvey lit another stogie. That guy's close to caving, he thought. I think I'll pay a little visit to his wife after he leaves for work tomorrow, see about this romance between her and the murder victim. She's bound to be upset that her lover is lying six feet under.

CHAPTER THIRTY

I HADN'T WANTED TO USE the few sleeping pills that were left, but out of desperation the night before, I swallowed a couple, and hoped it would give me time to tell the man that my psychiatrist would not be writing any further prescriptions. My heart ached with the thought of losing him, but I didn't know what else to do. I attempted to speak with some of the night nurses after their shifts, days earlier, but there was nothing that could be done. One of them nicknamed the new night supervisor, "The Warden" and said it was impossible to bend the rules now.

I continued to stop by my mother's nursing home, now that the habit had been established. She was usually asleep by the time I arrived, but when she was awake, she didn't recognize me. Her last examination showed that she had fluid in her lungs, and her heart was failing. I couldn't bear the thought of her dying without me making the sacrifice of seeing her daily.

It was late when I walked into her room, but she had her eyes wide open. "Peggy, sweetheart, is that you?" Immediately, I was moved to tears.

"Yes, Mom, it's me. Peggy, your daughter. I came to visit you. I'm surprised you're still awake."

"Yes, I am. I'm very tired, Peggy, but I had to wait up for you. Thank you for coming all these days. I know it must be difficult for you with your husband and children needing so much of your time."

I didn't see the need to explain that Rob was nearly always at work now, and the children were busy in college. "Yes, but I'm never too busy for you."

"Peggy, I want you to open my nightstand drawer. Inside, there will be some crumpled tissues. I can't give you much these days, but still, I have a present for you."

"A present, for me?" Tears streamed down my face, and I was glad the darkness of the room hid my sadness. My mother had nothing left to give, so she wanted me to have some tissues. I opened the drawer, and found them stuffed in the back of her drawer. "Thank you, Mom. I always need to blow my nose and never have anything handy."

"No," she whispered. "Your present is inside the tissues. Open them."

Inside was a large handful of pink pills, more than enough sleeping pills to get to the man.

"How did you...?"

"Sweetheart, I may be old, but a mother always knows. I saw you take them when they used to leave them on the nightstand, but now they don't do it anymore, so I forced myself to stay awake, until the night nurse put the pill in my mouth. I refused the water, and made a swallowing sound. She left immediately, and I quick popped them from my mouth and wrapped them up, one by one. Are you having trouble sleeping?" she asked with concern.

"No, Mom. I need these to travel to a faraway land. I can't imagine how you knew I needed them."

"We old people know more than you think. We watch, we hear, we listen. Hide them on your way out, dear. Now, I really must go to sleep."

"Mom, you can't imagine the gift you have just given me. I am forever grateful. You have just changed my life."

Before I could say anything else, she was quietly breathing, and fast asleep. Whether this one night of lucidity was a gift from the universe, or kismet, I will never forget our final exchange of secrets and love.

The night nurse called within minutes before my arrival home, giving Rob the news. "I'm sorry to inform you, Dr. Prescott, but your wife's mother passed away minutes after she left her tonight."

When I walked in the door, Rob met me, putting his arms around me, holding me tightly. "I don't know how to tell you this, honey, but your mother just died. The nursing home just called."

I suppose he imagined that I would fall to pieces, but instead, I smiled, and thought to myself, this is exactly perfect. She was given one last presence of mind to help me, as she always had. Then I began humming my favorite song on my way to the shower.

CHAPTER THIRTY-ONE

It WAS NOW A FAMILIAR journey, the cobblestone street leading to the dirt path, up to the man's cabin, but, when I arrived this time, the cabin was dark. The man and his dog didn't greet me on the front porch, and when I knocked on the door, there was no answer. I peered through the windows, and saw multiple packing boxes stacked high in the living room. I knocked again, my heart frantic that he had already left me, that he could wait no longer. I raced around to the backyard, and there he was, huddled underneath a blanket, sitting in an Adirondack chair, his back to me, his head looking skyward. I held my breath, afraid to make a move, in case he was already dead. At once, I felt in the pit of my stomach the pain of his departure, the agony of living without him. My pain was visceral, hollow and empty. My tears streamed down my face, until sobs filled the air. The sound of my crying stirred the man, and he turned toward me, his face darkened by the night, his eyes dimmed with age, but still, when he saw me, he rushed to his feet and held me tightly.

"Oh, my God," I said, "I thought it was too late, I thought you had already died."

"I thought you left me."

"What's happening, why is everything packed up? Where is the dog?"

"Peggy, I'm nearly thirty-three years old. I'm not a young man anymore, not here in Hope. When you didn't return, I knew it was almost time. The dog was sent away first, to a holding place, but he will be cared for properly, until we meet again."

"No, no. It's okay. My mother gave us a chance to be together again."

"I know you think you can change destiny, but you can't. All we can do right now, is to enjoy what time we have left."

"No. I don't have to leave you. I have enough pills to keep coming back."

"It's no use. I've done this a thousand times before. It never becomes easier, but I have to keep in mind that someday we might meet again."

"No! I can't go on without you. You said that if we died together at the same time, we can stay together forever."

"I've already told you, that if we arrange to die together, if it is preplanned, we will be breaking the contract. We will never see each other again."

I became inconsolable at that thought, punching at his chest and grabbing onto his shirt for dear life. "When will it happen? What will happen?" He held me close because he knew it all seemed impossible. I searched his eyes, "There must be something we can do, some way of begging for what is surely our fate. You have to do something!"

Suddenly, he swept me up, and led me inside to the warmth, toward the bedroom, and I found myself willing, without hesitation. We went from crying to kissing to undressing, with the moonlight bouncing shadows and light on our nakedness, our passion everything I imagined and more. This was a gift, to wash away the past, and right the wrongs. The man I knew, or possibly invented, had an ethereal presence, manly, but graceful, sensitive yet strong, defying logic, and yet, as I was with him, he allowed me to be open to all possibilities, to accept some universal secret that I hadn't yet grasped. I had managed to cross through the barrier that had once separated us. My love for him was timeless, endless, and although it defied all semblance of natural law, it redefined the concept of eternal love.

Afterward, our breathing synchronized, I whispered, "You are real, aren't you?"

"Peggy, sweetheart, you didn't invent me. I am here, flesh and blood. I have held you, comforted you. You know that I exist."

By now, I had all but undermined my determination to be true to my family. As I lay in bed, the man beside me, I thought about Rob. He was a good husband, innocent to the fact that I married the wrong man. If I stayed with the man, my family would be splintered, and my children destroyed, their memory of me permanently tarnished. I had to leave the man, but it couldn't be tonight, not when my head is nestled against his chest, the beating of his heart matching mine, the smell of him, beckoning me home. "Someday, when you die, will you decide to come back to Hope, to wait for me again?"

"My love for you is unending."

The man looked tired, worn out, frail. I looked past him, past the window frame, past the trees, past the clouds. "Let's take a vacation together," he said, "We could go to the beach like we used to, or picnic at the lake, or hike the Appalachian Trail. We could take in the sights in Canada, and kiss under the mist of Niagara Falls." He sensed my hesitation. "My birthday is in a few days, and I really want to spend it with you." I didn't have the heart to deny him.

"You always wanted to learn to ski. We'll go up to the mountains and play in the snow. We can sit in the hot tub that overlooks the entire town, and make love by the fireplace. I could finally teach you how to ski. Remember that's something we never were able to do before when we were together."

I looked past the moon to the place I imagined I must be. "Of course, I said. "I want to go with you wherever you go."

CHAPTER THIRTY-TWO

ROB WAS EXTREMELY ALARMED BY my emotional state, or lack of tears as it pertained to my mother's passing, so much so that he put a call in to Dr. Sherman, worrying about my aberrant behavior, thinking perhaps, Dr. Sherman should cut back on my medication, unaware that he already had.

Dr. Sherman returned Rob's call mid-morning the next day, but Rob was in surgery by that time, and the two played phone tag until the better part of the afternoon. Finally, they connected. "Hello, this is Dr. Sherman."

"Hello, Dr. Sherman, Rob Prescott here. I wonder if I might have a few moments of your time."

Dr. Sherman was instantly annoyed, after all, time was money, and he didn't care to have to give up any moments of his time, for free. He should charge for this call, he thought, but instead said, "Yes, Rob, how can I help you?"

"My wife asked me a few days ago if I would write her a prescription for more sleeping pills, because she was afraid to ask you. The pills are doing her a world of good, but I'd feel better if you could order her more, rather than me, since you're in charge of her case, and all."

"Your wife, behind my back, asked you to write her a script for medication that I recommended, knowing full well that I cut her off? Doesn't that strike you as odd, Dr. Prescott?"

"I agree it is a bit unusual, but so is her behavior. It's been strange these last few weeks. You recall that initially I told you that Peggy is opposed to taking any medication, which includes vitamin supplements, and yet, she is almost frantic at the thought of not having enough of these pills."

"Yes, that is a bit odd. Anything else?"

"Yes, her mother just passed away, and she seemed fine with it."

"It might be of interest to you, that your wife has already attempted soliciting further pills from me, and is, I believe, addicted to them."

"That may be so, but frankly, I would appreciate it if she could have another prescription for my sake. She has been no trouble, and sleeps like a baby when she is medicated."

"I see. You and your wife have quite a bit in common. Both of you seem to put quite a bit of value on the sleeping pills and none on her therapy. I am not as insulted as I am stupefied that there is so little emphasis on the art of psychoanalysis. In any event, you are back to work, I hear. No problems with her being alone?"

"No, she seems to be fine."

Dr. Sherman was disgusted with what he considered to be a dependent, sniveling wimp of a man, doing his wife's bidding. As far as he was concerned, Rob was just another example of the castration of men by women. "I do not want you to interfere with her treatment, Dr. Prescott. Just as I would not show up in your operating room and take over your surgical expertise, I expect that you will show me the same respect in my treatment plan of your wife."

"Of course, of course. That's why I'm calling. I want to know what to tell her, because if I don't do what she wants, she's going to throw a fit."

This man should be embarrassed by the subservient manner in which he is behaving, thought Dr. Sherman. Perhaps it is the doctor who should be in treatment, rather than his wife.

"I don't want you to tell her you spoke with me, nor do I want you to give in to her requests. Put your foot down, be a man, and tell her she can settle her discrepancies with me, during her session tonight. Truly, Dr. Prescott, you are as much to blame as she is, with her lack of progress. You are enabling her, and keeping her dependent upon you. As it is, she has refused to so much as skim the surface of the home invasion, and now she is attempting to control therapy. I am in charge here, last I looked, and as her psychiatrist, I, and I alone, will determine what she needs. Otherwise, I will be happy to discharge her to your care." Dr. Sherman sucked in his breath, worried that if Rob took him up on his request, his bank account would suffer greatly.

Rob quickly backed down, but not before apologizing profusely. "I don't want to step on your toes, Dr. Sherman, you're doing a fine job. She's much, much better thanks to you."

When the call ended, Dr. Sherman made a notation of the phone call in her file. What was omitted, however, was a sinister plot that was formulating in his brain, a plot that would have her on her knees, squirming underneath his manipulative mental torture.

CHAPTER THIRTY-THREE

DETECTIVE HARVEY HAD BECOME PROFICIENT at making himself at home in the hospital, dining in the cafeteria, lingering in the parking garage, strolling up and down the hospital hallways, passing time in the gift shop, and always making certain that Rob Prescott noticed him, cheerfully aware that Rob's usual, complacent demeanor was slipping rapidly. Even the busy medical staff was aware of Rob's lack of patience which had never been part of his personality before. Whispers of the home invasion and Dr. Prescott's potential guilt spread quickly, with almost everyone taking one side or the other. As his wife, sadly, I felt myself slowly disconnecting with Rob, spending more time thinking about the man, and how much I wanted to vacation with him. Try as I might, I was no longer a faithful wife. Dr. Sherman had a long list of my character infractions. He could now add infidelity to the list. Every night I counted the sleeping pills, rationing the last of them, but needing more.

My appointment was still five hours away, but I didn't believe I could hold my sanity together for that long. I needed an emergency appointment immediately. Dr. Sherman was bound legally by confidentiality, and I needed to unburden myself.

I dialed Dr. Sherman's office, and connected with the secretary. "Dr. Sherman's office, can I help you?"

"Yes, hello, this is Peggy Prescott. I was wondering if Dr. Sherman would be able to squeeze me in earlier than my evening appointment. I really need to see him now."

"I'm sorry, Mrs. Prescott. The doctor is booked all day. What seems to be the problem? It's only a few hours until your next appointment. Surely, you can wait."

"I don't think I can wait. Is there any way you could switch someone else's appointment for mine? It really is an emergency. Or perhaps he could make a home visit."

"Dr. Sherman does not make home visits. He will see you tonight, as scheduled." When she hung the phone up, the receptionist said under her breath, "These rich people have some nerve, always wanting things their own way. As if we are going to make an exception for her."

Dr. Sherman had been within earshot of the conversation, and made up his mind. Looking to his receptionist he said, "Please call her back and give her a two o'clock appointment. Then cancel the scheduled two o'clock patient and tell him I've taken ill."

The receptionist slammed her coffee down on her desk. "But Dr. Sherman, if you give in to her, there's no telling how many other favors she's going to ask for, and besides, when you go against what I've told her, it only undermines my authority."

Dr. Sherman walked over to her desk, his face inches from hers, his tone measured, but controlling. "I didn't realize, Valerie, that when I hired you, you had the impression that you could decide how and when I conducted my practice. You've been here, how long now? Four years, isn't it?"

Valerie needed this job, and knew she had crossed an invisible boundary. This would not be the first time she had witnessed his anger when he was challenged. "Yes, sir, Dr. Sherman. I apologize. It is not my place to introduce my suggestions into your practice. Please forgive me. I'll be happy to call her back and schedule her in an hour."

"Thank you, Valerie. I appreciate your cooperation. As well, why don't you take the rest of the day off."

"But..."

"This is not a suggestion, my dear, but a directive. Good day." He already made a mental notation that this insubordination would have to be dealt with immediately. If there was one thing he was not about to tolerate, it was a woman who didn't know her place. Now, the fun would begin, he thought. He would make his secretary's life so miserable that she would quit, thereby relieving him of having to pay severance pay or unemployment. He gave himself less than one week to see his plan to fruition.

When Valerie called back, I detected her hostility, poorly masked by her sweet words and disingenuous concern. "Dr. Sherman will be happy to see you in an hour, if that is alright with you, Mrs. Prescott."

"Thank you, I'll be there." Dr. Sherman wasn't receptive the first time I explained about the man and how close we had become, but it was now interfering with my marriage, and consuming almost every waking moment. Even phone calls with my own children had become almost secondary to the magnetic pull to return to him. If Dr. Sherman was correct, if this was simply chemicals, interfering with my brain function, if he wasn't real, I had to know, everything was hinging on it. I knew I couldn't remain stable, if my dream life continued spilling over onto my earthly life, and if, indeed, there was no man, then I was in need of desperate treatment, perhaps even hospitalization. Could I have invented him, someone who possessed qualities more than my husband was willing to give, someone who believed in love above all things?

If he did exist, somehow, in some other universe, what would be the harm to have more time with him, to have more sleeping pills, enough to get me through the fear of losing him while Dr. Sherman and I worked this out?

CHAPTER THIRTY-FOUR

AFTER DR. SHERMAN DISMISSED VALERIE from her duties, he closed and locked the office door, dashing to his car and down the road. He knew I would be coming to my two o'clock appointment in a few minutes, and he made it a point to leave me waiting and wondering why there was no one at the office. He parked a few blocks away, but within eyesight of my car. He had to give me credit, he thought, for persistence. I waited more than half an hour, checking my watch, recalling my conversation with Valerie, and her call back to me, confirming my two o'clock appointment. Eventually, I left, and went home. I was exhausted and mentally unstable. I couldn't be inside my own skin, and the only thing I could think of was to take a sleeping pill, just one, to take the edge off. I took a nap, and some hours later, without meeting the man, I was awakened by my husband's voice as he entered the bedroom.

"Wake up, Peggy, I have something to tell you." Rob couldn't help but blurt it out, "Arnie Stimmel has been shot. He's dead! I found out last night when I ran into the detective, but I couldn't bring myself to tell you right before you went to sleep. I couldn't concentrate on work so I came home.

I'm glad you're still here. It's nearly time for you to go to your six o'clock appointment with Dr. Sherman. I can't believe it. He's dead!"

My six o'clock appointment? Wasn't that cancelled? Wasn't it supposed to be moved to two o'clock? I tried to piece things together as the fog of sleep left my brain. I was so confused, and now, Rob is telling me that Arnie has been killed. I began shaking, sobbing, deep, from deep inside, the news too much for me to bear. "Arnie's dead? I don't know what to do, what to say. How could it happen?"

"I don't know."

"Oh, my God. It's just too much. Arnie's gone!" I held my head in my hands, screaming. "It can't be true, I don't want it to be true!"

"I can't believe you're taking this so hard. You hated Arnie. I thought you'd be happy, or at least, relieved, that you'll never have to deal with him again."

"Rob, that's ridiculous. Of course, I didn't hate Arnie, and I certainly would never have wished him harm. He was awful in a lot of ways, but there's a part of me that felt close to him. He was a good friend to me."

Rob began pacing, his hands outstretched as he talked, "A good friend to you? He wasn't your friend, he was mine. You said you despised him, remember?" Rob had to think about this carefully. If Peggy was taking Arnie's death this hard, perhaps the detective was correct in his assumption that Arnie and Peggy were in fact, having an affair. He couldn't believe it, wouldn't believe it. "I think we're both better off without him, don't you agree?"

I stared at my once mild-mannered husband in disbelief. If Rob couldn't feel anything but reproach for the man he considered his best friend, maybe, I thought, he did have something to do with his murder. Maybe Arnie was right, when he said he was worried that Rob had something to do with my home invasion. Maybe the only way to shut Arnie up was to kill him, so that Rob would have nothing to worry about. "Who are you?" I asked Rob on my way out the door. I needed Dr. Sherman more than ever.

For the second time that day, I went to my appointment with Dr. Sherman, but the office was dark and locked tight. My eyes were swollen from crying over Arnie's death. When I returned home, Rob had gone out. I lay on the bed, but fell asleep quickly, still in my clothes, and without my sleeping pill.

The next day, I realized Rob had not been home. Nothing made sense, not Arnie's death, not my two missed appointments with Dr. Sherman, or my husband's unexplained absence. My eyes were nearly swollen shut, and my hair was a mess. My clothing from the day before was crumpled from sleep, and my mascara had smeared down my face. Before I could shower, the doorbell rang, and I saw Detective Harvey peering in the kitchen window. I didn't want to speak to him, and yet, I knew I might need him now more than ever. I opened the door. "Hello, Detective. I'm sorry, Rob isn't home. He must have gone to work," I lied.

The detective noted her disheveled appearance, and thought that the once-attractive Peggy Prescott had aged before his eyes. He was struck by her gray roots, and the black smudges streaked down her face. He took a closer look. The whites of her eyes were red, and her eyelids were swollen and hooded over her eyes. There was no doubt that this woman had spent a significant amount of time crying. Obviously, he thought, it had to do with Arnie. He wondered exactly how much she knew, and how. "You look upset, Mrs. Prescott. Everything alright?"

I was taken aback, not knowing if he was fishing for information, not knowing if he had locked up my husband for masterminding my home invasion or Arnie's death. "I'm alright. I just woke up from a bad dream."

"You slept in your clothes?"

I looked down at my crumpled shirt and tried to smooth it. "Was there something you wanted, Detective?"

Harvey decided his best approach was to catch her off guard. "Mrs. Prescott, Arnie Stimmel is dead."

His tactic didn't work. "Yes, I heard."

"I'm surprised you know. News must travel fast in your circle of friends."

"Rob told me, but, I'm sure you already know that."

"Is that right? When was that?"

"l don't know that I should be talking to you, Detective."

"Why not? Has your husband instructed you not to speak with me?"

"My husband doesn't want me speaking to anyone, unless he is with me. You know, just to make certain that I don't get any upsetting news that I can't handle in my condition."

The detective was pensive for a moment, attempting to worm his way into the kitchen. "And what condition is that?"

"The home invasion. My mental state." With that, I couldn't stop the flood of tears that came again.

My tears meant nothing to Detective Harvey. He's witnessed them over the years, real tears, crocodile tears, manipulative tears, and grieving tears. He considered the question carefully, formulating his words to have the greatest impact. "Which home invasion are you speaking of, Mrs. Prescott? Yours or Arnie Stimmel's?"

I could barely catch my breath. "Arnie died in a home invasion?" Rob never said anything about that. My mind was racing. Rob must have known something, done something, and if he hircd thugs to kill Arnie, what was to say he didn't hire the same thugs to kill me, but for some reason, they left me to die on my own? Arnie must have been correct, I thought. Rob really did want to dispose of me, but if Arnie came to save me, and now he's dead, there will be no one else to protect me from my husband. My knees buckled and the detective grabbed my arm in order to steady me, leading me to the kitchen table.

"Sit down, Mrs. Prescott. I can see you're very upset. I guess I'll leave you to your grieving. That is what you're doing, isn't it? Grieving over Arnie Stimmel?" Then Detective Harvey turned and said, "If I were you, I'd be sure to lock the door on my way out. These days you can't be too careful. You never know when the enemy might show up."

CHAPTER THIRTY-FIVE

DR. SHERMAN'S DECISION TO FIRE Valerie was a small price to pay, when he weighed it against the amusement he would have, toying with Peggy Prescott. Besides, he thought, why not save the money and let an answering machine do the job. Dr. Sherman put a call into Peggy at home the next day. "Good morning, Mrs. Prescott. Apparently, your little emergency turned out to be a non-event, I suppose. At least, that is what I have to assume when you missed your emergency two p.m., which, by the way, I gave you out of the goodness of my heart, cancelling a patient to fit you in, a patient, who, I might add, would have been more respectful about my time."

I was caught off guard, both by the phone call, the accusation that I had no regard for my psychiatrist's time, and more importantly, the fact that he was unaware of my attempt to come to my appointment. "Dr. Sherman, I showed up at two o'clock, or a little before, and the door was locked. I knocked and waited, but after several minutes I drove away. I would never not show up for a time that you had allotted for me."

"And, yet, you did. If you do not wish to continue with your treatment, please let me know. I have many more appreciative patients that would love to fill your spot."

"No, you have to believe me. I was there!"

"I do not have to believe you, or do anything else that you seem to want to order me to do. I was here, with my secretary, Valerie, the office was open for business, and we waited for you to show up. You never did."

I could have sworn I had driven to his office yesterday. I distinctly recall making the appointment with Valerie, but now, he was suggesting that I was either lying or had no memory of what I had done with my time. I thought I went to his office, but if he said I never showed up, then where was I?

"Dr. Sherman, I really needed to speak with you yesterday, and now, it seems that my days, even my hours, cannot be accounted for. May I please have an appointment for some time today? I cannot wait for my regular appointment tomorrow."

"I'm sorry, Mrs. Prescott, but the poor chap whose time you took yesterday, the time for which you never showed, was put on the end of today's very busy schedule. I don't mind working hard, as you are aware, but I'm not planning on staying here half the night. I apologize, Mrs. Prescott, but I'm afraid you can't be counted on to keep your word. Therefore, I will see you tomorrow night at six."

I was barely congenial, worried about my lack of memory, concerned that Dr. Sherman might throw me out of his practice for wasting his time yesterday, and frantic to stockpile sleeping pills. I begged Rob to prescribe more.

"I am no longer going to do what you tell me to do, Peggy. You have to respect my medical license and the agreement that we both made with Dr. Sherman that you would be treated by him. Do you recall agreeing to that?"

"Yes, but..."

"Good, then that's all we have to discuss on the subject."

That night was long, as was the next day, until my appointment, for which I arrived ten minutes early, sitting in the waiting room, rustling the outdated magazine pages, creating noise to make certain that Dr. Sherman knew I was here. At precisely six o'clock, he opened the door to his inner office, and without a word, ushered me inside. I sat down in the brown leather chair opposite his desk, and waited. He said nothing. Finally, I spoke first. "I'm sorry about the misunderstanding."

"I don't think there was a misunderstanding, as much as you wanted control over my receptionist, and then me. Let me make something clear to you. You will not now, and not ever, control this office. Do we understand each other?"

"Yes, and I hope I didn't get Valerie in any trouble."

"Valerie is not your concern. Now, what is on your mind, so imperative that you have attempted to turn my appointment book upside down?"

"I have to make certain that you are locked in secrecy to whatever I tell you," I said.

Dr. Sherman stood from behind his desk, walked slowly around my chair, then to the window, looked out, and walked back to his chair and sat down. My face was lined with such a serious expression, that he managed to hide his amused smile, by putting his hand over his mouth, forcing a cough. "I can't believe we must go over this again, Mrs. Prescott, but I suppose, since this hour does belong to you, you can use it any way you like. I will tell you this again, and please, I beg of you, let this be the final time. I am bound by law to keep your confidence. If I utter a word to anyone, of anything you tell me, you would have grounds to sue me, and I might be required to either spend a year in an ethics class under supervision, or relinquish my license, entirely. I hope you take this in the way it is meant, but you are certainly not worthy of my license."

I took a deep breath and blurted out, "I am deeply in love with the man in my dreams. I need to leave Rob and go to the man permanently, but I can't do that without your help."

"You want me to help you leave your husband?" Her words sent Dr. Sherman into what he could only think of as his first out-of-body experience. He pictured hurling himself across his desk directly toward her, pressing his thumbs into her windpipe until she suffocated. He was at the end of his patience, both with his job, and especially, with Peggy Prescott. He wrote copiously, now into his seventh notebook, considering that she was certifiably insane, a condition which he somehow missed, but now saw clearly. He thought that if he gave her even one shred of attention in this matter, he would be an accomplice, a co-conspirator in what he considered to be her elaborate fantasy.

When he focused, he realized she had continued speaking, most of which he missed. "…not leave my husband, but just to bring me back to Hope, where I want to live permanently." Her insanity was ruining everything, he thought. He was capable of treating the worst of cases, but this woman's mental state was dangerous. The money he could have made from her case, treating her over years, was suddenly dissolving before his eyes. She needed hospitalization, long-term. He could not erase the images that were swirling around in his mind, of yanking her teeth from her mouth, ripping her lips off, biting her tongue, so that not another word could be spoken. He continued to write, page after page, while she sat there, lamenting over a fictious man. He was sickened to the point of wanting revenge, not only for himself, but for all men, who had been deceived, cheated on, and then robbed of everything they had worked for, monetarily and emotionally. He had to regain control.

"All right, Mrs. Prescott. Allow me to join you in this fantasy. Let's say there is a man. Is he aware that you are married and the mother of two children?"

"Yes, that's the thing. He does know, but he isn't upset or jealous. It doesn't affect him that I still sleep with Rob, because in Hope there are no negative emotions, no jealousy, no anger."

"Hope?" Dr. Sherman opened an eighth notebook, in the attempt to write down every word of her delusions. "Oh, that's right. Hope is the mystery town where all the sniveling crybabies go, to wait to be reunited. You have quite the imagination, I'll give you that. As I see it, you are without any sort of conscience as you continue to 'cheat' on your husband. That behavior, Mrs. Prescott, is blatant and shameless."

"But, when I'm with Rob, I do love him, and since he doesn't know about the man, it isn't like I'm hurting him. Besides, I don't always remember Rob when I'm with the man. Sometimes I don't even know I'm really married."

Dr. Sherman wanted to throw his hands around her neck and ring it until her eyeballs bulged from their sockets. "Let me give you an analogy, Mrs. Prescott. If I'm drunk, and kill someone, but I don't remember it the next day, is that a defense?"

I sat quietly without responding.

"I'm asking you a question, that you refuse to answer. Here, I'll give you a hint. No, it is not a defense. The judge will have me dragged to the electric chair, despite my plea for mercy based upon my lousy memory. Do you understand my analogy, Mrs. Prescott?"

"Analogy?"

More notations, more silence, than words fashioned out of frustration. "Yes, surely, you have had some sort of relationship with the English vocabulary."

"You're angry. Are you disappointed in me?"

"Not at all. To the contrary, I expected nothing more from you. Your love for your husband is in words only. I find no loyalty there."

I jumped to my feet. "That is absolutely not true! I do love Rob with all my heart. I don't know how things are so mixed up, and I don't know how I can love two men at the same time, but I don't see how you can hold me accountable for my actions, when they are so pure."

"Let's suppose that your husband finds out about this affair you say you're having? Do you think he would understand the fact that you spend your nights having sex with another man?"

"Of course not, but if what you're saying is correct, then I'm not in a relationship, sexual or otherwise, because according to you, this man does not exist."

"Yes, but according to you, he does, and if that is the case, then that is the very definition of infidelity."

"Rob isn't someone who can take care of me, physically, I mean. He doesn't know how to fend for himself. I don't even know if he can protect me, but the man has talents that are, I don't know, manly. For instance, he can cut and stack wood, build furniture, paint a house. He has a dog he loves and cares for, among lots of other things."

"Your comments are quite interesting, and also quite superficial. The word on the street is that your husband is a master magician at reconstructing faces and bodies, a genius at his craft, hailed by those whose lives have greatly benefitted under his care."

"Yes, I see where you're going with this, Dr. Sherman, but in everyday life, stuff happens, things break, and Rob would have no idea how to remedy those situations."

"So, you believe that your mystery man is a king among hired hands?"

"You make him sound awful, and unflattering. I don't think you understand what I'm trying to say. Rob and I share space, and that's about it. The man and I share thoughts, visions, and dreams."

Thankfully, the hour was coming to a close and Dr. Sherman needed to wrap things up. "Mrs. Prescott, you indicated when you first began this hour-long rant, that only I could help you. What do you mean by that?"

"I need more sleeping pills. Please, I'm begging you."

Dr. Sherman was genuinely concerned, not for his patient, but for himself. He should have cut her off sooner, stopped prescribing weeks earlier, and certainly, should have never increased her dosage. It seemed, he thought, that she had quickly become addicted to them, sooner than he would have thought possible. If anyone was to get a hold of her therapy notes, he could not defend his lack of caution with medicine as potent as this. She's hallucinating, he thought, and it's not going to be on my watch that she does something stupid. "I believe these ridiculous fantasies that you are having is the result of chemically induced hallucinations, and if you recall, what we should be concentrating on, is your anxiety as a result of the home invasion."

"I don't think I need to revisit that home invasion situation. That's not what I need right now."

"Mrs. Prescott, I do not appreciate you using this office, and specifically me, as a forum to laud your betrayal of your husband. As well, you are seriously disturbed, more unstable than you know, or that I ever suspected, I hesitate to admit. Serendipitous that they did more than allow you to sleep, wouldn't you say?"

I said nothing, angry and ashamed, but he took my silence as ignorance and said, "Oh, that's right. I am quite certain you have no idea what the word serendipitous means. I'll try to use only mildly intimidating words when I speak to you in the future. I implore you, please use your free time to bone up on the English language."

When the session ended, Dr. Sherman opened his desk drawer, retrieved an unopened bottle of scotch, and poured himself a glass, neat. He pondered his next move. His sure thing, the endless supply of money, wasn't worth it. He had allowed his patient's condition to deteriorate before his eyes. She might tell her husband everything, about the man, her hallucinations, and blame it on his prescriptions. It would serve her no good to confide in Rob, but, he thought, women ultimately can never keep their mouths shut. He decided his best move was to pre-empt her, and call Rob Prescott himself.

He picked up the phone, but didn't make the call to Rob Prescott immediately. He had to be smart, think of all the angles. He would align himself with the good doctor. After all, he reasoned, there is a certain unspoken code of ethics that men should follow, he thought, and he would not turn his back on Dr. Prescott, regardless of his oath of confidentiality to his patient, but then it would come down to a matter of trust. Could he trust Rob Prescott to keep secret the betrayal of his patient's confidentiality, or would he, himself, be exposed when Rob, in a blind rage, and perhaps, unable to control himself, accuses Peggy of cheating, with the man, knowledge that could only have come from Dr. Sherman?

He picked up the phone again and this time, dialed. A second glass of the scotch leveled the playing field between an illustrious surgeon and a lowly psychiatrist, not always revered by the medical community. This was too much of a burden to bear, he thought, involving the height of deceit, the most premeditated of betrayal, the most vicious of lies, and the immoral sexual acts of Peggy Prescott, albeit, imagined. Suddenly, he thought, he and Dr. Prescott had more in common than either of them initially realized, and that fact alone, trumped the ethical standard of confidentiality, as far as he was concerned.

CHAPTER THIRTY-SIX

DETECTIVE HARVEY HONED IN ON the hospital parking garage, since history had proven that location made the greatest impact on Rob's agitation. Though to date, he hadn't been much more than a visual nuisance, this evening would prove to be quite different. As Rob exited the elevator on the underground floor, he spoke with several nurses, all of whom seemed to be enjoying Rob's company. Harvey hid discreetly in the corner, behind a large SUV until they had all said their goodbyes. "How's it going, Dr. Prescott?"

Rob was in no mood for social congenialities, anticipating that it would be just a matter of time that he would be arrested for the murder of Arnie Stimmel, based upon little more than his message found on Arnie's answering machine. He had to give Arnie credit for having the last laugh, even when he was six feet under. "Got a minute, Doctor?"

"Not for you, Detective." At that exact moment the phone rang, and he picked up the call absentmindedly, their eyes still locked in a stare down.

"Dr. Prescott?" The voice on the other end of the phone said. "This is Dr. Sherman. I would like to have a word with you."

Rob checked his watch. It was nearly eight p.m., at least an hour after Peggy should have arrived home after her appointment. "Is this an emergency, Dr. Sherman? Is Peggy alright?"

Dr. Sherman smiled with what he was about to drop onto the doctor's lap. "Peggy is just fine, but I thought we might meet for a drink somewhere private, so that we can discuss how things are going."

Rob turned his back on the detective. "That sounds good, but the timing is bad, if you mean tonight. I've got a detective trailing me, and, as a matter of fact, I think he might be planning to arrest me."

"Arrest you? For what, if you don't mind me asking?"

"The murder of Arnie Stimmel."

Dr. Sherman quickly disconnected the call, without saying goodbye. He wanted no part of this drama, not at all, and he certainly didn't need his phone traced to Robert Prescott if he was part of a murder investigation. This guy has more on his plate than a cheating wife, he thought. He wondered if the detective was within earshot. He revisited the conversation, realizing that Rob had said his name, hoping that the detective didn't make the association. Talking to a potential murderer, especially after hours, when there was no emergency, would surely be a red flag, to what, he wasn't sure. He wiped the perspiration from his brow. "Close call," he said aloud. I could have found myself in deep trouble tonight. Certainly, the Psychiatry Board would have found plenty to hang him with if he exposed his patient's notes to her husband, and if he had met Rob for a private conversation, Rob surely would have told the police the content of their meeting. Dr. Sherman thought he might have even been called as a witness in a murder trial, as someone who knew Rob Prescott intimately. It would have all come out, the fact that Peggy Prescott suspected Rob and implicated him in her home invasion, as well as having a boyfriend, of sorts, even if the man was imaginary. No, this was amounting to nasty business and something he wanted nothing to do with.

He drove home, lit his pipe, poured himself a scotch, and began to lay out the characters. There was Peggy, the insane, cheating wife of a prominent physician, there was Rob Prescott, a workaholic husband who may or may not have had something to do with the murder of Arnie Stimmel, and perhaps, the home invasion involving Peggy Prescott. Then there was himself, hired on to help the miserable women with her anxiety, to which he did relatively useless therapy, and prescribed a large quantity of sleeping pills, which would be verified by the pharmacy. If Rob Prescott was a murderer, perhaps he might kill his own wife, or worse, come after Dr. Sherman himself, to destroy any notes that might implicate him in his wife's home invasion. Perhaps her husband even wanted him dead. Maybe he had a motive to have her killed, but the thugs he hired botched the job, and now, Dr. Sherman himself might be a target. Perhaps, his thoughts continued, Robert Prescott had a bad temper, a jealous nature, and maybe even a history of spousal abuse, with his wife protecting him for the money. After all, if he went to jail, she wouldn't be able to support herself without his income.

God, I hate this profession, he thought. I'm on the hook for what my patients say, and I'm on the hook for what they don't say, most of whom are crazy out of their minds, dragging him into their world of sordid obsessions. Then, again, Robert Prescott didn't fit the profile of a killer, unless he had spent a lifetime creating a character that was gentle and mild-mannered, law abiding, and self-sacrificing. If the detective was correct, and, according to Peggy, suspected Rob of foul play, he was already in too deep, simply by association. He wanted out.

Sherman poured another glass of scotch to the rim of the glass, no ice, allowing the warm liquid to numb his throat. He considered his position in all this, what the press might do with it, and if, in fact, there was a murder case, Peggy Prescott's notes could be subpoenaed. He would decline, of course, and nothing but a court order could make him turn the notes over. In all his years of practice, a judge had never issued a court order, so he would be okay there. There was no way he could explain that the good doctor's wife had taken on a dream lover, right under Dr. Sherman's charge.

Now, rather than wanting to keep Peggy Prescott as his patient, he wanted nothing to do with her, but how would he get her to leave? He had insulted her, criticized her, belittled her, and yet, she still kept her appointments. That's the way it always worked with these crazy broads, he thought. First, they don't want to come, then they don't want to leave. He'd have to make her existence so miserable, that she would terminate therapy, but it would have to be subtle, nothing traceable. He took a deep breath, poured himself yet another scotch, with most of it landing on the table, and attempted to devise a plan. The liquor set him on a path of paranoia. Peggy Prescott owned him. He saw himself for what he had become, a money whore for the unloved and unwanted. He hated Peggy Prescott, that was a given, but more than that, he hated Rob for botching the job. If only the thugs he hired had completed the murder.

CHAPTER THIRTY-SEVEN

WHEN ROB TOLD ME THAT Detective Harvey was continuing to harass him, and fingered him for the murder of Arnie Stimmel, I feigned surprise. "How could he think you would have anything to do with his murder? He was your best friend. Didn't you tell him that?"

"Did you tell him that?" Rob's stare told me that he might know more than I think, that the detective might have hinted that he already suspected him, but I revealed nothing.

I loved Rob, not the way I loved the man in Hope, but I needed Rob. Suppose Dr. Sherman was correct? What if the man only existed in my mind, on drugs, hallucinations that have no substance in the light of day? Rob didn't deserve this. He did nothing wrong. I had caused this wedge between us, a crack in the very foundation of what we once promised each other, now pinning us against each other. I had to find a way to glue us back together. I blamed Dr. Sherman for my disloyalty, the way he provoked me, the way he made me seem crazy, until I believed that I was.

I vowed my loyalty to Rob. I would stand by his side. He looked so broken. "Rob, let me help you," I said. "Tell me what is going on."

"I left a threatening message on Arnie's answering machine. The police in Maryland found it, called Detective Harvey, and they're both working the case, pointing fingers at me. But the only reason I left that message was because Arnie told me he was with you that day, while I was at work, that the two of you had sex in our bed, that the two of you had something going on right under my nose." Rob began breathing heavily, his eyes flashing rage, his fists clenched. I was afraid for him, and I was afraid of him. "I thought you were going to leave me."

"So, you had Arnie killed?"

Rob looked at me with tears in his eyes. "I can't believe you just asked me that. You've known me for more than twenty-five years. How could you think I am capable of taking someone's life?"

I thought of my own situation, my own deceit. "No one ever knows anyone, Rob, and that's a fact."

"What do you mean by that? I know everything about you, and you know everything about me."

There it was, another lie. Another reason not to believe him. Arnie told me about his affair with the nurse so long ago, and yet, Rob is looking me straight in the eye and lying. "So, did you do it, or didn't you?"

"Of course not! We're a team. We belong together. Nothing can tear us apart."

I felt sorry for him. He seemed so lost, so hopeless. "I will stand by you, Rob, always. I know you. I know your heart. You would never hurt anyone." My words sounded convincing, even to me, but there was still the part of me that doubted him. I should never have allowed Arnie to fill my head with words that turned me against my own husband, especially in light of what I was doing with someone else. That was the turning point for me, the realization of what I had become, and I decided right then and there that I would put all my effort into therapy, and getting well. I would talk about the home invasion with Dr. Sherman regardless of how painful it would be. My affair had to be over with the man.

Rob held me. "Thank you, Peggy. Thank you for always being there for me. I don't know how our lives have gotten so out of control, but I blame Arnie for everything. I despise him, you have no idea how much."

I shuddered at his words, once again fighting suspicions that there might be a side of Rob that I don't know, because there is certainly a side of me that he will never know. Rob poured us both a glass of wine. "Let's forget about all this now. Tell me, how are your therapy sessions going?"

"Fine, I guess."

"That's good. I was a little worried when Dr. Sherman tried to call me, but I was with the detective, and I couldn't talk. I tried calling him back several times, but he never answered his phone."

"Dr. Sherman called you?"

"Yes, after eight, after you left his office."

I couldn't imagine what Dr. Sherman would want to speak to Rob about, unless he was going to disclose my affair with the man. I wouldn't put it past him, but what would he gain? I could sue him, but that wouldn't put my marriage back together. He had all the ammunition. It would all become public if I did sue him for breach of confidentiality, all my private thoughts, so many months, page after page of my life, played out in his notes. I had to make this right. "I think I'm making progress in therapy. Thank you so much for paying for all my sessions the past few months."

"Don't be silly, honey. You don't have to thank me. I would happily give you every penny I had if it helped you to get well. There is nothing I wouldn't do for you. Nothing."

More suspicion. If he would do anything for me, then he might very well be capable of killing Arnie, especially if he thought Arnie was going to break up our marriage. I had to see the man one last time, and tell him of my decision to be faithful to Rob. There were not many pills left, so I rationed them, taking only two and went to sleep.

The man was waiting on his front porch. Even when I stood right in front of him, he was unable to see me. No matter how I tried, I couldn't get his attention. My arms grasped for his, but they made no contact. Dusk became night, and he turned, finally, and went inside. "Don't go," I screamed, "I'm here. I'm right here."

I woke up drenched in sweat, distressed, crying, unable to connect with him. My sobs awakened Rob, who pulled me close. "A nightmare, honey?"

"No, Rob. I just need more time. I have some things I've left unfinished. You have to trust me. You just have to."

"Of course, I trust you. You're the only person in the world I can trust."

His words pierced my heart. "Dr. Sherman thinks you're too good for me, and he's right. I am an awful person."

"Honey, you're still half asleep. You'll feel better in the morning."

Rob began stroking my hair and back. I knew what he wanted. He was a man of habit. It was always the same, stroking my hair, massaging my shoulders, nuzzling his face into my neck, nibbling my ear. He wanted sex, plain and simple. I felt sorry for him, but repulsed at the same time. I had to end it with the man before I could be with Rob sexually again. "No, Rob, I'm sorry, not tonight."

"Sex will make you feel more relaxed. Besides, honey, it's been a long time."

I was trying, I really was. I wanted to be the wife Rob deserved, but not tonight. I was torn, ripped apart by what seemed so real, but perhaps was just a figment of my imagination, and a chemical reaction. Sex with Rob was out of the question right now. I rolled over and went to sleep, knowing that I would go to the man once more, to our promised vacation, and to celebrate his birthday. When it was time to leave him, I would explain that I would never return, and that he should move on to whatever lies beyond the town of Hope.

CHAPTER THIRTY-EIGHT

DETECTIVE HARVEY WAS JUST POWERING down his computer and signing off for the night, when his phone rang. It was ten minutes past five in the evening, and he let the machine pick up. "Hey, Sergeant Barney Bristol here, Baltimore, P.D., remember me? Anyhow, I wanted to touch base on that nasty Prescott case..."

Harvey picked up the phone. "Hello, Bristol, Glen Harvey here. What's up?"

"Not much."

"Okay, well you called me, and it's ten minutes past closing time, so what's on your mind?"

"Well, now, I called to tell you something that you're not going to want to hear." Then silence.

Detective Harvey turned the lights back on and lit a cigar. This wasn't going to be quick, he thought. "Don't you ever go home, Barney?"

"I don't have much occasion to keep an eye on the clock, since the missus left me. I pretty much just try to keep busy."

"Oh, sorry to hear that. It's gotta be rough. I'm going through the same thing. So, about the Prescott case..."

"Well, Chief, here's what I called to tell you. Except for the message on Stimmel's answering machine from your boy, Dr. Prescott, we got nothing else. No fingerprints, no blood spatter that doesn't belong to the victim, no clues whatsoever. I was kinda hoping you had something on your end to help me out."

"Bristol, don't you think if I had something on my end, I'd have called you by now?" God, this man was irritating as hell.

"So, what should we do now, Chief?"

"The first thing you need to do is to stop calling me Chief. Right now, I'm going home to try to patch things up with my wife, and since I haven't been home for days, for all I know she's probably moved out, and I wouldn't blame her."

"Yup, sorry to hear you're having women problems, it's going around. Like I said, my wife walked out on me not too long ago, my uncle's having the same problems with his wife. Last Saturday, he comes walking in the house and--"

"Bristol, you idiot. Can you stick to the business at hand? I'm running low on patience, I'm starving, and I'd like to go home."

"Oh, okay, Chief, uh Detective Harvey. Sorry, but I'm not too good with names. My sister was the same way...oops, there I go again. Sorry. My buddies always cut me off too. You know I'm kinda slow on a lot of things, but I got one thing goin' for me. I'm a real good police officer."

"No kidding, if you're such a great cop, why haven't you figured out a way to help me nail Prescott? I want him behind bars so bad I can see it in my dreams. You know Prescott's good for both home invasions, right? If we don't get him off the street soon, we can add a dead wife to his resume."

"Well, now, that comment sure hurt my feelings just now, but I will try harder, Detective Harvey. You'll see. You'll be real proud of me. I'm going over all the evidence you sent me from scratch, and see if we missed anything. You want to come help me?"

"Come to Maryland?"

"Yessir, I can pick you up at the airport anytime, day or night, no advance notice needed and there's a spare room I can put you up in. Real comfortable mattress."

"Nope. No can do. I have a fear of flying."

"Well, ain't that something? I had a friend who was afraid to fly, couldn't even drive to the airport, and guess what happened?"

"I'm sure I don't know, nor do I care." He put out his cigar and turned off the lights. "Sorry, Bristol, I can't do this anymore. It's turning my stomach."

"I bet you have that stomach bug that's been goin' around. I had it last week, couldn't get off the toilet for two days."

"If there's nothing else..."

"Well, there is one more thing. Last night, I was watching television. Law and Order. I just love that show, how about you?"

"Yeah, sure."

"You can really learn a lot from those real-life television shows. Anyhow, there was this murder, and they kept looking at the husband, but they couldn't pin nothin' on him. Then one guy, the smart one, says what about the wife? See what I mean?"

"Sorry, I'm not following. You think that Mrs. Prescott went to Baltimore and shot Arnie Stimmel in the head?"

"Course not. Now you're just playing with me, right? I'm just saying, maybe the wife knows more than we think. After all, if she turns her husband in, there goes his salary, and the house, the boat, the car, the whole shebang. Maybe she's protecting her assets."

"Keep watching TV, Bristol. You're bound to come up with something. I gotta go."

"Oh, I get it, that stomach bug again. That'll keep you on the pot, for sure. Best get some of that hemorrhoid cream on the way home, all that strainin' and such, next thing you know you're sitting on your insides."

Harvey slammed down the phone. Sergeant Bristol muttered to himself, "Poor guy, sour stomach. He must have had to race to the bathroom real bad for him not to say goodbye."

CHAPTER THIRTY-NINE

THE DAY OF MY FINAL meeting with Dr. Sherman, I told him about our vacation, our plans to ski and enjoy the mountains. "The man has been so kind to me, I owe it to him to show up one last time, and to share his birthday plans. Don't you agree that's the correct thing to do?"

Dr. Sherman faced the window to the street, watching the cars coming and going. The sky had a purple tint, and the wind picked up. Must be a storm brewing, he thought. It wasn't until he heard his name for the second time, that he realized he had drifted off into his own fantasies, unaware that Peggy was waiting for a response to her blabber, that he had, for a while, successfully tuned out. "I'm sorry, Mrs. Prescott, your question, again?"

"I said, I think honoring my promise is what I should do. It's important."

"Important to who? You are not as important as you think you are, and you certainly have no importance to me. May I say, Mrs. Prescott, that among your other horrid character traits, we must include the following, you are a first-class narcissist."

Although I was familiar with the word, apparently, my expression said otherwise. "Yes, Mrs. Prescott, yet another word you may add to your ever-increasing vocabulary. I shall help you with the definition. It means that you are self-centered, self-involved, and unaware of the needs of anyone but your own. Your husband has been through hell trying to help you, his best friend has been murdered, your children seem to be nothing more than an afterthought, your incessant need to spend your husband's money knows no bounds, and your insistence in arguing about the necessity of the sleeping pill matter has been nothing short of exhausting. Now, you're planning to romp in the snow with your lover. You have no right, knowledge, or experience in the field of psychotherapy, and yet, you persist in inserting your amateur theories, as if you're an expert. That, my dear Mrs. Prescott, is what is known as a textbook narcissist."

I left in tears, but that did not affect Dr. Sherman in the least. After the session was over, he remained in his office, staring at the peeling leather chairs and his scuffed mahogany desk, a couple of side tables and mismatched lamps. His former wife was kind enough to allow him to keep his office furnishings, which he turned into a surrogate home of sorts, making it as comfortable as possible for his patients and their burdens of misery. He despised every one of them, the sniveling men crying about being taken advantage of by their wives, and ungrateful women who believed they were entitled to their husband's paychecks, passwords and private thoughts. The infidelity, the lies, the fights that left children in the midst of their selfishness. It was a wonder that anyone would plunge into relationships, he thought, never mind the institution of marriage. The few moments it took to promise unending love, was nothing more than the backdrop to years of repairing the permanent damage of divorce.

His medical diploma stared him in the face. "My entire life has been a complete waste of time," he thought. He was lost in his own despair, when the glare of headlights shining in the unshaded window interrupted him. A male shadow got out of the car, and walked to Dr. Sherman's office door, knocking. He looked familiar, but in the dark, Sherman couldn't be too sure. Another knock sent him to open the door, cautiously, only to find Rob Prescott. "Dr. Prescott, is everything alright?" He immediately assumed Prescott's wife had committed suicide, although he had no indication of that from their earlier visit. He was hard on her, no doubt about that. Perhaps he went too far. Should that be the case, he most certainly would find himself in front of his ethics board. I would have to defend myself, he thought, his word against her own. He stood upright, supported by his ego, and said, "Please come in. To what do I owe this unexpected pleasure?"

Rob followed Dr. Sherman into the inner office, his eyes staring at the opened bottle of scotch on the desk. It was dark, with the exception of the desk lamp, and he assumed Sherman was packing up for the night. Rob stammered, "I was just driving by, in the neighborhood, and well, I thought maybe I could come by, if you were still in your office, and well, here you are."

Dr. Sherman's anxiety was mounting. What did this guy want? "Yes, I see. Please, sit down. How can I be of assistance?"

Rob sat down, got up, then sat down again. He wrung his hands, first one way and then the other. "I'm in a bit of trouble. I did something wrong, something completely out of character, and I need to talk to someone about it. Confidentiality is a must."

So, it wasn't about his badgering of Prescott's wife. That was good news, but not good enough. Dr. Sherman wanted out. Out of this conversation, out of this office, and out of this job. He believed that Rob Prescott was about to confess to the murder of Arnie Stimmel, and he couldn't be a party to that. Rob's protection by confidentiality would not be upheld, and the very association between he and Rob Prescott would cast shadows upon his name. If Rob confessed to the murder, he would not think twice about killing Dr. Sherman to prevent him from notifying the police. He wasn't ready to die. "I'm sorry, Rob, I'd like to help you, but you're not my patient, and anything that you tell me would not be kept confidential."

Rob thought for a moment, then said, "Fine, give me the paper-work. I'll sign it, and to make it official, charge me whatever you want. I'll pay cash."

"No, that would be unwise. I'm sorry, Rob, since I'm treating your wife, initiating a professional relationship with you would be considered a conflict of interest. I would, however, be pleased to refer you to a colleague."

Rob backed up against the far wall, causing Dr. Sherman to back up against the other, suddenly noticing the andiron by the fireplace, just within Rob's reach. After a momentary pause, Rob walked toward Dr. Sherman, shook his hand, and said, "It's just as well, I shouldn't have bothered you about it."

"Maybe you should talk to your wife, and get whatever worry you have, off your chest." Besides, Dr. Sherman thought, she would be pro-tected against having to testify against her husband in court, should it come to that.

"You don't understand. It involves my wife, I was unfaithful, I betrayed her, and I am consumed with guilt over it."

Dr. Sherman misread the issue at hand, prematurely believing Rob was about to confess either to the home invasion or the murder of his friend Arnie, when all the while, he wanted to unload guilt over his cheat-ing. He almost started laughing out loud. This was comical, he thought, two people cheating on each other, one willing to unload guilt, the other feeling no guilt at all. "You had an indiscretion? My dear man, no man ever admits to an indiscretion. That's marriage 101, deny, deny, deny." Dr. Sherman turned out the lights in his office and walked Rob to the door, saying, "That advice is free."

CHAPTER FORTY

Rob passed Detective Harvey in the hall, coming from the direction of the administration office. "Have a good day," Harvey said with a smirk on his face. Rob continued on to the operating room, but found that he had been replaced on the board by another surgeon for the seven o'clock case.

"Dr. Prescott," the unit secretary said, "I've been told to send you up to the top floor, to the Chief Attending."

He got off the elevator on the fifth floor, and nearly bumped into the CEO. "Dr. Prescott," he said, "Please have a seat in my office."

Rob walked inside and sat down, "What in the hell is going on? Why is my name erased from today's surgical schedule?"

The CEO shuffled some papers on his desk, then straightened them, causing more tension in the air than there already was. "Is there anything you'd like to tell me, Dr. Prescott?"

Rob's irritation spilled over into his tone of voice. "Yes, I want to tell you that I'm supposed to be scrubbing for my first case of the day right now, and instead I'm sitting in your office without a clue as to what in the hell is going on."

The CEO stared at Rob and spoke slowly, enunciating each word firmly. "What is going on, Rob, is that people are talking, gossip is spreading, and speculation is running rampant. The talk on the street is that you may not be as focused as you should be, what with your, shall we say, legal entanglements and intrusions."

"What other intrusions?"

"I just concluded a visit from Detective Harvey. He has insinuated that you may have some legal problems to sort out. I can't allow you to operate on patients, if you are not one hundred percent mentally fit."

"What are you talking about? I'm as mentally fit as you are, maybe more. I can assure you that I've never been better."

The CEO sat back in his chair, "Look Rob, I like you. You're a great surgeon and a good man, but there's no denying that you and your family have been under quite a strain these past few months. The nurses have reported that your attitude in the operating room is less than stellar, and you certainly are acting testy with me right now. I think it would be best for all of us, if you took some vacation time."

"I've barely been back to work. I don't need more time off from work. I need to work."

"I hate to pull rank, Rob, but I have to protect the reputation of this hospital. How would it look if news got out that you are being investigated for a crime, and we continue to allow you to come to work? I'm sure all this can be ironed out soon, and you'll be back before you know it, but right now, my loyalty has to be to this hospital and the patients we serve."

"Can you tell me what the detective told you?"

"I'm sorry, Rob, but I'm not at liberty to disclose his statements right now. Let me just say that it was enough to cause me concern."

Rob sat there for a few minutes, hoping there would be more conversation, but when it was clear that the meeting was over, he got up and left, cleaned out his locker and went home.

In the meantime, back at Detective Harvey's office, the suspense to finally arrest Rob was closing in. Harvey called Sergeant Bristol in Maryland, who picked up his phone on the first ring.

"Bristol, Crime Bureau."

"My God, don't you folks have secretaries? You just waiting by the phone, hoping for some action? This is Detective Harvey, down in Florida. Got a minute?"

"Howdy, Detective. I knew it was you, the minute you started talking. My secretary up and quit a few days ago, said she was gonna take some time off to get some schooling. Her exact words to me were, "If you can do this job, any moron can." I don't think she needed to be that hard on herself, what do you think?"

"Not sure she's talking about herself, but that's just me."

Bristol, missing the sarcasm, picked right up where they left off last time. "So, what's on your mind, Detective? You still got that stomach trouble?"

"What? No, no stomach trouble. I'm close to making an arrest. Tying up a few loose ends, but I think I'll have enough to get him."

"No kidding, that's great. Who are you fingering?"

"Dr. Prescott, of course. Good God, don't you have any recall. The plastic surgeon, Stimmel's friend, turned his worst nightmare."

"Sure, I got recall, but I don't think your evidence is going to hold up. Not in front of a judge. What we call it in Baltimore is circumstantial evidence, you know, no real link to the crime."

"That's what they call it everywhere, you moron, but circumstantial evidence still flies if you pick the right jury, you know what I mean?"

"Sure thing, Chief, but how you gonna know how to pick the right kind of jury?"

"I'm going for a jury of all men. Men who have been jilted by their lovers, men whose wives divorced them and ran off with someone else, men who know when another man has reached his last straw. Men are black and white in their thinking, dumb, smart, educated, or high school dropouts, they all have one thing in common. They can't stand a lying, cheating woman. All we have to do is show the jury that Dr. Prescott, the hard-working, dedicated family man that he is, found himself with a cheating wife who slept with his best friend. That's a man who would hire a couple of thugs for the home invasion. He wanted her dead, no doubt in my mind, but the thugs got soft. It didn't go the way he planned, so if he couldn't kill the wife, he'd have to kill the boyfriend."

"Well, sure, when you put it like that, it does sound reasonable, but won't these men feel sorry for the guy?"

"Jurors are known to take their job seriously. You can take a pot-smoking, good-for-nothing, out of work loser, put him on a jury, and suddenly he's a genius with the law. I've seen it time and time again. After a trial, when the jurors are interviewed, they all sound like they have Ph.D.'s, quoting the law verbatim. Then, they go back to their pot-smoking lives and clip coupons, but for those couple of days during a trial, they're on top of their game. I think they'll convict him, maybe even give him the death penalty. We've got a little place here by the name of Stranton, where they give out lethal injections like candy."

"Seems like you've been thinking about this case a lot."

"Every day and night. I just needed to figure out the plan, and now I have. Besides, my job is riding on this case. I want you to go through the files again, A to Z, then send me what you have."

"Should I put it in a brown envelope?"

"What?"

"You know, the way they mail those porno magazines?"

"Bristol, you're a real piece of work, I'll give you that. Just mail what you have FedEx overnight and do it as fast as you can. I need your files yesterday."

CHAPTER FORTY-ONE

WHEN ROB ARRIVED HOME, I had already taken a bath and was getting ready for bed. "You're home late, were you stuck in the operating room?" I asked.

Rob didn't stumble over his lie. "Yes, a bad car accident just west of town, nobody killed, but a family of four pretty smashed up. I think they'll all be alright in a few weeks. Right now, though, I'm beat. Ready for bed? Unless you want something more?"

"No," I said, a little too quickly. "I just can't have sex right now." They'll be plenty of time for sex with my husband after tonight is over, in the weeks and years to come, after I leave the man forever, but right now, I just wanted to get to the man as quickly as possible. Rob opened a bottle of wine, offered me a glass, and got annoyed when I declined. He managed to finish off the entire bottle himself. With the final amount of sleeping pills in my bathrobe pocket, I went upstairs, took a long drink of water, and swallowed all of them at once, falling into a deep sleep.

The man was waiting for me. We embraced tenderly, and then he said, "It's time." The man smiled, though he felt like crying, but this was no time to be sad. Love is never a reason for sadness, he thought. "Today is your big day. I'm going to teach you how to ski."

Just like that, the man and I were immediately transported to a beautiful lodge at the base of the mountain. Vacationers and locals were milling around, carrying their skis, preparing to enter the lifts, or sitting in outdoor chairs with mugs of hot chocolate.

"Let's get our lift tickets and enjoy the day," the man said. His voice sounded weak, weary, but happy to be here with me. I knew I would have to break the news to him, that I chose Rob and my family over him, but I couldn't bring that up now. He would find out soon enough.

We began walking toward the lifts, but a passing skier, carrying his poles and skis said, "Doesn't look good. The lifts are down for now. They're calling for new snow and possible avalanches. They've got to get the all-clear before the mountain opens again."

"Avalanche?" the man said. "Usually, this time of the year, is not common for avalanche conditions."

"Yes," he said over his shoulder, "Highly unusual. I'm bummed. This is my last day here, and I was looking forward to trying out the diamond slopes. They said they might allow people on the lift later on, depending on conditions, but it doesn't look promising."

The man turned to me. "We shouldn't take a chance if the conditions are unstable."

"I was so looking forward to it," I pleaded. "Couldn't we at least climb some of the mountain and look down at the town below?"

"Let's wait and see if the lift starts back up. If it does, we'll hop on, before they change their mind."

"I'm not afraid," I said, "After all, it's only snow."

"An avalanche is a lot more than snow. It is a fury of impacting energy that can kill. Most people don't realize this, but a major avalanche is the size of eighteen to twenty football fields of snow, barreling down the mountainside. It's just too dangerous. Let's just wait and see what happens."

"Couldn't we outrun it, even if it does happen?"

"Unlikely. An avalanche follows a track, taking trees, rocks and people with it. If someone is fortunate enough to know to run horizontal to the avalanche, and out of its path, there's always the possibility of survival, but to actually outrun it, no, an avalanche can travel as fast as one-hundred twenty miles per hour. No human can outrun that."

We decided to check into our room while we waited, making love, taking our time, our passion insurmountable. He looked into my eyes and said, "You are the part of me that was worth it all." I wanted to breathe in this moment forever. The strength of his arms holding me as if everything would be ok. But deep within, where I wouldn't allow my mind to go, was the inevitable tick of dread. Time, like a marching soldier, battling on.

Suddenly, we heard, a group of skiers cheering just outside of our window. "It's up and running!" they yelled. We hurriedly dressed and followed them. The chair lift began moving slowly up the mountain, scantily filled with skiers, the risk takers, with the more cautious skiers congregating at the foot of the hill, preferring to wait out of an abundance of caution. "I've seen this happen before," one of them said, "an overly zealous chair operator giving the okay, when conditions are still precarious. It's all about the money. No skiers, no money."

The man stood by my side, conflicted. I made the decision. "Let's go, we came this far, and who knows how long I can stay," I said, thinking of the sleeping pills.

The man agreed, knowing his time was limited, but saying nothing.

"Let's go all the way to the top," I said. "We can carry our skis for a while, while we take in the view on our way down to a lower slope."

Again, the man agreed, but he was no longer making rational decisions. His chest felt constricted, and his oxygen level was dropping. The pain in his chest was almost debilitating, and he knew, his time was running out, yet he said nothing.

The view from the top of the mountain was breathtaking. The sky crested like a wave, muted grey and blues blending into each other. We took off our skis, deciding to walk down a path out of the way of skiers. We held hands as I rambled on, about the view, about our lives, about our timeless love. I was so engrossed in conversation that I hadn't noticed that the man's steps were becoming shorter, weaker, his breathing labored, stopping to rest frequently. We had walked at least a mile by now, and heavy snow began falling again. "We need to get back down to the lodge," I said.

I tried to hurry him, but he wasn't able to move any faster, finally falling to his knees, looking up to the heavens, pleading, "Not now! Please, just a little longer." His eyes held immense sadness.

"What's wrong?" I yelled. "What's happening?"

The man's voice was suddenly drowned out by what sounded like a freight train. It was the unmistakable sound of an avalanche, heading our way. "Run," he screamed over the noise, "Run, Peggy!" I stood still, not moving, "Please, Peggy, you have to go. I love you, and I'll see you again. I'll be waiting for you the next time you come to me, I promise, but for now, save yourself!"

I was conflicted. I knew I was ultimately going to go back to Rob, but on my terms, not like this. I looked into the man's eyes and saw fear. "I can't leave you here to die."

"You can't stay, and I'm dying anyway. I won't live much longer, but you have to save yourself, if you ever want to see me again."

I stood up, tears running down my face, turning back one last time, knowing our time together had come to an end. "How will I find you?"

"You will feel me pulling you toward me, and if you are able, you'll find a way to come." The man's face was ashen gray, his breath coming in short, shallow bursts, then long pauses. I knew I had to leave him, to run, like he begged me, to save myself for my husband and my children, especially if we were ever to meet again. I gave him one last kiss, but his eyes were almost shut and his breathing all but stopped. I remembered what he told me, to run in a path horizontal to the avalanche. I had to go, now. As I attempted to leave, my boot wedged into a tree root, just visible above the snow line. I turned this way and that, but I couldn't unleash its grip on me. I tried to take my boot off, but there was no time left.

"No," I cried. "No!" My heart was torn in two directions, feeling a tremendous loss for the man, but also a desperate need to save myself for my family. I strained again, trying to wiggle out of my boot, but my foot wouldn't budge. Panic gripped me, and I knew I was about to die. The deafening wall of snow was nearly upon us. I threw myself over the man, to protect him, bracing for what was to come. I closed my eyes and saw the faces of both men before it hit. The man whispered his love for me just before his words, and my cries, were silenced by the mountain of snow that covered us. Hovering birds witnessed our final moments, as the treetops bowed in prayer.

Forever closed in.

CHAPTER FORTY-TWO

DR. SHERMAN, STILL IN HIS pajamas, bent down to retrieve the morning paper outside his door. The headlines hadn't been kind to Rob Prescott, and today was no exception. Splashed across the front page in bold type, for all to see, was 'Plastic Surgeon Trial Ends Today'. Underneath the headline, was printed, 'Prosecution Seeks Death Penalty'. The column was written by an ambitious reporter who suggested several motives for the killing of Peggy Prescott at the hands of her husband, Dr. Robert Prescott. Speculation had been growing for weeks, and it was nearly impossible for him to get a fair trial, in this town, or any other. Locals and gawkers alike, filled the streets, standing on the Prescott's lawn, taking pictures of the Prescott house, and talking among themselves. Everyone wanted a piece of Dr. Prescott.

The reporter was explicit in describing the details of her death, going on to say, that although Mrs. Prescott had not been dismembered, it was assumed by the authorities that the husband had stored her in a fish freezer for an undetermined amount of time, only to move her back to the marital bed to be 'discovered' by him. Detective Harvey's words were quoted, saying that it was because of the arrest, that 'Dr. Prescott was off the streets, and the community was once again safe'. Of course, the defense attorney tried to punch a hole in his testimony, attempting to capitalize that the DNA recovered from the semen in Mrs. Prescott's body did not match Rob's DNA, but nonetheless, from the look on the faces of the jurors, that fact didn't appear to hold much merit. The paper also stated that 'Detective Harvey was held in high esteem by his superiors, remarking about his dedication, while attempting to crack the case.'

To his credit, Rob never veered from his story, swearing that he was telling the truth about finding his wife dead in bed. No one, of course, believed him, including his own children. He was a man who was at the brink of losing everything and everyone he ever loved.

Dr. Sherman threw the paper down onto the kitchen table and paced the floor. He knew Peggy told him that she was about to vacation with the fictious man at a ski resort. He laughed at her and called her crazy, but, in fact, impossible as it was to even begin to imagine the events that might explain her frozen state, he didn't want to get himself involved. If what she told him was correct, crazy as it seems, then the DNA would have been a match for the mystery man.

He looked at the newspaper dated months earlier, a newspaper he saved, with headlines about the freak snowstorm and avalanche. Coming forward now, would not only mean that Dr. Sherman would be the laughingstock of his colleagues, but that he would also have to substantiate this unfathomable theory that Mrs. Prescott, in fact, was able to be transported from one dimension to another.

He checked the clock. Court would be in session in one hour. Dr. Sherman wrung his hands. He knew the truth, the incredible, unthinkable, unbelievable truth. Peggy Prescott must have died in the same avalanche that made headlines in the newspaper, now living in a time and place that didn't exist. The trial would end today, and if he didn't do something, it would be too late. He quickly showered and dressed. He hadn't been a good example of a man for most of his life, but this was a chance to redeem himself, at least as he stood before God. He would finally care about another human being. He parked his car in front of the courthouse, struggling to balance two overflowing banker boxes, and walked inside. He emptied his pockets, placed his phone, belt and wallet inside the bin on the conveyer belt, to be X-rayed. The security officer checked his driver's license as a formality, and said, "Dr. Sherman, haven't seen you in quite a while."

"Yes, I retired about six months ago."

"Hey, no kidding? Good for you. Living the life, huh?"

"Something like that."

"What brings you here today? Subpoena to testify?"

"Nope, no subpoena, they don't even know I'm showing up. Prescott case."

The officer looked at the banker boxes, bulging at the sides. "What do you have there, therapy notes? Coming in to save a lost soul today, Doc?"

Dr. Sherman lowered his voice, reverently. "Souls always find their way back home. I'm here to save a mere mortal man."

THE END